BLOODY JOE

BLOODY JOE MANNION BOOK ONE

PETER BRANDVOLD

WOLFPACK
PUBLISHING
— EST 2013 —

Bloody Joe
Paperback Edition
Copyright © 2022 Peter Brandvold

Wolfpack Publishing
5130 S. Fort Apache Rd. 215-380
Las Vegas, NV 89148

wolfpackpublishing.com

Paperback ISBN 978-1-63977-898-0
Large Print Hardcover ISBN 978-1-63977-899-7

BLOODY JOE

CHAPTER 1

"Bloody" Joe Mannion, Town Marshal of Del Norte in the southern Colorado Territory, saw the glint of sunlight off steel an eye blink before he threw himself off Red's back.

He hit the ground way too hard for a man of forty-six years—none of them easy—and rolled instinctively to his left, toward an arroyo, as two bullets tore up rocks and sage just behind him.

The hammering reports of two rifles reached his ears above Red's shrill, indignant whinnies and drumming hooves as the lawman, who also had a deputy county sheriff's commission, dropped over the lip of the arroyo and rolled down the four-foot embankment. As he rolled, he glanced up to see another bullet pink a rock at the arroyo's lip. The rock smacked Mannion's chest, adding insult to injury, as he came to rest at the base of the cutbank.

He ground his jaws in fury. "I'm getting too damn old for this crap!"

Not bothering to take stock of his condition, fury overwhelming him and dropping a bright red veil down over his eyes—Mannion hated bushwhackers as much as back-shooters, card sharps, sky pilots, harpy women, and snake oil drummers—he heaved himself to his knees, set his hat on his head, grabbed both nickel-plated, ivory handled Russian .44s residing in soft leather holsters, and clambered up the embankment.

Joe Mannion was a big, broad-shouldered, sun-seared man who emoted great strength and toughness and a fair amount of wildness, for wild was the land he was from, right here in the Colorado Territory. Mannion's face was flat-planed and hard-lined, ever-so-vaguely Indian—his mother had been one-quarter Navajo and raised on one of the first ranches in the foothills of the Sawatch, along the Arkansas River. His father, long dead, had been a mountain man. Mannion's skin was ruddy, his eyes the deep cobalt of a mountain lake just after sunset. When angry, they blazed in sun-seasoned sockets.

He had a thick head of wavy silver hair stitched with some remaining dark brown; it hung down well past his collar from beneath his high-crowned, broad-brimmed, black Stetson. A long, thick, gray mustache mantled his broad mouth. On Mannion's six-feet-four inch, two-hundred and twenty-pound frame—not a pound of it tallow—he wore a brown corduroy shirt; red, neck-knotted bandanna; black denim pants; wide black belt with a brass buckle; and well-worn black boots.

He was breathing hard, cursing under his breath, spitting dirt from his lips.

Two more bullets tossed more rocks and gravel and a sage branch into the arroyo. The bullets were followed by the hiccupping reports of both rifles. The echoes of said reports hadn't died before Mannion lifted his head and both hog-legs over the top of the cut, aimed quickly, narrowing his fierce blue eyes, and fired into two large sycamores standing on each side of the old Indian trail he'd been following, tracking cattle rustlers.

He'd found them, all right.

The bushwhacker on the left, resembling a large, ungainly bird perched on a branch roughly halfway up the tree, gave a howl and threw away his rifle as Mannion's bullet punched him back sharply. He gave another howl as he lost his perch and toppled off the far side of the branch, turning two backward somersaults and losing his cream hat before landing with a resolute thud at the base of the tree.

The second bushwhacker, in the tree on the opposite side of the trail from the first gutless tinhorn, grimaced and clutched his left gloved hand to his upper left thigh as he fired his Winchester straight out before him over Mannion's head. The lawman cocked the big Russian in his right hand, aimed again quickly but more carefully this time.

The hog-leg bucked, roaring.

Mannion watched in satisfaction as the .44-caliber slug painted a purple welt in the dead center of the second spineless dry-gulcher's forehead just beneath the brim of his low-crowned, flat-brimmed black hat. The slug sent him the way of the first man, tumbling down...down...ricocheting off a lower branch with a crunching thud...then continuing down...down...before striking the ground with another resolute thud.

He lay belly down, arms thrown out to both sides, the blown-out back of his head resembling a pound of freshly ground beef glistening in the mid-afternoon sunshine raining down on this forbidding canyon in the remote reaches of the Sawatch Range, formerly a playground of death for the Ute Indians and whom Mannion had fought with some renown when he'd been stationed at nearby Fort Winslow.

But these days he rarely fought the mostly cowed Utes.

Now it was mostly bank, train, and stagecoach robbers as well as the occasional rustling, dry-gulching sons of bitches like the two that lay before him.

Frank Colvin's men. Local rustlers. The rest were likely holed up at the abandoned Scully ranch farther up the trail, in Bitter Water Canyon.

Mannion gave a ragged sigh, tramped back down into the arroyo to retrieve his Stetson. He reshaped it, dusted it off, set it on his head, and climbed up out of the arroyo. He paused to take stock of the two men before him, one on each side of the trail.

Only one was moving—the one on the trail's left side.

Mannion looked around for his horse, saw the handsome bay stallion standing off in some cedars to his left, reins dangling, looking guardedly back toward the scene of the lead swap, skeptically twitching his ears.

"It's all right, Red," Mannion said. "I've defanged these two serpents."

He gave a grunt and started forward.

He tramped, spurs chinging, toward the dry-gulcher lying on his back and breathing hard on the left side of the trail, ten feet away from Mannion now and drawing closer with each stride of the lawman's long legs.

He stopped and gazed down at the man before him— tall, lean, and sandy-haired with a long beak of a hooked nose, mud-brown eyes, and long, loosely braided mare's tail mustaches.

Mannion recognized him as a small-time outlaw named Gaylord Kimble. That sounded about right. Frank

Colvin ran only with the lowliest of small-time, long-looping outlaws. Kimble was one of those, for sure.

Had been, rather. He wasn't long for this world.

Mannion prodded the man's side with the toe of his left boot. "Colvin at the line shack?"

Frothy blood oozed from the hole in the dying man's blue work shirt and brown leather vest. He grimaced as his stomach expanded and contracted quickly. His eyes had a glassy sheen. He'd hit his head hard; likely cracked his skull, scrambled his marbles though Mannion had heard they'd been born scrambled.

Kimble lifted his head up off the ground and glared at the lawman. "You go to hell, Mannion, you bloody bastard. You killed me, an' you're twice as old as me. It shoulda been you!" If the ambush had been successful, they'd likely be dumping the big lawman in a deep ravine about now. Or into the shaft of an abandoned mine. Plenty of both out here in this rugged country. Most likely, Mannion would never have been seen or heard from again. He thought of Vangie and winced. That was the problem with being a lawman father. The danger was not only to you but to those you left behind.

He was all Vangie, short for Evangeline, had. She was all he had. Her mother, Sarah, was dead. Speaking of never being seen or heard from again...

Many *would* cheer his demise, however. Mannion was an uncompromising SOB. He'd admit that up front. You had to be an ornery SOB in his line of work and in this rugged country. Yeah, he'd made enemies. More than friends, in fact. That was all right with Mannion. He'd never had much time for friends excepting his two deputies, whom he supposed he could call friends—Rio Waite and Stringbean McCallister.

Mannion grinned coldly down at the dying man. "Ah, the fates do have fun—don't they, Kimble?"

"You keep ridin'." Kimble canted his head to indicate up trail and smiled coldly. "Death's waitin' for you in Bitter Water Canyon, you old devil."

Some said Colvin was fast with a six-shooter. He was also slippery. That's why he'd never actually been caught rustling and given a necktie party. Not yet. But if he was in Bitter Water Canyon and he was rustling Red Feather beef as had been reported, his trail would end there.

"I'll see you in hell, then." Mannion aimed his left-hand Russian down at a slant and narrowed his left eye.

"No, wait!" Kimble cried, both eyes cast in sudden horror.

The Russian bucked and roared. Kimble broke wind and lay still, his lips still stretched back from his yellow teeth in a grimace. He had a puckered purple hole in his forehead to match the one his friend had received from Mannion's other Russian.

The lawman replaced the spent rounds in both pistols with fresh from his cartridge belt, holstered the guns, snapped the keeper thongs in place over the hammers, and walked over to where the second bushwhacker lay on the other side of the trail. He kicked the man onto his back.

Eyes glassy in death gazed sightlessly up at Mannion.

"L.J. Hawkins," Mannion mused aloud.

That left Colvin and his three brothers—James, Loot, and Grayson. Mannion probably should have taken one of his two deputies along for this ride, but they were needed to keep the lid on the still growing Del Norte. This was a no-help kind of country.

Mannion pulled off a glove, stuck two fingers in his mouth, and whistled. Presently, Red came trotting up, reins bouncing along the ground, high-stepping, tail arched, friskily shaking his head.

"I tell you, boy," Mannion said, taking the reins and swinging up into the leather, "this little ride of ours just got a whole lot more adventurous." He patted his prized bay's left wither. "But we need a little adventure in our lives now and then—don't we, fella? You know we'd just be bored otherwise!"

As if in Mannion's five years as Del Norte Town Marshal he'd ever been bored. He'd been brought in originally to tame the town, for he'd been renowned for his uncompromising, devil-may-care town-taming skills from Texas clear up to Kansas. He'd more-or-less tamed Del Norte though he considered it a work in progress.

He booted the horse ahead along the trail and a half hour later found himself riding into Bitter Water Canyon —a narrow cut with a dry arroyo wending its way along the trail's left side, choked with rocks and scrub brush. The trail curved to the right, and as the rock wall, spotted with hieroglyphics painted there long ago by the ancients, pulled back behind Mannion, the canyon opened before him.

The old Scully ranch cabin—a small, brush-roofed, age-silvered, log affair—squatted ahead on the far side of the arroyo that cut across the trail fifty yards beyond. A small log stable and a connecting pole corral lay to the left of the shack. A good dozen white-faced beeves milled in the corral, half of them lying down, switching their tails at flies.

Earl Drake's beeves long-looped off his Red Feather range. Mannion would send for the rancher's riders when he'd cleaned up here.

To the right of the shack leaned a privy of vertical

pine planks and with a gray wooden door adorned with the traditional half-moon.

A blonde-haired woman in a sack dress was pulling a bucket of water up out of the well. Hearing the slow thudding of Red's hooves as Mannion put the horse across the wooden bridge that spanned the arroyo, she turned her head toward the newcomer.

A woman. Yeah, Mannion had heard that Colvin had a woman. A former whore and dance hall girl went the rumor.

She didn't look half bad, either. Not the kind of woman you'd expect to ride with Colvin. Not young but not old either, Mannion saw as Red clomped off the bridge and into the yard fronting the place. Just tired-looking with large brown eyes that held little interest in the newcomer or maybe in much else in her hard, worn-out life. A life that had come to this—running with a lowly, long-looping, back-shooting dog like Frank Colvin and his brothers.

It had likely either been that or growing fat and dead too soon as a percentage gal, damn the poor gal's rotten luck.

Mannion drew rein a good twenty feet from the woman standing by the well, holding the bucket as she stared blandly at him, the breeze touching the thick, curly blonde hair that hung to her shoulders and which the lens-clear mountain sun limned with a salmon sheen. She had an age-lined but delicately featured face with a wide, full mouth though the lips were badly scabbed. They shone with dried blood. One eye still shone with the remnants of a bruise.

Those large, flat, lusterless eyes were damn haunting.

Mannion unsnapped the keeper thongs from over the hammers of his Russians.

"Frank here?" he called to the woman.

She didn't say anything. She just stared at Mannion for a few more seconds before turning and walking with no urgency toward the cabin. She mounted the small wooden stoop fronting it, glanced once more over her shoulder at Mannion, then opened the door, stepped inside, and pulled the door closed behind her.

Mannion heard her muffled voice on the other side of the door.

Boots thudded and then the door opened again. Frank Colvin stepped out onto the stoop. He was a short, broad-shouldered man with thick, curly brown hair and a thick, curly brown beard carpeting his round, fleshy face. Some said the Colvins had some Mexican blood and it shown in Frank's complexion and brown eyes. He was dressed only in wash-worn red longhandles and boots. He wore two pistols in holsters thonged low on his thighs.

A wooden scraping sound and the squawk of leather hinges rose on Mannion's left. He swung his head in that direction to see Frank's bear-like brother, James, "J.J." for short, step out of the stable and into the yard, cradling an old-model Schofield revolver in the crook of each crossed arm. A floppy-brimmed hat shaded his bearded, bruin-like face in which two small eyes were set, gray as dead coals.

Another scraping rose on Mannion's right.

He turned to see yet another Colvin brother, Grayson, step out of the privy. Grayson was tall and lean, with curly, dark-brown hair like Frank's but with an oddly feminine-looking face. Grayson wore a checked shirt, tails out, pocket torn, and buckskin trousers. A battered, funnel-brimmed Stetson sat on his head.

He spat to one side as he rested the Spencer repeating rifle on his right shoulder, and grinned.

Footsteps sounded ahead of Mannion.

He turned his head forward to see the fourth Colvin brother walk up along the right side of the cabin. Loot Colvin was built like Frank, only broader and with a big, bulging belly. His brown beard was liberally stitched with gray. He wore a black hat, buckskin tunic, baggy sack trousers, and knee-high, Apache-style moccasins.

He had two guns strapped to his broad hips and held an old Spencer repeater in both hands up high across his chest. He stopped at the corner of the cabin and stared without expression at the newcomer, his flat brown eyes none so vaguely threatening.

"Well, well, well, brothers," Frank said, grinning at Mannion and unsnapping the keeper thongs from over both of his holstered Remingtons. "Look who's here—Bloody Joe his ownself! Come to die, didja, Joe?"

CHAPTER 2

"YOU ALONE, MANNION?" JAMES COLVIN CALLED FROM the privy, the breeze slowly opening and closing the privy door behind him.

"Nah, I got the cavalry from Fort Winslow out here," Mannion said. "We got the place surrounded. You best throw down those irons and come peaceful like or get shot to ribbons standing right there."

Frank grinned as he kept his gaze on Mannion. "Mannion always comes alone. Don't you, Mannion?"

Mannion sighed as he swung down from the leather. He slapped Red's rump. The bay galloped to the edge of the yard then stopped and swung back around as though to watch the upcoming festivities. "That's about the size of it. Still, toss down those irons, or I'll shoot you to ribbons standing right there. Fill you so full of lead, you'll rattle when you walk."

"There's four of us, Mannion," the bear-like Loot said. The breeze grabbed tufts of his thick, tumbleweed hair hanging down his thick shoulders, the sun glowing red in it. He jutted his square jaw at the lawman and pinched up his eyes. "An' Frank's fast. Faster'n you!"

"That right, Frank?" Mannion said. "You faster than me, Frank?"

"Sure as hell am," Frank said, smiling, holding his hands over the grips of his pistols. "I've been practicing. Besides, they say you've slowed down over the years. You mighta once been fast. Oh, you was fast when you first came to Del Norte. There's no denying that! But I heard Everette Dicks beat you at the draw last year out behind the Three-Legged Dog in Sapinero!"

His grin broadened, eyes flashing boldly.

Mannion inwardly winced. The man was right. He'd been beaten at the draw the previous summer. Dicks had triggered his Colt an eye wink faster than Mannion had triggered his Russian. Dicks had dropped the shot, though, and took Mannion in the left leg, laying him up for a good six weeks. Going down, Mannion had snuffed Dicks's wick with a lung shot.

It had taken Dicks two days to die, but he'd died, all right.

Still, the damage had been done. Bloody Joe was no longer as fast as he once had been. That had, unfortunately, emboldened his enemies. Just as it had emboldened the Colvins standing before and to both sides of him now.

Mannion had to admit a twinge of apprehension.

Might've been foolhardy, riding in here like this, with no one to back his play. He probably should've waited till good dark and then kicked in the door.

The trouble was in his mind if not in his body, he was still the same lightning-fast town-tamer who'd gotten Del Norte under rein five years ago.

Vangie. He couldn't help thinking of her now. He never used to do that, worry about leaving her. He'd been *that* good.

Maybe, like everyone else around him now seemed to think, he no longer *was*.

Or had Dicks been a fluke?

He was about to find out.

Frank kept grinning at him.

The breeze moaned around the yard, lifting dust.

Birds piped in the pines.

Then, suddenly, eerily, they grew silent, and the yard became as quiet as a church on a Saturday night.

Straight out away from Mannion, Frank Colvin's hands dropped in a blur of quick motion. His grin broadened and his eyes intensified as he raised both hog-legs.

Boom-Boom!

It was Mannion's twin Russians that spoke first, both bullets punching into Frank's chest and blowing him straight back into the cabin with a look of startled horror on his fat, fleshy face. The woman's scream was muffled by a blast from Mannion's right-hand Russian just as the fat Colvin brother, Loot, raised his Spencer and gritted his teeth.

The rifle roared as Loot, jouncing backward with Mannion's bullet in his belly, blew up a fist-sized chunk of ground six feet in front of him.

Mannion dropped to a knee as to his left as Grayson's Winchester carbine lapped flames, sending lead caroming through the air where the lawman's head had been a second before. The whip-cracking report was followed by the pop of one of James's Schofields, the echo of which hadn't died before the Russians bucked and roared twice more, quickly. James cursed as he twisted around and flew back against the stable, and Grayson screamed and tossed his Winchester high in the air and flew straight back into the privy. He took a seat over the hole and canted his head to one side, as though deeply tired.

Clicking the hammers of both hog-legs back, Mannion swung around quickly toward the stable then eased the tension in both trigger fingers when he saw James kneeling over a water trough as though in prayer at an altar, arms hanging straight down against his sides, unmoving. His face was in the water.

The lawman tightened his fingers over the Russians' triggers again when he spied movement in the corner of his left eye. He jerked around, spying a Winchester carbine aimed at him from just inside the cabin door. At first, he thought it must be Frank but too late he saw the twin blue eyes of the woman gazing down the barrel at him, saw her blonde hair fluttering against her pale, drawn cheeks.

Too late he saw the mildness of those eyes, the lack of killing intent, because by then he'd pulled the triggers of both Russians. They bucked and roared once more, punching two forty-four caliber rounds into the woman's cream shirtwaist, making it buffet against her chest.

She screamed as she stumbled backward, dropping the carbine onto the stoop. She stopped, getting her feet set beneath her. She glanced down at the twin holes in her chest, red stains growing over each breast. She lifted her head and gazed with a peculiar concentration at the lawman who'd killed her.

She took one uncertain step forward then dropped to her knees with a sharp, "*Oh!*" hair bouncing on her shoulders.

Her gaze still held Mannion's. Her lids closed over her eyes, and she fell straight down onto the stoop without breaking her fall. She lay there, belly down, arms stretched out above her head.

Mannion gazed at the woman in shock, heart

hammering his breastbone, smoke curling from the barrel of each hog-leg still aimed straight out before him.

Slowly, he lowered the irons to his sides, and cursed.

"Now...while in the hell," he said under his breath, "did you do that?"

———

THOSE EYES, MANNION THOUGHT AS HE RODE THROUGH a broad valley with misty, blue-green, pine-carpeted ridges rising on both sides of him, the woman's blanket-wrapped body tied over the back of the horse he trailed behind him by its bridle reins.

It was one of the Colvin Gang's mounts he'd found in the stable.

Those eyes. Those damn eyes.

He kept seeing them as he rode, shadows stretching out from the southern ridge on his right as he walked the horses south toward Del Norte, which lay on the other end of the valley, between the San Juan Range to the south and the Sawatch Range to the north, behind him now. He kept blinking his own eyes in a futile attempt to rid them of the haunting image of the woman's sad, desperate blue orbs as they'd stared down the barrel of the Winchester at him, waiting for him to kill her.

That's what she'd done. She'd made him kill her.

Yeah, sad, desperate eyes. But there'd been a vague cunning in them, too. She'd known he'd have no choice but to shoot and thus, killing her, put her out of her mental misery but also leaving him baffled.

And haunted.

Those eyes had looked just like Sarah's eyes in her last, desperate days—weary, exhausted, troubled beyond the human will to endure.

It was almost as though Sarah had returned from the dead to kill herself before him once more.

Only, this time *he'd* killed her. She tricked him into killing her, honing his guilt for having been unable to help her to a fine edge.

"Why, lady?" he said aloud, shaking his head as he scowled toward the distant smudge of Del Norte sprawled across dun plateau ahead, the snow-capped peaks of the San Juans rising beyond it. "Why'd you do it? Why'd you make *me* do it?"

Of course, he knew. Like Sarah, she'd thought she'd run out of options.

Those eyes.

Now he had two pairs of eyes to see one last time on his deathbed, haunting him even during his own last gasps.

He'd dragged the Colvin brothers off into the brush behind the old ranch. The predators would take care of them. He'd wrapped the woman in the blanket and tied her over the mouse brown dun's back to take her back to Del Norte to give her a better burial than what he'd given the men.

Why?

She'd been no captive. She'd run with them. Likely *been* one of them.

Still, he couldn't leave a woman as he'd left the men. Even after she'd tricked him into killing her. He had to give her a proper burial.

Sentimental, Bloody Joe?

Not like you.

"No, not like me," Mannion said aloud, shaking his head, puzzled by his own wash of feeling when in the past he'd prided himself on his lack of sentiment except in his dealings with Vangie, whom he felt the need to shower with attention and affection to help compensate for what had become of her mother.

And maybe to compensate for his inability to love Sarah as deeply as he should have and for generally being absent when, as a town taming marshal in Kansas, she'd been going through such mental misery in the months after Sarah had been born.

Those eyes. Those damn eyes...

Again, he blinked and shook his head and watched without really seeing Del Norte grow before him until, after the sun had dropped behind the western ridge silhouetted against it, he rode into its ragged outskirts with a lumberyard and stock pens and gray log cabins and chicken coops crowding the trail to each side of him.

And then the street widened as he entered the main business district bustling even now at nearly seven o'clock at night with clattering ranch and mine wagons and the thudding horses of ranch hands heading for Del Norte's dozen or so saloons and hurdy-gurdy houses. A mule team and a big Pittsburg freight wagon was parked before the broad loading dock of Wilfred Drake's Mercantile.

The tall, thin Drake himself stood on the dock in a long, green apron, a pencil tucked behind one ear as he stared down at a clipboard in his hands while three beefy, deeply sunburned, bearded men in the traditional work shirts, suspenders, baggy canvas breeches, and high-topped, lace-up boots of mule skinners back-and-bellied mining supplies into the Pittsburg's box.

Just up the street, a dusty stagecoach and sweat-silvered team sat in front of the San Juan Mountain Stage Line office while passengers disembarked and the burly jehu, Lyle Horton, hauled a portmanteau out of the driver's boot. As he did, he glanced toward Mannion just then passing in the street before him and narrowed his eyes at the blanket-wrapped body draped over the mouse-brown dun's back.

Horton laughed and yelled, "Who'd you ventilate today with them big Russians of yours, Bloody Joe? Hah! Hah! Hah!"

Ignoring the man, the severe planes of his face set grimly, Mannion continued riding until he rode up in front of the San Juan Mountain Hotel & Saloon on his right. He drew rein and gazed up at the woman staring down at him from the second-floor balcony of her office suite, two French doors standing open behind her, lace curtains blowing in the breeze.

Even pushing forty, Jane Ford was as lovely a woman as a man could find in this rowdy, remote ranch and mining supply town. She cut a striking figure this early evening in her cream and brown silk and taffeta gown with lace-edged, low-cut shirtwaist, black silk, diamond-studded choker adorning her fine, creamy long neck, silver hoop rings dangling from her ears. Her rich, curly, copper hair slid around her fine, wide-mouthed, brown-eyed face as she gazed down, arms crossed on her lovely breasts, at the Del Norte Town Marshal.

Her eyes went from Mannion to the blanket-wrapped body tied over the back of the mount behind him then slid back to Mannion, brows ridging skeptically, one beringed hand rising to absently finger the diamond stud in the choker at her neck. She opened her mouth to speak but then closed it without saying anything, only gazing down at him, her eyes peculiarly searching, as though she sensed the trouble in his soul.

Mannion gazed back at her, expressionless, then touched spurs to Red's flanks and continued riding, jerking the dun with its grisly cargo along behind him, heads on both sides of the street swinging toward him, men chuckling and shaking their heads fatefully as they tipped sudsy beer mugs to their mouths.

"There goes Bloody Joe makin' another trip to Boot Hill!"

"There goes Bloody Joe makin' Marvin Bellringer a wealthy man!"

Marvin Bellringer was the undertaker.

CHAPTER 3

MANNION'S JAILHOUSE AND OFFICE LAY TWO BLOCKS UP the street from the San Juan Hotel & Saloon, on the right side of the street, directly across from John Dunham's Tonsorial Parlor outside of which Dunham sat in a hide-bottom chair, wearing a green eyeshade and reading a newspaper.

At least, he had been reading a newspaper.

As Mannion had approached with his two horses, the barber had looked up, turned back to his newspaper, then looked up again quickly to give the notorious lawman closer scrutiny, taking in the second horse obviously carrying a body on its back. He slid his gaze to Mannion and raised his bushy gray eyebrows as if to say, "Here we go again," before quickly raising the newspaper again to hide his smirking, gray-mustached face.

Resembling a small bunkhouse, the office was a brick, tile-roofed affair with a small, unpainted, wooden front stoop. Hanging from chains beneath the porch roof, between two roof support posts, was a large wooden sign announcing in large black letters: JOE MANNION TOWN MARSHAL. A couple of years ago, some smartass had climbed up there in the night and added "Bloody" in sloppy red paint to the left of Mannion's name. Mannion had decided to leave it in surly defiance of the prankster's joke, not wanting to let on it had gotten to him.

Hell, it really hadn't.

Let it be a totem against crime. There was still plenty of crime in Del Norte, but Mannion and his deputies kept a lid on the place.

One of Mannion's deputies, Rio Waite, was out there now, one hip hiked on the porch rail right of the front door propped open with a brick to let the heat from the supper fire out. He was a thick, burly man with a fleshy face and keen blue eyes set beneath the brim of his badly weathered Stetson. A considerable paunch pushed out his shirt and brown leather vest and nearly turned the big, brass buckle of his cartridge belt upside down.

Waite, a retired ranch foreman in his early sixties, held a long, double-barreled Greener across his thighs in anticipation of trouble breaking out in Del Norte's watering holes and whorehouses, which could be depended upon to start occurring in another hour or two, this being Friday night and the hitch rails along both side of the main street were crowded with saddled ranch ponies.

Waite's cat, Buster, sat on the rail beside the chubby deputy, licking one front paw to clean behind his ears. In his black and white coat complete with a furry black bow tie, Buster looked nothing so much as an eternally tuxedoed fancy-dan with no debutante's ball to attend.

Buster's refined looks were deceiving, however. The tom was such a good mouser that Mannion rarely spotted mouse droppings in either the ground-floor office or in the underground cell block under the place. Buster would even catch mice and rats outside at night, and often leave his trophies on the stoop for Mannion's and the lawman two deputies' appreciation.

Rio and Buster lived in an old cabin directly behind the jailhouse. It had been abandoned when one of the early prospectors had pulled foot.

"Don't say it," Mannion said as he drew Red up to the hitchrack fronting the stoop.

"Not going to." Rio scrunched up his unhandsome face with bulging, baby blue eyes in ironic delight. "I knew you'd get your man, Joe. You always do!"

"That's what I told you not to say."

"Well, how'd you know what I was gonna say before I even said it?"

"Because everyone in town says it." Mannion swung wearily down from his saddle, tossed the reins around the worn hitch rail and turned to his deputy now running one big, brown hand down Buster's back. "This one isn't a man."

"Oh..." Waite frowned. "If it's not a man, it's..."

"Yeah." Mannion tied the mouse-brown dun to the hitchrack and said, "Come down here."

"Who you got there, Marshal?" came a voice behind Mannion.

He turned to see his other deputy, Henry "String-bean" McCallister, walking toward him from the other side of the street. Aptly named, Stringbean was a long, tall drink of water with a long, pale face and a wing of sandy red hair dropping down from the brim of his battered brown slouch hat to hover wing-like over his left eye. He wore an old-Model Colt low on his right thigh and held an 1878 Winchester rifle in his gloved right hand down low by his side.

"One o' them rustlers?" Stringbean asked as he drew

to a stop in front of Mannion. He was long and tall, but he was still an inch or two shorter than the town marshal's six-feet-four. "Why'd you bring one back to town?" He glanced at Rio and grinned. "You always say the coyotes need to eat, too."

Rio had walked down off the stoop, Buster standing now with his back humped, watching him with interest. Waite crouched now over the blanket-wrapped body and peeled the folds of the horse blanket away from the face. He glanced up at Stringbean and said, "This one's a woman." He glanced at Mannion. "A purty one."

Mannion glanced down at the woman again. Her eyes were still half-open. He'd tried to close them, but they'd stubbornly refused. They stared up at him accusingly.

Those damn eyes.

"She was one o' them rustlers?" Stringbean asked Mannion, skeptically.

"I doubt she helped with the rustling, but she was in with them—that's right."

"She throw down on ya, too?" Rio asked, straightening.

Mannion's eyes were still on the woman. "She wanted me to believe she was. She aimed a rifle at me, had me dead to rights." He turned to Rio and raked a thumb down his unshaven jaw in bitter perplexity. "But she didn't pull the trigger."

Both deputies frowned at him, curious.

Rio said, "You mean..."

"She wanted me to shoot her." Mannion looked down at her half-open eyes again and added, "Wanted to die." Again, he remembered the hopeless look in her eyes but didn't bother describing them to his deputies.

He turned to Rio and then to Stringbean. "Either of you ever see her before?"

Stringbean hiked a shoulder and shook his head. "Uh-uh."

"Not me." Rio smiled at Mannion. "And you know me, Joe. I know most o' the women in town."

"At least the working ones," Mannion said dryly.

Turning to Stringbean, he said, "Take her over to Bellringer. Tell him I'll pay for a decent burial."

"Now," Rio said, frowning his astonishment and his boss. "Imagine that! An outlaw woman, no less!"

"You wanna pay personal?" Stringbean asked, equally perplexed. "Not just send the bill to the town council, like usual?"

"No." Mannion shook his head as he gazed down at those haunted eyes again. "I want to pay for her myself."

"Have it your way, Marshal." Stringbean untied the reins from the hitchrack. "I'll take her over to Bellringer."

As he led the horse and the woman away, he glanced over his shoulder at his fellow deputy and shrugged. Rio turned to Mannion, still frowning curiously, searching the lawman with his eyes.

"You all right, Joe?" the deputy asked him. "You look a little green around the gills."

"I'm fine. Just a little trail weary's all."

To avoid the deputy's gaze and anymore questions— he didn't want to talk about why he felt obligated to pay for the woman's funeral because it perplexed him a little himself—Mannion glanced into the street. His gaze landed on seven riders riding into town from the south— all dressed in traditional trail attire. One man glanced at Mannion as he and the other six rode side by side, chinning and laughing, then quickly turned his eyes away from the lawman, pretending he hadn't seen him. He laughed a little too loudly with the others.

They split up to ride around a parked ore dray sitting outside the blacksmith shop and then rode on past Mannion and his deputy, pointedly keeping their gazes aimed straight ahead.

"Say," Rio said, lifting his chin to indicate the riders now dwindling on up the street to the north, "ain't that them curly wolves you—"

"Kicked out of town last weekend—yes?" Mannion finished for the older man. "That's them, all right."

He'd kicked them out of town for starting a brawl, busting up a saloon as well as a whore's jaw. Mannion turned toward the riders just then pulling their horses up to the San Juan Hotel & Saloon, and felt the anger burn in him. He squeezed his fists down low by his sides.

It was a satisfying burn, distracting him as it did from the haunted eyes of the woman who'd made him kill her. He didn't usually like his anger. In fact, he was often afraid of it. Too often it ran off its leash and was too hard to get reined in again. He'd been that way all his life though he'd tried hard for Vangie's sake to get himself in check.

Oh, well. It was one very good reason he'd made such an effective lawman for most of his adult life after he'd finished fighting the Indians, prospected for gold in the Southwest, and worked as a shotgun guard for a stagecoach line. That was before he'd headed to Kansas hoping to get a job with one of the big Texas ranches that had just run a herd up to the railhead in Abilene. They usually needed a few riders for the winter, and most of the punchers who'd trailed up from Texas stayed in Kansas to stomp with their tails up, pockets filled with money.

Instead, a town marshal had pinned a deputy's badge to Mannion's shirt after witnessing Joe's gun work when a drunk gambler had drawn on him, accusing him of dealing from the bottom of the deck. While his smoke had still been billowing, Mannion had flattened the gambler's partner with two quick jabs to the mouth and a devastating roundhouse he'd brought up from his knees.

He'd bare-knuckle fought for extra money on weekends in the army.

"With a temper like that," Marshal Dan Rowe had told Mannion, who'd still been steaming over the accusation, "and with the way you can shoot—accurate and without hesitation, I might add, ha-ha—I'd just as soon have you with me as *agi'n* me!"

Rowe had proven a great mentor to the young firebrand town tamer until Rowe had been shotgunned out of the privy flanking his jailhouse early one morning by a pair of Panhandle punchers he'd braced for drunk and disorderly the night before. Mannion had run them down and killed them hard. That's when he'd acquired the nickname, and it had stuck to him tighter than a skin on a snake ever since.

"Reckon I'd better head over to the San Juan," Mannion said now, watching the seven riders tie their horses to one of the several hitchracks fronting the hotel and saloon—easily the largest building on the main drag —and walking up the steps of the broad front porch fronting the place.

They were talking and laughing. One took off his hat and playfully slapped it against the shoulder of the man walking beside him.

"You want I should back your play, Joe?" Waite asked as the seven filed through the batwings on the saloon side of the building.

"Nah," Mannion said, sliding his rifle from its scabbard and setting it on his shoulder. "Just stable Red for me, will you? Have Kellogg give him a good rubdown and a bait of oats."

"Will do. Be careful. One o' them is Whip Helton, an' you know how he is."

"Oh, I know," Mannion said. Helton was the rebel son of a thuggish but wealthy local rancher—as quick to rile as Mannion himself and good with a hog-leg. He was a known rapist though no girl had ever had the courage to testify against him. Mannion hated the man and the six he rode with on sight. All were border toughs of the worst kind.

No-goods on horseback. Just riding around the Colorado mining camps, gambling, occasionally robbing and rustling and shaking down prospectors and mistreating parlor girls, though no one had ever been able to pin anything on them.

Whip's father, Garth Helton, knew powerful men in powerful places. And most folks were afraid of him and the gunnies he had working for him.

Mannion took his rifle into the office and racked it. For close order work, he relied on the Russians.

He came back out, descended the stoop. Buster sat on the rail now, watching him and curling his tail.

"Hold the fort, Buster," Mannion said as he turned at the bottom of the porch steps and strode south along the street.

He kept to the boardwalks, occasionally nodding to men he knew or who knew him, which was most of the town, of course. A man with Mannion 's reputation always turned heads.

Approaching the San Juan, he mounted the steps, crossed the porch, and pushed open the heavy oak batwings, the left door owning a fancily carved 'S' in its panel, the right door with an equally fancily carved 'J'.

The broad drinking hall before him was packed. The big, mahogany bar with elaborate back bar mirror which owned another, larger 'S' and an 'J' in gold leaf, lay to the rear of the room. The broad, red-carpeted stairs that rose to the second and third floors lay to the bar's right. Between Mannion and the bar were a good thirty or forty tables, smoke rising from the gamblers and drinkers to hover around the crystal chandeliers.

A conversational roar echoed.

Mannion's gaze had just found the seven men he was looking for when he noted movement on the stairs to the right of the bar. He looked that way to see Jane Ford descending the stairs just as she saw him, turning her head to face him.

She stopped, one beringed hand on the banister to her right, and regarded him with that vaguely puzzled, searching gaze she'd bestowed upon him earlier when he'd first ridden into Del Norte.

She continued down the stairs and came across the room, weaving around the tables, occasionally smiling and nodding at the clientele, and briefly responding to friendly queries or appreciative comments. Mannion smiled. The lady always received a warm welcome no matter how long she'd been gone. Like Joe himself, she was a bit of a loner, and running such an establishment was trying on her nerves.

He noted that as she moved with panther-like grace toward him, long, pleated skirts with a glistening metallic sheen caressing her long, fine legs, every male head in the place turned to appreciate her, lights from the gas chandeliers glinting in her rich, curly red hair part of which was piled in a neat bun atop her head, the rest left to hang in long, copper waves down over her shoulders. The gown's bodice was cut low, allowing an inviting glimpse of deep, freckled cleavage.

She was deep into her thirties but there wasn't a trace of gray in her hair, and her face was as soft and supple as a woman ten years younger. The small lines around her eyes gave her a seasoned look.

She stopped before Mannion, placed her hand on his forearm, and wrinkled the skin above the bridge of her long, fine nose as she looked up at him with that curious expression again. "Drink, Joe?"

Mannion affectionately caressed her hand on his arm. They'd been lovers for over a year now though that had come as much of a surprise to him as to her. Beyond being basically solitary, they couldn't have been more different. Hailing from a rich St. Louis family but having come West on her own to seek wealth and adventure, she was cultured and refined as well as ambitious. But maybe their differences are what had attracted him to her—that and her obvious beauty, of course—and what had attracted her to him.

Some women are fascinated by bold, dangerous men, and Mannion was all of that. Some bold, dangerous men were intrigued by beautiful, high-strung yet independent women, and Jane was all of that, as well.

Mannion shook his head. "Not here for relaxation at the moment, Jane."

"Joe, what's wrong?" She canted her head a little to one side and squeezed his forearm.

When he turned his own curious gaze on her, she said, "You don't look yourself. What happened? Who was that dead man you brought to town? One of the rustlers?"

The reason she'd asked was because it was damned

rare for Bloody Joe to bring any outlaw back dead or alive. He usually fed them to the carrion eaters.

Mannion didn't respond to her query. He turned his gaze back to the seven men sitting near the bottom of the stairs.

Jane turned her own gaze that way. "Who are you look—"

Just then a great clatter rose in the room, echoing above the roar of conversation. One of the seven cow punchers—Whip Helton himself—had taken out an Arkansas toothpick and was stabbing it quickly into the table between his splayed fingers, grinning with childish delight, the commotion making the beer in his and the other men's schooners lick up and over the rims.

The others around him were laughing.

"Oh, my gosh—my table!" Jane said, cupping a hand over her mouth as she stared at Helton.

Anger burning in Mannion once more—deliciously, shoving out all thought of the woman who'd tricked him into killing her—he gentled Jane to one side then, clenching his fists low at his sides, headed for Whip Helton's table.

CHAPTER 4

"You stick that into the table one more time," Mannion said as he stopped before the curly wolves' table and spread his boots a little more than shoulder width apart, "I'm gonna cut off your fingers, dry them, and wear them from a thong around my neck."

Helton looked up at him and feigned surprise.

"Well, if it ain't Bloody Joe!" the baby-faced firebrand said, grinning, his dung-brown eyes flashing with delight. He was of average height and wore a Spanish-style red shirt with green piping on both breasts. Girlish, long, straight, dark-brown hair hung down his back, and he wore a gold spike in his left ear. A brown leather hat was on his head, rawhide chin strap dangling to his chest.

Leaving the Arkansas toothpick stuck in the table, he leaned back in his chair and crossed his arms. "To what do we owe the pleasure, Marshal?"

The room had fallen silent. The only sounds were the rumble of wagon traffic outside and a dog barking in the distance.

"You seven devils are barred from town. *Were* barred for a month. Now it's *two* months."

Mannion glanced over his shoulder at Jane Ford, who stood behind him and a little to one side, her face flushed with anger at the poor treatment her table had received at the hand of the thuggish Helton—every bit the lout his father, old Garth Helton, was. "After you pay the lady for the table. How much, Jane?"

"Those tables are solid mahogany," Jane said tightly, her voice quavering with anger. "They are fifty dollars apiece."

"*Fifty dollars?*" Helton said in wide-mouthed shock. He rose from his chair, placed his hands on the table, and leaned forward, jutting his bony chin defiantly at the lady. "For a *table*? Lady, you and your man here can both go to *hell*!"

Suddenly, Mannion's wolf was off its leash.

Gritting his teeth and narrowing his eyes in fury, the Del Norte Town Marshal pulled the toothpick out of the table and rammed it point down through Helton's left hand. Just as Helton opened his mouth to scream, Mannion reached up, grabbed a handful of the firebrand's hair, and slammed his head down on the table with a loud, crunching *bang!*

"*Whoah!*" exclaimed one of the onlookers behind Mannion and Jane.

The firebrand screamed as he lifted his face and broken, bloody nose from the table.

As he did, two of his cohorts lurched to their feet and slapped leather.

Mannion had anticipated the moves.

Both of his Russians were in his hands. He extended them both across the table.

Boom! Boom!

The man who'd been sitting directly to Helton's right flew back over his hair and dropped with another thunderous boom. So, too, did the man sitting one man away from Helton, on Helton's left, but not before triggering his own gun into the ceiling.

"*Jesus!*" exclaimed another onlooker.

"Kee-RIST!" exclaimed Helton, nasally, lying belly down on the table. His hand still impaled by the Arkansas toothpick, he looked at the dead men on his right and left.

Mannion slid his gun around at the other four, who'd dropped their hands toward their own hog-legs. After seeing the tragic fates of their pards, however, they had wisely decided to leave the guns in their holsters. They sat tensely regarding the two big, smoking, silver-chased Russians bearing down on them.

"Hands on the table, boys," Mannion said, teeth still gritted.

Helton was staring in horror at the knife pinning his hand to the table. He poked his right finger at it, yelling, "*Oh, Lordy me! Oh, Lordy me!*"

"Lordy me, hell," Mannion said. He holstered his right-hand Russian and pulled the toothpick out of the table as well as out of Helton's hand.

The firebrand screamed and, clutching the wrist of the wounded appendage with his right hand, dropped back down in his chair with a bark of sliding chair legs.

Mannion walked around the table to stand before him, fists on his hips. "Pay the lady."

"Look at my hand, you crazy son of a bitch! I need a doctor!" He was blowing a fine spray of blood through his broken nose.

Mannion kicked the firebrand's chair, almost knocking him over backward. "Pay the lady!"

"Joe," Jane said, knitting her brows in reproof at him.

Mannion ignored her. "I said pay the lady!" he said as

he again kicked the firebrand's chair, evoking a horrified yowl as Helton grabbed the arms with both hands, even the one with the bloody hole in it. "You crazy bastard—I don't have that much on me!"

Mannion glanced at the other four. "Pool your money or you'll all be my guests tonight in the town lockup."

Sobbing, Helton shoved his good hand into a pocket of his black denims and looked at his four remaining accomplices. "Help me pay the man! I gotta get over to the damn sawbones before I bleed dry!"

Reluctantly, the other four leaned back and dug into their pants pockets. Between the four of them, they had only thirty-eight dollars.

"That's enough, Joe," Jane said.

"No, it's not."

Mannion walked over to the first man he'd shot, and, dropping to a knee beside him, plundered his pockets for four dollars and six bits. On the other man he found a silver cartwheel.

Mannion held the coin up and smiled. "Well, look here—this fella's right flush! Too bad he's not alive to spend it."

He laid the money out on the table before Jane.

"The extra's for the trouble."

Jane drew her mouth corners down at him in mute admonishment.

Mannion looked at the four cowpunchers giving him the wooly eyeball and canted his head at the sobbing Helton. "Get your friend out of here. He's getting blood all over the place. Get your dead out of here, too. You won't be invited back to Del Norte for three months. When you return, you'd better be on your best behavior, or you'll rot in my basement cell block!"

Grumbling curses, the four rose from their chairs.

Glaring at Mannion, Helton rose from his own chair and strode across the room, practically running, weaving between tables, then stopped before the batwings. Holding his injured pa like a tender little bird against his chest, he looked back over his shoulder at the Del Norte Town Marshal.

"This ain't over, Bloody Joe!"

He pushed through the batwings and was gone.

When the other four had carried the two dead men away, Mannion looked around the room. His fury had taken such control of him that he hadn't realized the place was still as quiet as a cemetery. Not only that, but a good third of the customers were gone.

The rest were looking at him as though he were some African wildcat escaped from a circus.

Feeling his cheeks warm with chagrin, he turned to Jane. She stood at the table before the pile of coins and greenbacks, staring up at him, her eyes hard and cold.

"What's gotten into you, Joe," she said tightly, quietly. "That was too much even for you."

She didn't wait for him to reply but turned to the bar where her two night aprons stood, as frozen as everyone else in the room, and called, "Lonnie...Phil—free drinks on the house!"

The remaining customers shuttled their wary gazes from Mannion to the lady of the San Juan. They cheered and clapped.

Jane plucked the coins and greenbacks off the table, gave Mannion another disgusted look then headed for the bar.

"He ruined your damn table," Mannion said, incredulously.

She kept walking, stiff-backed, toward the bar.

———

GRUMBLING CURSES AT HIMSELF, MANNION PUSHED OUT through the San Juan's batwings and onto the stoop. He stopped at the top of the steps and adjusted the set of his hat, looking around the street, where the traffic was dwindling and slowing as the long shadows of dusk stretched across it.

Well, at least he wasn't still staring at the poor woman's eyes.

No, now he was remembering the shocked gazes of the San Juan clientele when he'd finally come up from his roaring. The shocked, disgusted look on his lover's face. He'd likely lost Jane. He'd blown his top in front of her before. She knew how he was. But he'd never quite gone this far, pinning a man's hand to a table, shooting two others.

At least, never in the San Juan. Never in front of Jane.

He'd always prided himself on never starting dustups. Only finishing them. But he'd started this one, all right. And finished it too. In grand ol' Bloody Joe fashion.

He dropped down the porch steps and into the street.

From far away on his left, a man called, "Mannion!"

A familiar voice. Ah, shit.

Mannion turned quickly right and began taking long strides, heading north.

"Mannion!" came the call again.

As he walked, Mannion ignored the looks he was tossed from the small crowds of cowboys, townsmen, muleskinners, and miners—men of all races, even a few Chinese—standing in front of saloons, talking and taking some air while they drank. Word about what had happened in the San Juan had already spread. Of course, it had.

Like a wildfire.

"*Mannion!*"

The man's voice, louder this time and accompanied by the quick tapping of running feet. With a weary sigh, Mannion stopped and turned around.

Mannion grimaced as he watched the little, bespectacled gent in a three-piece suit walking quickly toward him on his short legs and brogan-clad feet. The Del Norte mayor, Charlie McQueen, approached with a stiff smile on his plump, bearded face, his round, steel-framed spectacles glinting in the fading light beneath the narrow, curled brim of his bowler hat.

"Mannion! Mannion! Mannion!" the little mayor said, stopping in front of Joe and leaning forward, breathless, letting his hands hang straight down to the ground. He straightened, cheeks flushed, and thumbed his glasses up on his nose.

Breathing hard, he said, "I was just heading over to the San Juan. Saw you leaving. I called but you must not have heard me."

"That a fact?" Mannion said, lifting his hat and running a hand through his hair. "Well, no, no, I didn't hear, Mister Mayor. What can I do for you? Been a long day, an' my daughter's likely getting ready to send a posse out for me."

McQueen gave another strained smile and hooked his thumb to indicate behind him. "I was over at the Longhorn." He gave a chuckle but there was little mirth in it. "I heard...heard what you did to Whip Helton."

The mayor laughed but it wasn't a serious laugh.

He said, "Boy, he really had it coming—didn't he? Ain't he a keg of dynamite with a lit fuse?"

Mannion gave a dry snort and did not respond. A keg

of dynamite with a lit fuse was how he'd heard himself described a time or two.

The mayor, several inches shorter than the lawman, looked up at him, his soft, bearded face twisted in shock. "Did you *really* pin his hand to a table with a *knife*?"

Mannion bunched his lips with a grim smile.

"What'd he do?"

"He was vandalizing one of Jane's tables."

McQueen gave an exaggerated grimace, sucking air through his teeth. "Oh, I see, I see." He grimaced again, looked down, then, lifting his head again, thumbed his glasses up on his nose. He placed his hand on Mannion's arm, sidling up to him, and said confidentially, "Joe, just between you and me, that sort of thing isn't going over as well anymore as it once did."

"What isn't?"

"The, uh...well, the way you *handle* things."

"The way I *handle* things."

"Yes, the way you *handle* things."

"I don't understand," Mannion said. "You brought me over here from Kansas five years ago to tame the place down. Well, I've tamed it down, but it still needs tamping from time to time. If you don't let the bad guys know that their hurrahing ways won't be tolerated—well, then, by God, you'll have to tolerate them, Mister Mayor."

McQueen grimaced again, this time at Mannion's raised voice.

"Yes, but, but..." Taking Mannion by the arm, he led him two steps into a break between a small café and a Mexican-run tobacco shop then glanced over his shoulder to make sure they were alone. "You see, Joe, we have several new men on the town council. They weren't here when Del Norte was really stomping with its tail up, so they don't understand."

"They don't understand..."

"Your somewhat, uh...shall we say *heated*...ways...?"

Mannion turned to face the little man directly. "What are you saying, Mayor?"

Again, McQueen adjusted his glasses. "What I'm saying is that—well, quite frankly, Mannion, a couple of the newer members...and a few of the newer *businessmen* here in Del Norte...have...well, they've called for your *head*, Mannion!"

CHAPTER 5

"Ah, so the tinhorns want Bloody Joe's head, eh?"

"Frankly, that's a fact." Again, McQueen glanced over his shoulder to make sure they were alone then, keeping his voice low and confidential, said, "You see, Joe, your more, uh, *roughhewn* ways frighten some people. The *important* people here in Del Norte. They want Del Norte to be a *civilized* place. They believe *civilized* equals *prosperity*."

Mannion knew just who those "important" people were. One was the banker who'd moved to Del Norte from somewhere back East—Morgan Howell. He was definitely one of them. Probably the barber, Dunham, too. Dunham never talked much, friendly-like, when Mannion went in for a shave and a haircut. He talked friendly with most of his other customers. A couple of times Mannion had even glimpsed the barber giving him the wooly eyeball in the mirror when he'd been running a straight razor down the lawman's neck.

Nowadays, Mannion kept a close eye on the man in the mirror and one hand on a gun handle.

Another discontent was probably the mercantiler,

Wilfred Drake. Yeah, throw Drake into the same bucket of worms.

Mannion wrapped an arm around the mayor's shoulders and said in the same quiet, confidential voice the little man had used on him: "Mister Mayor, you tell those hoopleheads they can take a running leap right into the burning lakes of hell! Tell that to 'em from Bloody Joe, will you?"

McQueen tilted another pained expression up at the taller man. "Joe, *must* you be so intransigent?!"

Mannion stared down at him, one brow arched.

"Obdurate...intractable...*stubborn!*"

"Why didn't you say so the first time?" Mannion gave a stubborn smile. It was genuine. He felt stubborn...intractable...obdurate...intransigent. All of those. He felt foolish for having blown his lid in such grand fashion in the San Juan. Especially in front of Jane. Still, he had a stubborn streak a mile wide. He would not give ground. He was like a Brahma bull in the Texas Big Thicket that way. He *couldn't* give ground.

"I tamed this town my way, and nobody complained about how I did it. I've been keeping towns on their leashes for over twenty years, and every town councilman I've ever run into has always doffed his hat to Bloody Joe." Again, Mannion smiled. "Give those new members Bloody Joe's message, Mister Mayor. If they want my head, they can come get it themselves."

He gave the man's shoulders a punctuating squeeze then stepped out of the break and continued his journey north along the boardwalk.

After a block, he swung east down a side street which after another block became a two-track trail. It was getting dark enough now that he could see the windows of his and Vangie's little, white-frame house shimmering in a grove of aspens off the trail's left side. She'd set the lamps in the two front windows for him.

A warm feeling came over Mannion as he swung off the two-track trail and followed the secondary trail toward the neat house sitting before him, surrounded by a freshly painted white picket fence. Vangie had painted the fence herself recently. Mannion tripped the latch on the front gate then followed the brick path he'd laid himself when he and Vangie had first moved to Del Norte from Kansas, when Mannion had needed a change of scenery, and he'd built the house with Vangie's help though she'd been only twelve.

He climbed the three steps to the front porch and stopped. He'd glanced through the window to the left of the front dor.

Vangie was in the kitchen, rolling out a pie crust on the food preparation table just beyond the window. Mannion smiled as he watched his lovely daughter, who reminded him so much of Sarah it made his heart ache at times. It was a good ache, though. Vangie owned her mother's best traits—a warm heart, a giving soul, a keen wit, deep intelligence. She was a good housekeeper to boot.

All the things Mannion himself was not.

As she leaned forward across the table, rolling out the pie crust, she tucked her bottom lip under her front teeth. Sarah used to do that. Vangie's ivory cheeks were prettily flushed just like Sarah's had been when she'd toiled in the kitchen. Like Sarah, Vangie wore her hair in a French braid down her back, but strands of it danced against her cheeks, some clinging. Mannion figured that Vangie wore her hair in a braid because she'd seen pictures of her mother wearing her own hair that way. It was Vangie's way of being close to the mother she'd never known, who'd died when Vangie was only a little over a year old.

One way that Vangie was different from her mother was that she rarely wore dresses. Vangie preferred flannel shirts, denims, and boots—riding attire. She was a horse girl through and through, whereas Sarah had always been afraid of the beasts. Every minute that Vangie was not working in the house, cooking or cleaning or doing laundry, she was outside, toiling in the garden beds around the yard or out in the corral with her two horses, Willow and Jack.

One thing about his daughter that worried Mannion a little was that she was a loner with no close friends to speak of. At seventeen, she'd never had a beau. Several boys had come calling, and Vangie had gone out to sit with them on the porch and to accept the flowers they'd brought her, but they'd never stayed long. So far, Vangie had taken a stroll with only one of them, and only once. She'd never spoken of any of them to Mannion.

Like her mother, she could be moody and withdrawn, sometimes acquiring a haunted cast to her gaze, a tight set to her mouth, betraying an inner turmoil. The moods never seemed to last long, however, and considering what had become of her mother, Mannion was grateful. Vangie seemed to prefer the company of horses to that of people. In that way, she was like her father. She had a close bond with Willow and Jack—a bond Sarah hadn't had even with her preoccupied husband—and for that Mannion was grateful, too.

She'd be all right, he thought. She might have some of her mother's moods and her father's reclusiveness, but she was a sweet soul. And she had her horses. She'd be all right. She'd meet a nice boy and get married in her own sweet time. As far as Mannion was concerned, she could take her time. He didn't know what he'd do without her.

Now as he watched her through the window continue to roll out the dough, Vangie glanced out at him, as though sensing a presence on the porch. She looked back down at her dough and then snapped another look out the window, frowning curiously. She set down the roller, leaned closer to the window and pressed her hands against the glass around her face, blocking out the lamp-light's reflection.

When she saw her father on the porch, she smiled broadly, showing her white teeth.

"Papa!" Mannion heard her call through the window.

She turned quickly away from the window and disappeared. Quick footsteps sounded from inside the house, growing louder. Mannion stepped up to the door and a moment later it opened and Vangie threw herself into his arms.

"Oh, Papa—it's late and I was getting worried!"

"Oh, heck, darlin'," Mannion said, wrapping his arms around the girl. "You know me. I can never make it home at a decent time." He held her out away from him, smiled down at her. "Did you keep a plate warm for your old pa?"

"Don't I always?" Vangie said with feigned snootiness, narrowing her brown eyes—her mother's eyes—and planting a fist on her denim-clad right hip. She swung around and flounced into the kitchen, her men's small-sized stockmen's boots clomping on the walnut puncheons. "Right this way, kind sir. Did you rundown the bad guys?"

Mannion removed his hat and pegged it, removed his cartridge belt and six-shooters, and pegged them, too. He ran a hand through his hair. "Don't I always?"

"Of course, you do. You're my father, after all." Vangie walked over to the range and pulled a speckled black pan down from the warming rack. "You wash up and I'll set the food out for you."

"All right, honey," Mannion said, yawning, the day's travails weighing heavily on his aging body now as they had on his mind. He'd started feeling the effects of his tumble from Red's back not long after he'd left the abandoned ranch.

He walked over to the washstand abutting the wall to the right of the range and the wet sink with a handpump running up out of the floor. The water in the porcelain pitcher was warm. Vangie always warmed it for him when she expected him home soon.

"Tell me about your day, Papa," she said as she spooned the contents of the pot onto a china plate, steam rising around her with the mouth-watering aroma of beef stew.

Unbuttoning a shirt sleeve, Mannion said, "You know I don't like to talk about it, honey."

"Did you bring any of them back alive, Bloody Joe?"

Mannion glanced over his shoulder at her, gave her a tolerant grimace.

She smiled crookedly at him.

"Oh, Papa, I'm just joking," she said, setting the pot in the wreck pan in the sink then reaching for the coffee pot steaming on the range. "I know you don't like to talk about it. You don't like to talk much about anything."

"Talk's cheap, darlin'," Mannion said with a weary smile.

He washed and toweled off and, leaving his shirt-sleeves rolled up to his elbows, moved over to his customary place at the head of the table. Filling a glass with buttermilk from a crock jug she'd retrieved from the springhouse when he had been washing, Vangie watched him.

Mannion slid out his chair and sat down. "Looks delicious, honey," he said, gazing down at the nicely marbled and charred beef chunks, carrots, potatoes, onions and peas swimming in a rich, dark-brown gravy. Vangie had set a small plate with two slices of sourdough bread and a small bowl of butter on the table fronting his plate.

Now she set the glass of buttermilk down before him, as well. She frowned down at him, planting her fist on her hip. "What's eating you, Papa?"

What was eating him? he thought. *What wasn't?*

It had been a long day. He'd killed a woman who'd wanted killing, made a fool of himself in the San Juan in front of his woman, whom he'd probably lost, and the town council was gunning for his head.

That last didn't bother him all that much. Members of the town council every so often came gunning for his head. But when they got to thinking about what the town might be like without Bloody Joe to keep the proverbial wolves on their leashes, they had dramatic changes of heart.

He didn't like to let on to Vangie when something was bothering him, however. He might have been a hard man outside the Mannion house, but inside he wanted nothing more than to protect his singular daughter, his sweet soul of a girl whom he loved more than life itself, from the larger, dangerous world beyond their neat house and freshly painted picket fence.

"Come on—out with it, young man," she said, tapping the toe of her boot impatiently on the floor.

"Young?" Mannion laughed, spooning a bite of the succulent stew into his mouth. Chewing, he said, "I haven't been young in quite a spell, darlin'."

"Don't change the subject."

"This is delicious, honey," he said around another mouthful of food. "Why don't you let me eat it?"

"All right." Vangie grabbed a porcelain mug off a shelf and filled it with coffee at the range. She returned to the table and sat down in her usual place, to her father's right, and said, "I'll be waiting right here when you're done."

Mannion scowled at her as he slathered butter on a slice of bread. "You know I don't talk about my work, honey."

"I want you to talk about it this time."

Mannion dunked the bread in the stew and took a bite. "Why?"

"This time's special, I can tell. You're not yourself. Your eyes are dark and you're talking even less than usual." Vangie sat back in her chair, crossed her arms on her chest, and gave a pained, deeply worried look. "I'll be danged if you don't *look* old, Pa!"

"Ha! Don't doubt that a bit." Mannion looked at his daughter holding her steady gaze on him. She'd seen it, too. Just like Jane had. Even Rio had.

He hadn't realized his malaise had been so obvious. His cheeks warmed with embarrassment. He was not a man who normally showed his feelings to the world. He prided himself on his poker face, in fact.

Mannion was surprised that as he gazed back at his daughter's gently pleading eyes, he felt a softening in his resolution to remain silent about the woman he'd killed. Not only that, but he felt himself feel the *need* to talk to Vangie about it. Talking it out might unburden his heart.

But then he'd only burden Vangie's heart.

On the other hand, maybe he didn't give his daughter enough credit for her toughness. Maybe he'd been worried for so long that she'd have Sarah's same weakness —a rot in the core of her soul—that he'd failed to see how strong she was.

She was strong, wasn't she? There was strength in that steady, brown-eyed gaze.

Also, she was no longer a child. At seventeen, she was almost a woman.

Why not open up to her, Mannion? Maybe she'd open up to you more. She did a lot of talking but it was usually only about the horses or what food she was going to cook for him that night, about that wicked wind that had come up and frightened Willow so bad she'd leaped the fence and galloped into the country.

Never about things she felt.

She hadn't because he hadn't.

He had the urge to open up to her now.

My God, Bloody Joe—what has come over you?

Those eyes. Those damn eyes.

Sarah's eyes...

That stopped him cold. Vangie had not seen her mother's eyes in those last days. She'd been a baby in a crib. Mannion had seen those eyes every morning and evening. He'd seen them one last time—and what a haunting image they had burned into his brain! —just before she'd gone.

It had been a Sunday morning. He'd slept in. By the time he'd risen the sun was up. Sarah's side of the bed was empty, the covers thrown back. Yawning, Mannion had walked to the bedroom window just in time to see her standing in the fork of the old cottonwood in their back-yard, just below the window. She must have sensed his gaze—his shocked and befuddled gaze as he'd stared down at his wife standing in the tree, her nightgown billowing in the breeze, a red ribbon in her hair.

A noose around her neck.

A nightmare image, for sure.

Around her, green leaves flashed gold in the Kansas sunshine.

She'd looked up at him, given him that haunting look not unlike the look of the woman he'd killed as she'd stared down the barrel of the rifle at him. The next second, Sarah had stepped off the tree and into thin air, the rope tied off at the base of the tree quickly taking up its slack.

Mannion had pounded on the window: "*Sarah, noo!*"

Then the baby had started crying.

His guts tightened as he sat staring at that seventeen-year-old baby now—his daughter. He must have given an involuntary wince, because her brows knotted more tightly and her gaze became even more intense, more concerned.

"What is it, Poppa?"

Mannion feigned a smile. "You'd best finish your pie and go to bed." He leaned forward and resumed eating. "Getting late."

CHAPTER 6

MANNION COULDN'T SLEEP.

He tossed and turned.

Just when he'd been about to finally nod off, a storm had blown in, thunder rumbling like kettle drums, lightning flashing in the windows, lighting up his entire room, the dresser, the armoire, his gun rack, hat tree, the elk head on the wall over the door, the oval, gilt-framed ambrotypes, one his and Sarah's wedding photograph, on the red-and-gold papered walls.

As he lifted his head from his pillow in deep frustration, another blast of near lightning lit up the room. In that flash, he saw Sarah standing at the foot of his bed, looking down at him with the same expression she'd given him just before she'd dropped to her annihilation.

In the next flash, Sarah became the woman he'd killed, aiming a rifle at him, staring down the barrel with those eyes cast with all the sadness of the universe and a self-satisfied cunning—pinning it all, the universe's malaise as well as her own, on him.

"Damnation!" Mannion groused, tossing the covers back and dropping his feet to the floor.

He stood. The rain lashed the house with a wind-driven roar, rattling the windows. He walked heavily to the armoire, opened a door, and pulled out the bottle he kept for sleepless nights. He plucked out the cork, took a pull, then another, deeper pull. He started to return the cork to the bottle then reconsidered.

Holding the bottle by its neck, he walked to the window and gazed out into the murky, rain-lashed night, the lightning illuminating the yard in which he and Vangie had transplanted wild berry shrubs, firs, and a few Ponderosa pines. Vangie's old tree swing still dangled from a sycamore, jerking this way and that in the wind.

Mannion looked at the sycamore to which the swing was attached. He shuddered when the sycamore became the cottonwood, and Sarah was once again in the fork, the noose around her neck, just now looking up at him as if sensing him here.

She'd just turned away from him and started to drop when Mannion swung around sharply with a gasp, taking another deep pull from the bottle and raking his hand down his face, squeezing his eyes closed to rid them of the nightmare image of his young wife's suicide.

His heart banged in his chest.

He was about to take another pull from the bottle when he tensed, frowning. He'd heard something. Voices maybe, beneath the roar of the rain. He turned to gaze out the window again.

Lightning flashed, showing only the jostling of branches and the tree swing and the bending of the grass in the wind.

No one would be out in this weather.

Mannion turned from the window, took one last pull from the bottle. He had to get to bed.

He pulled the bottle down, looked at it, reconsidering.

What the hell? He'd had a miserable day.

He set the bottle on the table beside the bed, crawled into bed, adjust his pillows, then lay back against the headboard, drawing the covers up. He took the bottle and cradled it in the crook of his arm.

Long damn day, long damn night.

The whiskey, however, took the bite out of both.

He smiled, took another pull, then another...

He must have nodded off. The sudden clamor of breaking glass jerked him out of a heavy slumber. He blinked and looked around, startled and disoriented.

Vangie's scream cut through the sudden silence in the wake of the storm.

"Papa!" she yelled.

"Vangie!"

Mannion threw the covers back and bounded out of the bed, which he vaguely noted was wet. There was a heavy thud and he realized he must have knocked the bottle over during his drunken slumber, and now he'd knocked it onto the floor. Ramming a corner of the bed table with his bare left foot, he gave a yowl and, limping, ran to the door.

"Papa!" Vangie screamed from downstairs. She slept down there, in the bedroom off the kitchen.

Instantly, Mannion smelled smoke.

"Fire, Pa!"

Smoke roiled in the dark hall. Mannion saw the ominous orange of flickering flames playing amongst the shadows as it issued up through the stairwell.

There was another crash of breaking glass followed by a heavy thud.

Again, Vangie screamed.

Mannion ran forward, got his feet entangled, and dropped headlong to the floor so hard his ears rang. "*Damnation!*"

"Papa!"

He looked up to see Vangie's slender shadow running up the stairs, the orange light of the flames flickering in her hair.

"The house is on fire, Papa! We have to get out of here!"

She ran to him, nightgown billowing around her bare legs. She dropped to a knee and grabbed his left arm with both hands. "Papa!"

"Oh...oh...Christ!" he said, blinking to clear the exploding stars from his vision.

"Good God, Papa!" She must have realized he was drunk. "We have to get *out* of here!"

She grunted as she pulled hard on his arm and half-rose, trying to bring the big man up with her. Her hair swung down to cover her face.

"I'm com...I'm comin'..." Mannion said, pushing up with his hands.

As he did, the smoke grew thicker, burning his eyes. Vangie was coughing and now Mannion was too as his lungs filled.

From outside, he heard men whooping and hollering.

His brain still a whiskey-sodden fog, he was slow to realize that the men howling outside like moon-crazed coyotes were tied to the fire. When he did, rage ignited in him, and he was more easily able to heave himself to his feet.

"Okay," he said, coughing against the smoke, tears running down his cheeks from his burning eyes. "Okay...let's go..."

Vangie held him tightly around the waist as he made

his way unsteadily down the stairs, trying to move faster than he was able in his condition. A couple of times, he almost fell.

When they gained the parlor at the base of the stairs, his guts turned when he saw the flames licking up over the settee and climbing the wall on his left, curling and burning the paper. On the parlor's right side, velvet curtains billowed over the two large windows in the wind. Broken glass lay on the floor at the base of the billowing drapes.

Raw fury burned through Mannion. Some bastard had thrown a torch or a whiskey bottle with a whiskey-soaked rag for a wick into the house!

"I got you, Papa...I got you," Vangie said as she led him through the parlor toward the door leading to the backyard.

"Hold on!" he said, suddenly stopping and again almost falling in his drunkenness. "My guns! Go on outside and run, Vangie!" he yelled as he stumbled his way toward the door leading to the kitchen.

"There's no time, Papa!"

"Get outside and run for it, daughter!" Mannion bellowed, hearing men laughing outside beneath the roaring of the flames. He knew he was likely sending his daughter to the wolves, but it was either death by wolves or death by flames.

Gasping for air and coughing, Mannion stumbled into the kitchen, which was also on fire, the air thick with smoke, the area around the food preparation table and the wall above it covered in leaping flames. Glass from a broken whiskey bottle and a burning rag shown beneath the flames near the table.

Cursing with fury, Mannion grabbed his guns and

shell belt off a wall peg. He grabbed his hat, as well. He didn't know why. The move was automatic.

When he had the gun belt looped over his shoulder and his hat on his head, he stumbled back out into the parlor where Vangie was waiting for him, a shadowy figure engulfed in smoke, flames licking up over the ceiling above her now. She had her arm hooked over her eyes and was bent forward, coughing.

"Good Lord, girl!"

Vangie lowered her arm and yelled thinly, "Hurry, Papa!"

Mannion ran toward her, so overcome with drink and smoke, his eyes burning, that he tripped over the leg of an end table.

"Christ!" He dropped to his knees, the guns and belt falling down his arm.

"*Papa!*"

Vangie ran over, helped him to his feet and, arm in arm, strangling on the smoke, gasping for air which they found damn little of, they stumbled to the back door. Vangie fumbled it open and pushed her father through it. Mannion tripped over the threshold and fell to a knee on the back porch. Vangie grabbed his arm again, pulled him up, and led him down the back steps and into the yard.

When they were well away from the house in which the fire roared and cast an eerie orange glow into the darkness, revealing trees and shrubs and a dimly star lit sky, father and daughter fell together on their hands and knees in the grass cold and wet from the rain, violently coughing, tears running down their cheeks.

To Mannion's right, Vangie screamed, "*Papa!*"

Mannion jerked his head toward her. Horror engulfed him when he saw a grinning, horseback rider pulling her up onto his horse, the horse neighing and shaking its head, sidestepping. Another rider rode up around the first rider and the screaming and flailing girl.

The second rider curveted his chestnut horse to face Mannion. Whip Helton smiled down at Mannion from beneath the brim of his leather hat. The white bandage over his nose and the one wrapped around his left hand glowed in the darkness.

Hooves thumped and horses blew. Mannion looked around to see the other three men he'd braced in the San Juan ride up around him. The eyes of their horses glowed orange in the light of the growing conflagration behind Mannion.

Beyond Whip Helton, Vangie was desperately fighting the man who'd drawn her up onto his blaze-faced dun horse. The man was laughing as he pinned her arms to her sides and pulled her taut against him, nuzzling her neck. Vangie screamed in revulsion.

"That's...my...daughter..." Mannion tried to yell against the smoke still constricting his throat, terror gripping him, heart pounding. He glared up at Whip Helton smiling down at him. "Turn her loose, damn you!" He coughed violently, cleared the tears from his eyes with a sleeve of his balbriggan top. "She has no part in this!"

Helton held up his bandaged hand. "Doc said I've probably lost the use of this. So, she does now, Bloody Joe!" Helton pulled the six-shooter from the holster thonged on his right thigh, swung it over the horn of his saddle, and clicked the hammer back.

He narrowed his eyes, flared a nostril, and hardened his jaws.

Vangie turned from where she was being pawed by the man who'd drawn her up onto his horse, tears glistening in her eyes which glinted with the orange flames of the fire consuming her and Mannion's house.

She slid her gaze to Helton then to then to the gun in his hand and then to Mannion. "Papa!" she sobbed as the man's hands roamed her chest, working their way up under her nightgown, kneading her breasts, throwing his head back and howling.

Heart racing in panic, Mannion reached for one of his guns on the ground before him. He pulled it out of its holster and had just raised it but not yet drawn the hammer back before he saw Helton aiming his own six-gun at him.

Helton canted his head toward the sobbing Vangie and the laughing rider, who had swung her around so that her back was against his chest, his hands violently molesting her under the gown as he buried his face in her neck. Her high-kicking legs were bare and pale and glistening wet in the firelight from the rain-sodden grass.

"She's all ours now, Bloody Joe," Helton yelled above the loudening roar of the burning house. "You know me —I'll treat her right!"

He winked then narrowed the eye gazing down the barrel of the six-shooter in his hand at Mannion's head.

Flames lapped from the barrel.

After a brief, thundering pain, everything stopped right then and there for Bloody Joe.

CHAPTER 7

COLE SHRAKE REINED HIS DAPPLE CREAM TO A HALT ON a grassy, pine-peppered rise, hooked his right leg over his saddle horn, and gazed down into the broad valley before him.

"My, my, my," Shrake said, thumbing his black Stetson up off his forehead. "Ain't that an impressive sight? Hard to believe one man can own so much." He whistled, and then a smile stretched his knife-slash mouth. "And have so much to lose..."

He chuckled as his gaze encompassed the headquarters of Garth Helton's Spur Ranch. The main house sat up a slight rise to the right of the working part of the ranch—the bunkhouses, the cook shack, the several corrals including a round breaking corral, blacksmith shop, and even a shed where Helton had beer brewed by a professional brewer he'd called in all the way from Germany because he didn't care for "the slop" they served around here, especially in Del Norte, a town he had a love/hate relationship with.

The main house was part chateau and part hunting lodge to which every autumn Helton invited friends from

back East and even Europe to spend a month of drinking
—mostly drinking, Shrake had heard—and hunting
mountain lions, elk, and grizzly bears. It was a big, hulk-
ing, two-story affair. It resembled two long bunkhouses
set one atop the other, with a broad front porch and a
balcony off Helton's second-story office.

The land around the headquarters was gently undulat-
ing, tall, lime-green grass and sage aproning gradually to
high hills and bluffs topped with pines and firs. All of it
was capped by a cobalt sky as clean this fine late-summer
morning as a freshly scrubbed baby's ass. Not a cloud in
sight.

Only a few black specks of grazing cows shone on the
slopes around the headquarters. Most were still running
loose up in the high country. They'd be gathered and
brought down in a month or so, the cattle of Helton's
neighbors cut from the herd (though Helton had a reputation for being too greedy to not overlook a few, Shrake
smiled as he remembered), the new calves branded, and
the steers driven to market.

Something flashed in the sun on the second-floor
balcony fronting the double front doors of Garth
Helton's office. Shrake squinted until he saw the tall,
broad-shouldered, potbellied figure of Helton himself,
master of his universe, clad all in black—black shirt,
black vest, black pants—lower binoculars from his eyes
and beckon impatiently with one long, thick arm.

Shrake chuckled. The old man had spotted him ogling
the compound. Even in his sixties and going to seed, the
old man didn't miss a thing.

Shrake toed the empty stirrup, turned the horse
toward the valley, and clucked. Horse and rider dropped
down the grassy apron slope at a trot then, bottoming
out in the valley, rocked into a gallop until Shrake and

the dapple cream rode through the portal in which the name HELTON and the Spur brand—a Spur tilted inside a box—had been burned into the stout overhead crossbar.

As Shrake crossed the yard, he nodded to a man standing on guard duty in the shade of a willow tree, holding a carbine in his folded arms and smoking a cigarette. Shrake followed the two-track trail outlined in rocks up the rise and saw a tall, familiar, blonde-headed figure on the front porch. Landry Helton, at nineteen the Heltons' youngest daughter and the only one left at home —at least when the only other child, the twenty-five-year-old Whip, wasn't off sowing his wild oats with a nasty bunch of local hardtails.

Landry was also barefoot, Shrake saw as he drew within twenty feet of the two hitchracks set to either side of the porch steps. His loins warmed. The girl had the cutest little pink feet Shrake had ever seen and, being somewhat of a ladies' man, he wasn't too proud to admit, he'd seen a few.

Shrake smiled up at the girl who'd stopped sweeping and was standing at the top of the porch steps, leaning forward on the broom, both hands closed over the end of it, her pert chin resting atop them. Clad in a too-tight, lace edged day dress that complemented her figure just fine, she smiled crookedly down at him.

"Hello, there, Mister Shrake," she said saucily. "What brings you out to the Spur, if I might ask?"

"Why, you, darlin'," Shrake said, keeping his voice down as he swung down from the dapple cream's back. He was a tall, mustached man clad nearly all in black himself save a brown leather vest over his black, bib-front shirt with white piping scrolled on the sleeve cuffs. He had two big pistols on his hips and a pretty Henry rifle in the oiled boot of his saddle. "Don't you know that by now?"

The flaxen-haired blonde gave a caustic snort and then curled that smile again with one half of her full-lipped mouth.

Shrake tied the reins at the hitch rack, climbed the steps, and stopped on the porch beside the girl. He leaned down to whisper into her ear. "You're lookin' mighty fine today, Miss Helton."

Landry placed one bare foot atop the other. "Why thank you, Mister Shrake." Her smiled stretched to include her entire mouth. "Maybe we should have a picnic later, Mister Shrake? I know a good spot on Porcupine Creek. It's just beautiful! We could take Ivanhoe!" Ivanhoe was her dog.

Shrake glanced around to make sure no one had overheard then leaned down to the girl and, with a wink, said, "Now, haven't I told you I never mix business with pleasure?"

She glowered up at him. "You're just a tease, Mister Shrake. I hear the only girl you got eyes for is that half-breed girl over to the Yellow Butte Road Ranch!"

Shrake opened his mouth to respond but closed it when Garth Helton's voice thundered from inside the lodge: "Shrake, stopping chinning with my daughter and haul your freight up to my office pronto!"

Shrake turned to the chateau's two stout oak doors, the Spur brand burned into each. "Comin', Mister Helton!"

He turned to the girl again, winked and pinched his hat brim to her. "Some other time, Miss Helton."

Landry giggled and resumed sweeping.

Shrake glanced at the chateau's closed doors then turned to the girl again and smiled again, intimately. She might have been fun, but Shrake didn't mix business with pleasure. Besides, he knew that if Garth Helton caught him in a dalliance with his daughter, he'd likely stretch hemp. He swung around, opened one of the two big doors, and stepped into the house, doffing his hat as he did.

"Hurry up, Shrake!" thundered Helton's angry, raspy voice once more.

Shrake smiled and started forward. An impatient man was Mister Helton, the lord of the land in these parts. Under the circumstances, however, he had a right to be, Shrake supposed.

Shrake stepped up to the broad, varnished wooden stairway that rose ahead of him, splitting the house in half, and gazed up at the big, broad-faced, clean-shaven man of some sixty-odd years and with a thinning cap of salt-and-pepper hair on his square, rough-hewn head.

"You've heard, I take it?" Shrake called.

Helton stood at the top of the stairs, feet spread, fists on his hips, puffing a fat stogy turned up at one corner of his broad mouth. "I've heard," Shrake said, drolly.

"Who told you?"

"A little bird flew out from town."

Shrake nodded. It figured. Helton had a lot of spies, a lot of men on his side, wanting his favor.

The old man blinked once then swung around and walked through the open door of his office. "Get up here!"

Shrake sighed and climbed the stairs, taking one heavy step at a deliberate time, spurs chinging. He walked into Helton's office to find Helton sitting behind the giant desk to Shrake's right. The desk was piled high with account books and files and loose papers of every shape and size as well as bovine health and range management books and catalogues.

More of the same lay in precarious stacks, on the floor and on various tables, throughout the room. Old traps and tack and trophy heads adorned the walls.

An oil painting of Mrs. Helton hung on the far wall, to the left of the open French doors that opened onto the balcony and a view of all of Helton's holdings to the north. In the painting, Mrs. Helton was a much more attractive women than the thin, craggy-faced crone Shrake had spied ghosting around the house, crooning to her daughter, on previous visits, a perpetual drink in her hand.

Shrake couldn't believe the woman, who appeared in her fifties, at least, had birthed the lovely Landry only nineteen years ago, which meant Mrs. Helton was likely much younger than she appeared.

There was a liquor cabinet on the wall to Shrake's left, under a ticking cabinet clock. An open cut-glass decanter sat on the cabinet. Helton had a half-filled glass of straight liquor on the desk blotter before him.

Like wife, like husband. Or was it vice-versa?

Shrake had no idea how anyone could live with such a bellicose old bull as Garth Helton without swilling the who-hit-John.

Helton was crouched over his desk, both arms on it, encircling the drink like some precious thing he needed to protect. He looked up at Shrake severely and said, "Why in the hell did you not stop him? I pay you to keep an eye on the town and an eye on my son whenever *he is in town!*"

He slammed his large, thick, open-palmed hand down on the blotter with a thundering *crack!*

It was true. Shrake, a regulator who worked mostly

covertly, posing as a gambler in towns he traveled through or toward on his way to a kill, had been hired by Helton to keep an eye on Del Norte. To keep an ear to the ground, so to speak. Helton owned several businesses in Del Norte and intended to run a spur line up to Del Norte from the Atchison, Topeka, and Santa Fe Railway farther south. He also wanted to run a narrow-gauge line from Del Norte farther up into both the San Juan Mountains and the Sawatch Range. Many of the other ranchers in the area as well as mine owners and a few prominent citizens of Del Norte opposed the idea.

They weren't opposed to prosperity but the breed of man or men such an endeavor would draw to the country and possibly create a cesspool every bit as fetid as that which Del Norte had been before they'd called Bloody Joe Mannion in from Kansas to fumigate the place, so to speak. The town had started out as a hide-hunters', fur trappers', and miners' camp—a lawless place around which freshly dead bodies were piled up every morning. Not only were many of the good citizens afraid of the track-laying and gandy-dancing breed, but the general hubbub and the danger that would stalk Del Norte's streets likely every night as well as every day.

They'd seen Leadville, Deadwood, Tombstone, and Abilene in their "heydays". They wanted Del Norte to stay small and somewhat civilized, which it generally was due to Bloody Joe 's firm hand.

Gamblers and regulators and outlaws of every stripe would come to capitalize on the growing wealth and job opportunities. More saloons would rise along the main street of Del Norte, creating competition for those already in existence. Helton wanted to know who was against him and who for him in town, so he could act accordingly. The old bulldog was ruthless when getting what he wanted and in taking down those opposed to his ambitious dreams of a vast fortune.

Shrake was also supposed to be keeping tabs on the old man's firebrand son, who'd been running off Helton's leash for years, not only embarrassing the family but causing trouble for the old man, as well. Shrake wondered how many fathers he'd had to pay for the daughters who'd had the grave misfortune of finding themselves in Whip's goatish sights.

Shrake held up his hands in supplication. "I know, I know. But the thing is, boss, Whip was barred from town. For a month. I wasn't expectin' him to be *in* town, so I took a little trip."

"Yes, out to Yellow Butte where I'm told you're fawning over some half-breed half your age."

That annoyed Shrake.

Was the old man keeping an eye on him the way he was keeping an eye on Del Norte and his son? Or the way he was *supposed* to be keeping an eye on Whip Helton, that was...?

Helton raised the cigar to his mouth, lowered his lids halfway down over his large, brown eyes, and took several puffs, saying around each puff, "Yeah, I know where you are and what you're doing at any given time. If you think I trust you when I don't trust any man on God's green earth, you've got another think coming. Hah!"

He slammed his hand down on the blotter again. "And I was right not to."

"I wouldn't go that far. It was an honest mistake."

"You got lazy." The old man smiled coldly inside the smoke wreathing around his big, granite-like head. "You got, shall we say, *restless*." He stretched his lips back from his large teeth and the stogie clamped within them.

Shrake sighed. He didn't know how to respond to

that. The old man was right. He'd gotten both lazy and "restless". He felt genuinely chagrined. He'd always prized himself for his professionalism. At least in getting the job done but he'd never been above having a dalliance with a pretty, plump whore. Especially a half-breed, when he could find them. The pretty ones were rare. He had a weakness for those, he had to admit if only to himself.

"What a damn mess," Helton said, flopping back heavily in his chair, making the swivel squawk.

Shrake asked, "Did the little bird who told you all that happen tell you *all* that happened?" Some fellas were too weakhearted to give the old man all the facts. Especially when the facts were as bad as they were here.

Helton took another puff off the stogey and turned his head to stare pensively out the open French doors, the curtains over which billowed in the cool morning breeze. "He burned Mannion's house, shot him, and took his daughter." He paused then turned his dark eyes to Shrake. "But Bloody Joe pushed him mighty hard, I hear. Broke his nose, stuck a knife in his hand. Whatever my son has turned out to be, he's still a Helton, by God. You don't assault a Helton and expect to get away with it. At least," he added, turning to the open doors again. "At least, that bloody devil is dead!" He pounded the arm of his chair. "That makes the whole situation a helluva lot less complicated. We just have to make sure that..."

Helton stopped when he looked up to see Shrake slowly shaking his head. Dread in Helton's voice: "What is it?"

Shrake glanced at the open decanter on the cabinet behind him. "Uh...may I?"

"No. But you can sit down. I'm getting a neck ache looking up at you."

Shrake sighed then dropped into one of the two

chairs angled in front of the old man's desk. As a veteran hired killer, he deserved more respect than he was getting here. He wouldn't have put up such indignities if he hadn't been getting well paid—in extracurricular benefits out at Yellow Butte, especially. At least, he hadn't deflowered the old bull's daughter. He hiked a boot on one knee and hooked his hat over it.

"Don't tell me he's alive," Helton said softly, dreadfully.

"He's alive, Mister Helton," Shrake said, grimly. "Bullet just grazed his noggin. Whip must've been three sheets to the wind. Mannion'll be laid up in the San Juan, in his lady friend's suite, for a week or two with one helluva headache. But I overheard the sawbones say he should make a full recovery."

Helton cursed and pounded the desk again. He puffed the stogie almost manically, fingering his bottom lip as he gazed pensively out the open French doors again...at all his precious holdings that would hurt like hell to lose all because his son couldn't keep his wildcat in its cage.

He turned to Shrake. "Do we dare kill him?"

Shrake thumbed his chest. "Do you mean do *I* dare kill him? Hell, I'll feed him a pill he can't digest anytime you want."

"No, I mean what might be the repercussions?"

"Well, for one thing you're killin' a right famous man."

Helton held up a long, crooked—likely a rope accident—index finger. "*In*famous. Notorious."

"On the other hand, he has plenty of detractors amongst the mucky-mucks in Del Norte. From what I've heard in the saloons, a good many of them would *hire* him killed. He's become an embarrassment. A fossil, some call him. Holdin' the town back."

"My friends wouldn't take too kindly to what he did

to my son," Helton opined. "They need my friend-ship...my backing. Several want to invest in my ventures. They know they'd become rich men if my dreams for Del Norte come to fruition. If I pulled out, took my busi-nesses elsewhere, they'd lose a lot of money." He looked at Shrake. "They know that."

"What about the girl?"

"What about her?"

"Kidnappin' is illegal, Mister Helton. And, uh..." Shrake let the sentence trail off to an ominous death.

"And, uh, what?"

Shrake raised and lowered an arm to an arm of his chair. "What if he kills her?"

"He's my son. I'll get him off. Say it was an accident. He can't go to jail." Helton turned in frustration to the open French doors again. "He can't go to prison. God, how would it look to my investors back East? Besides, he's my only son. My God...what's become of that crazy kid? Screw loose, that's for sure." Turning to the regulator again, he said, "That's all it is, though. Something's missing up here." He tapped his temple and then said in a low, conspiratorial voice, "Run's in Berenice's side of the family. It's no fault of mine."

"No, no, of course not."

"Damnit!" Helton pounded the arm of his chair. "The problem will be Bloody Joe. He'll kill Whip...all because he couldn't keep his hands off one crazy girl. She was probably making eyes at him in town, giving him the wrong idea. Kind of odd, I hear. Speaking of crazy." Helton looked at Shrake again and again tapped his temple.

"Word going around is she's touched, like her mother was. Suicide, you know."

"Really?"

"Hanged herself. In Kansas. Of course, Bloody Joe likely drove her to it. But the seed had to be here." Yet again, the old man tapped his temple and gave the regulator a slow wink.

"Oh, of course!"

"Do you have any idea where my son is?"

"No. Do you?"

"No, dammit. I wish he'd come home where I can protect him." Helton turned thoughtful again. "This is all gonna take some figuring." He pensively bounced his hand off the arm of his chair, puffing the stogie. Again, he turned to Shrake. "In the meantime, Bloody Joe's long reign of terror has come to an end. If not...well. If there's one man who can ruin me, it's Bloody Joe!"

"He's only one man, Mister Helton. You have a whole outfit."

"Yeah, but Mannion's a holy terror. There'll be a reckoning for what Whip did, mark my words. He'll find a way."

Again, he bounced his big hand off the arm of his chair, staring out the doors, puffing the stogie. The wind blew the curtains inside. "Yes...yes...yes," he said finally, slowly, turning to Shrake again, his eyes wide and bright with savagery. "Kill him. Kill Bloody Joe. That'll end it right then and there. If the town suspects it's me who did it, they're all too afraid of me—too *greedy*—to do anything about it."

"Yessir, Mister Helton."

"Get out of here. Get it done. As fast as possible."

"Yessir, Mister Helton."

Shrake rose to go.

CHAPTER 8

THOSE EYES.

Those damn eyes.

They peered through a red curtain of misery at Bloody Joe. First the eyes of the unknown woman, then Sarah's eyes. Accusing eyes. Cunning eyes.

Then they were Vangie's terrified eyes as she gazed down at him, kicking her wet bare legs, struggling in vain to free herself from the man holding her, molesting her under her nightgown, nuzzling her neck then tipping his head back and yowling like a moon-crazed coyote.

By sheer force of will, even in his painful unconsciousness, Mannion shifted his gaze from Vangie's remembered image to that of the man who'd pulled her up onto his horse. A long-haired man in a ragged bowler, a scraggly blond mustache mantling his thin-lipped mouth. Like Whip Helton, he was in his mid-to-late twenties. He had a bulge in his nose from where it had been broken and not set correctly, and acne scars marred his gaunt cheeks. Mannion remembered the man looking down at him while he'd ravaged Vangie, his bulging blue eyes ablaze with lust and mockery.

Luke Nordekker.

That was his name. It floated up out of the depths of Mannion's unconsciousness. Nordekker had ridden for the Kitchen Sink at one time before he'd been fired for stealing hay and selling it to nesters though Mannion hadn't been able to make the charges stick. Unemployable in these parts, Nordekker had thrown in with Whip Helton's gang of thieves, murderers, and rapists. Mannion remembered he wore a long, denim jacket, rode a blaze-faced dun, probably stolen, and had two pearl-gripped Bisley revolvers on his hips.

Also probably stolen.

Mannion would remember those images. He resolved to remember them even in the depths of his painful unconsciousness, grinding his teeth together in silent fury. Such memories would come in handy soon. Very soon.

By sheer force of will, he heaved himself up toward the mouth of consciousness. He was like a man swimming in a deep lake with lead tied to his ankles. Furiously, he clawed at the water, tracing broad strokes with his arms, desperately kicking his encumbered feet, grunting with the effort, the watery grunts echoing in his ears as he toiled.

He propelled himself up...up...up to the surface of consciousness, finally breaking free, taking a long, deep, gasping breath and opening his eyes.

Jane Ford sat before him, clad in a ruffled white shirtwaist, her copper red hair pinned atop her lovely head. Her lustrous brown eyes stared down at him with deep concern and sorrow. She was just then pulling a wet cloth away from his face. She held a bowl of water on her lap.

He glanced around. He was in Jane's four-poster,

canopied bed in her third-floor suite at the San Juan Hotel and Saloon.

Sitting on the bed beside him, Jane dropped the cloth in the water and placed her pale, freckled, beringed hand on Mannion's chest, pushing him back against the deep feather pillow.

"Joe, rest easy."

"Vangie," Mannion croaked, sitting up, pushing against the woman's hand so that she increased the pressure to hold him down.

Jane put some steel in her voice. "Rest easy, Joe. Doctor's orders. Stringbean took a posse out. Doc Bohannon was just riding back into town after delivering Mrs. Ferguson's baby. He saw the fire. He got to you just as the attackers were galloping away. He saw Vangie on one of their horses, heard her screaming."

Mannion winced against the throbbing pain in his right temple. He raised a hand, felt the bristle of fresh sutures. "How come...I'm not...?"

"Dead?" Jane shrugged. "God knows. Somehow, the bullet just grazed your skull. You must have turned your head just before you were shot. Still, the doctor thinks you might have a fracture. You're going to need to rest, Joe."

"Rest?" Mannion pushed Jane's hand away from his chest and sat up, his face a swollen red mask of rage. "They took *Vangie!*"

Again, Jane placed her hand on his chest. "I know, Joe. I'm so sorry, but—"

With a sudden, involuntary flick of his left hand, Mannion pushed her hand away. She gave a shocked yell, eyes widening, as she dropped over the side of the bed and struck the floor with a resolute thud and a startled grunt. The washbasin struck the floor and overturned, spilling the water onto the carpeted floor beside her.

Sitting up, Mannion dropped his feet to the floor and looked down at the woman sprawled on the floor beneath him. His lower jaw sagged in shock, and his heart contracted with self-revulsion.

"Oh, Jane...Jane...I'm so—" He rose from the bed and extended a hand to her then immediately drew it back and clutched his temple. He staggered first right and then left, the room pitching around beneath his bare feet. Part of the problem, he knew, was that he was hungover. He'd been dead drunk, and that's how he'd let those savages take Vangie...

"See?" Jane said where she lay with her head and shoulders resting back against the wall where she'd fallen, arms thrown out to both sides, hands flat against the floor. "You have to stay in bed, Joe!"

He staggered again to the right, trying to get his feet set beneath him, left hand closed over his throbbing temple. "I can't...can't...leave her to those devils..."

Jane rose to a sitting position, the bun atop her head loosening and tumbling onto her shoulder. Mannion turned to her, staggered over to her, crouched over her, extending his hand. "Oh, for Heaven's sakes, honey, I'm—"

She thrust her hand up, palm out. "Joe, no—don't help me or you're gonna end up down here on top of me and you're way too big!"

She pulled her lips back from her teeth and pushed herself to her feet.

A little breathless, she smoothed her skirt and blouse, repaired the bun, and stood regarding Mannion sadly. Her face crumpled with sorrow. She stepped forward and wrapped her arms around him and buried her head in his chest still clad in the balbriggan top he'd worn the previous night. "I'm so sorry, Joe!"

She wrapped her arms around his waist and squeezed.

She pulled her head back from his chest to gaze up at him. "Who were they?"

"Helton."

Jane's face crumpled again in anguish. She placed both hands on his broad face. "Oh, God, Joe!"

He placed his hands on her shoulders. "You think it's my fault. I see it in your eyes. I pushed him too hard. Maybe I did. But he shouldn't have burned my house, taken my daughter. That's a line you don't cross." He didn't mention he'd been drunk, to boot. That was too much for him to admit to. He'd have to bear that cross alone.

"Oh, Joe..."

"He should have come for me and me only." Mannion swung away from Jane too quickly, had to grab a post of the canopied bed to keep from falling. "I'm gonna *kill that sonofabitch! Every last one of them!*"

His enraged baritone voice thundered around the room, echoing off the walls.

When the room steadied somewhat, Mannion pushed away from the bed and staggered toward the bedroom door.

"Joe, my God—you're not going out there like *that*?"

Mannion stopped, looked down at himself. He glanced over his shoulder at Jane. "What choice have I got? Every minute I lay in that bed, those devils get just that much farther away with Vangie."

He grabbed his hat off a peg by the door, set it gently on his tender head.

Jane hurried over to him, sandwiched his big face in her hands, and gazed up at him beseechingly. "Joe, you'll never make it. The doctor demanded one week of bed rest at the very least. If you go after them, Joe, you'll die!"

Mannion placed his hands lightly on her forearms. "I'll ask you again, honey, what choice do I have? They burned my house and took my daughter!"

Jane drew a steeling breath and stepped back. She smoothed her skirt against her thighs, worked on her bun a little more, drew another breath. "All right, all right." She reached up and laid a hand against his cheek. "I will fetch what you need. Tell me what and where."

"I have a spare set of duds at the office. I'll need my rifle." Mannion glanced around. "Where are my...?" His gaze landed on his six-guns hanging from a chair back. "All right. I'll need my rifle, a couple boxes of cartridges. Rio will help. We have some trail supplies there, too. My horse and my tack are at the livery barn." He frowned down at her. "Are sure you can handle all that?"

"What choice do I have?" She gave a dry chuckle though there was no humor in her eyes. "I can't have my man running around town in his underwear—can I? I'm supposed to be a respectable businesswoman, you know, Joe."

"I thought I'd lost you."

"I thought you had, too." Jane shook her head, frowning up at him. "Joe, I've never known any man like you. You're riddled with failings. You have a terrible temper, which you *cannot* control. You make a horse's ass of yourself. But..." Again, she placed her hand on his cheek. "You're the most passionate man I've ever known. You care and you care deeply. You hate deeply and you love deeply. What's more, though you've never told me, I know you love *me*. No man has ever loved me before, Joe. At least, not like you do."

"I didn't know—"

"That I knew?" She smiled, nodded. "I knew. No man could make love like you do without love in his heart." Tears welled in her eyes. "Just when I realize I love *you*, I'm going to lose you. Just my luck!"

She sniffed, brushed a tear from her cheek with the back of her hand. He opened his mouth to speak, but she shook her head, cutting him off, and turned to the door. "I'll fetch your things, Joe."

"Send one of the houseboys."

Jane shook her head. "No, I want to do it. I want to make sure to pack the right food." She drew her mouth corners down, eyes darkening with sadness. "It's probably the last thing I'll be able to do for you."

She stepped out and glanced back over her shoulder at him. "Rest until I get back. I'll have food sent up."

"I'm not hungry."

But she'd already closed the door.

———

"EASY, JOE, EASY," JANE SAID A HALF HOUR LATER.

She had one arm wrapped around Mannion's waist as she helped him down the carpeted stairs in the San Juan Hotel and Saloon.

"Not so fast, Joe!"

"No damn time to spare!"

He took a misstep and stumbled back against the railing with a grunt. "Oh!" He clutched his throbbing temple again, gritting his teeth.

"See, Joe? I told you. You have to take your time. You may have a cracked skull, for God's sake!" Jane looked up at him. She wore a knit shawl around her shoulders. "Are you sure you won't go back to bed?"

Mannion lowered his hand to his side. "Can't."

He turned toward the drinking hall below him in which a half-dozen mid-morning customers sat over their breakfasts of beer and raw eggs or, for the die-hards, whiskey shots, gazing skeptically up at the pair on the staircase.

"Here we go," Mannion said and continued down the stairs, Jane leaning close against him, her arm around his waist.

When they'd gained the bottom of the stairs, Mannion stopped for a breather then continued forward, weaving around the mostly vacant tables, all eyes in the room including those of the morning bar tender, Mort Crawley, on him, following his uncertain progress.

He felt buoyed by the fact of his gaining the batwings after tripping over a chair leg only once.

I've made it this far, he told himself, *I can make it all the way to wherever those devils have taken my daughter.*

It was empty encouragement, of course. He wasn't sure, given his pain and dizziness not to mention the weakness in his limbs, if he could even make it onto his horse.

As he and Jane pushed through the batwings and stepped out onto the San Juan's front porch, he saw his bay standing at the hitchrack to the left of the porch steps. The stallion had been craning his neck to watch a mule skinner's mongrel dog in the back of a freight wagon behind him but now, hearing foot thuds on the porch, Red turned his head forward.

Spying his rider, the bay pricked his ears, lifted his fine snoot, and gave a greeting whinny.

It was almost as though the stallion had sensed the trouble Mannion had been in the night before and had been worried about the outcome. Mannion wouldn't put it past the horse. He knew horses better than he knew most people, and he knew they had a prescience about things humans did not. Except for the gifted ones.

Sarah had been like that. She'd said she'd always sensed when Mannion had been in a tight spot, and she'd always been strangely stirred at odd times, finding out later that those odd times may very well have coincided with the passing of a family member.

Mannion smiled at his friend and closest companion outside of Vangie. "Hey, you old broomtail," he greeted the horse. "Hey, Rio."

His thickset, middle-aged deputy stood holding Red's reins and scowling up at his boss. He thumbed his weathered Stetson up off his forehead, shook his head, and brushed his fist across his chin.

"Doc says you're to stay in bed, Joe. Lookin' at you now, I can see why."

"Don't be an old lady, Rio." Mannion looked at Jane standing beside him. "I'll take the last steps myself. If I can't make it onto my horse, I'll go back to bed."

Jane sighed and removed her arm from around his waist. "Have it your way, stubborn man." She rose up on her tiptoes and planted a kiss on his cheek.

"Don't be thinkin' you're gonna get one of those from me," Rio said.

Mannion snorted a laugh and stepped forward. The porch was rising and falling around him but not quite as severely as the upstairs hall had been, nor the floor of the drinking hall. He thought he could make it. No. He *had* to make. He had to get Vangie back. And he had to turn Whip Helton toe-down with a cold shovel.

Same for the rest of his gang. Especially the bowler-hatted gent he'd seen pawing Vangie.

Mannion took another step, another...one more...then descended the porch steps without a hitch except for the burning throb all through his brain plate that made everything before him a little blurry. The world had become a mirage.

He stepped up to Rio.

"Which way'd they head?"

"South."

"Figures. Into the San Juans. Think I won't find 'em there."

"They think you're dead, boss, most like."

Mannion smiled. "Well, then, death's gonna pay 'em a call."

Rio said, "Stringbean's after them, you know. Stringbean's young but he's good. He'll get 'em. Hennessey's trackin' for him."

"How many's with him?"

Waite flinched at the question, glanced sheepishly down. "Five."

"Five's all he could get, eh?"

"Sorry, boss."

"The town knows Helton burned me out, don't they? They know they took Vangie."

Rio didn't answer either question. He kept his eyes on the ground.

Mannion looked around the street. Many dubious eyes were on him. Directly across the street, John Dunham was sweeping off his stoop but mostly he was watching Mannion. When the lawman turned toward him, the barber looked away quickly then stepped through the open door of his barbershop and closed the door behind him.

Mannion shuttled his gaze a little farther up the street to the north. It held on the dapper, little, bespectacled Mayor McQueen standing outside his brick law office, fingers in the pockets of his wool vest, gazing toward the San Juan. When his eyes met those of the town lawman, McQueen quickly dropped his chin and toed something on the boardwalk before him, pooching out his lips as though whistling.

"They've turned against me," Mannion said.

"It's not you so much. They're afraid of Helton."

"It's not Helton they should be afraid of," Mannion said. "It's me."

Rio lifted his eyes to meet his boss's gaze.

Mannion took his reins from his deputy and stepped up to his horse. He reached up to grab the horn then planted the bulk of his weight on his right rear heel as he lifted his left foot. "Here goes nothin'," he said, and toed the stirrup.

He hoisted himself with an agonized grunt into the saddle then sat there for a minute, grinding his molars as dynamite sticks of raw misery exploded behind his eyelids. His brain felt as though it were being tickled with red-hot, poison-tipped Apache arrows.

He thought he could even hear the warriors yowling raucously in his ears.

"Damn savages," he muttered, drawing a deep breath, willing the pain into the peripheries of his consciousness.

Instead of on the agony in his head, he concentrated on the broken-nosed face of Whip Helton and the bulging blue eyes of the wanton devil Luke Nordekker as the man's hands moved around inside Vangie's nightgown while she'd kicked and screamed against him.

Drawing another breath, feeling a little better though only incrementally so, Mannion looked up at Jane and smiled. "Thanks for the help." He wanted to tell her more than that but not in front of Rio. He had so much more to tell her, he suddenly realized now, though he wasn't sure why.

Why now?

She stood at the top of the porch steps, one hand across her belly, her other hand clenched into a fist against her mouth, silently sobbing. Tears ran down her freckled cheeks. Her deep brown eyes glistened with sadness.

"Anytime," she said in a voice quavering with raw emotion.

"I'm gonna hold you to that," Mannion said. He turned to his deputy. "Thanks, Rio."

Rio smiled up at him but there was only sadness in his eyes, as well.

Mannion reined the bay around and let him walk south for a block, wanting to ease into the ride, before he booted him into a trot.

Behind him, Jane came down the porch steps to stand close beside Rio, watching Mannion trot off into the morning shadows, his dwindling figure obscured by the mid-morning traffic of Del Norte until he followed a bend in the main drag and disappeared altogether.

Jane allowed herself a sob then canted her head against Rio's thick shoulder. "There goes death on a bay horse, Rio."

Rio gave a ragged sigh and raised a hand to pat the woman's back.

CHAPTER 9

"STRINGBEAN, YOU SURE YOU KNOW WHERE WE'RE goin'?"

Stringbean McCallister hipped around in his saddle to look back at the man riding directly behind him in his six-man posse. "No, but Mister Hennessey does." He turned his head to look at the broad back of the man riding ahead of him. "Don't you, Mister Hennessey?"

Five good citizens of Del Norte were all Stringbean had been able to convince to join him in riding after the bunch that had burned Marshal Mannion's house and kidnapped his daughter. Everybody in town pretty much figured it had been Whip Helton's bunch—what was left of them after the marshal had shot two in the San Juan the night before—and no one wanted to get crossways with the Helton family.

Namely, old Garth Helton himself. Everyone in this neck of the mountains knew what it meant to get crossways with old Helton. Nightriders in flour sack masks. Burning barns and houses, gunfire and hang ropes. Helton lived in these mountains the way men lived in them fifteen, twenty years ago. He did not change with the times. It helped that he knew men in high places who, because of the fortune he'd accrued after coming West from somewhere back East—first in mining and then in ranching and now railroading, to boot—backed his play.

Or they simply looked the other way.

Another reason Stringbean couldn't convince others to join his posse was because some had seen or heard what Marshal Mannion had done to Whip Helton the previous night, in front of half the town. At least in front of half the businessmen in town.

They thought the marshal had gone too far.

To Stringbean's way of thinking, maybe the marshal had, as he tended to do sometimes. Still, you don't mess with a man's family. No, sir. The family and a man's house are off-limits. Besides, Whip Helton and his bunch had been barred from town and they'd ridden into town in open defiance of the marshal's orders and were vandalizing a table in Miss Ford's establishment. They knew the marshal. They'd had to expect they'd be running up against him.

To Stringbean's way of thinking—and he admitted to being partial when it came to the marshal—those miscreants had gotten what they'd deserved.

The big man riding ahead of Stringbean turned his white-bearded red face and keen blue eyes back to Stringbean and said in his heavy Irish brogue: "Have no worries, me lads. If ol' Brian Hennessey can't track these mongrels, no one can."

Hennessey sold Harvest windmills for a living, but back during the Apache Wars he'd ridden for General Crook. He'd been a packer and a tracker, and he claimed to be able to track a June bug across a stormy lake. Stringbean believed him. Hennessey had helped Marshal

Mannion and Stringbean in the past when they'd gone after bank or stage robbers. Every time, Hennessey had led the marshal and Stringbean right into the outlaws' lairs and, being handy with a long gun, he'd helped take them down, as well.

Stringbean had faith that Hennessey would lead them to Helton or whomever had burned the marshal's house and taken his daughter. The doctor thought for sure it was Helton and his unwashed, hardtail pards.

"Why is it I feel like we're being led to the wolves?" asked another man riding behind Stringbean. This was George Bottoms, a shoe salesman in Del Norte who'd also once been an army man and still hunted elk in the mountains so knew his way around a rifle himself.

"Have a little faith," intoned Hennessey, tipping his head back and lifting his right hand and spacing his thumb and forefinger a half-inch apart. "Ay, just a wee bit of faith, my friends!"

The others riding behind Stringbean were the muscular twin well-diggers, Lyle and Steve Kowalski, and the Mexican roofer, Ernesto Gomez, who felt he owed the marshal a favor for saving his life when two drunken drifters had threatened to hang him for merely being Mexican and they'd wanted a little fun late one Saturday night behind the Come One, Come All hurdy-gurdy house on third street in Del Norte.

The posse was following a dry streambed up into the first front of the San Juans. The bed was cut deep and paved in solid stone with occasional loose rocks and boulders impeding the posse's course. The bed rose gradually, the banks to either side rising a hundred feet in places. Stringbean knew from experience that though the bed was dry this time of the year, in the spring, when the snow melted in the higher reaches, it was a rushing torrent, and you did not want to find yourself on the wrong side of it while hunting spring turkeys.

Beyond each bank, a mountain rose steeply, thick with columnar firs and pines in which birds piped, hawks screeched, squirrels chittered, and crows cawed raucously, unhappy with the intruders they've discovered in their remote mountain home. The air was winey with the smell of pine and mountain sage and damp rock where springs bled out through cracks in the chasm walls, forming narrow, twisting and turning rivulets.

Stringbean glanced at the hard stone floor of the riverbed beneath his zebra dun's clacking hooves then turned to peer forward again at the broad back of Brian Hennessey. "I don't understand what you're seein', Mister Hennessey. I mean, with all due respect—and I know you must be seein' somethin' or you wouldn't be leadin' us this way—but how can you see a thing on such a hard surface. Why, the floor of this cut is dang near solid granite, most places!"

"I think he's imagin' sign," quipped one of the Kowalski twins, Lyle, riding behind Stringbean.

"No, no, senores," called Ernesto Gomez, the short, stocky Mexican riding between the twins, who kept their distance from each other due to the fact that, from what Stringbean had been able to make out from their short, hushed but fervent bouts of sporadic arguing, they'd had a falling out over the Del Norte mercantiler's, Wilfred Drake's, comely clerk. "I saw several day-old horse apples farther back along the bed. It helps if you keep your eyes on the ground and not merely sit your saddle imagining the witchery you might experience if Senorita Lisa Anderson ever dropped her drawers for you!"

The jocular Mexican, who'd apparently also picked up on the subject of the twins' row, wheezed out a laugh.

Stringbean glanced over his shoulder as both twins—big blond men in their mid- to late-twenties—each good with a hunting rifle—cast the Mexican riding between them indignant scowls.

The shoe salesman, George Bottoms, who'd once ramrodded for a ranch in New Mexico until he'd taken an Apache arrow in his knee and had decided to adopt a more sedate lifestyle, said, "I'll let Hennessey watch the ground. Me, I'll be watching those ridges to either side of us, thank you very much. I still got this creepy-crawly feelin' we're bein' led to the wolves. At any moment, we're liable to spy a rifle angled down from one of those rock walls, only too late to do anythin' about it!"

Hennessey reined his horse to a sudden halt and curveted the beast, causing Stringbean and the other riders to tug back on their own reins, stopping their mounts in kind. "You fellas keep your voices down, an' mind ol' Brian now. We don't know how far ahead those said *gun wolves* are. They might have holed up in that old trapper's cabin under Crow Ridge. If so, my weary darlin's, they might just have, as dear George is so afeared of, a rider or two scoutin' their back trail. Now, I know you're bored and you're wishin' you weren't here—"

"Like the rest of Del Norte," grumbled Steve Kowalski, riding behind the Mexican, his heavy shoulders slumped in the saddle. He leaned to one side to spit chaw onto a flat, pale rock with a *splat!* then rubbed the back of his gloved hand across his blond-bearded mouth.

"Yes, yes, like the rest of Del Norte," agreed Hennessey. "The ungrateful cowards they are, too. Bloody Joe might be an uncompromising man, an' I'll give the ol' devil his due on that, but what other man could have tamed the mire of unwashed humanity Del Norte had become before he'd ridden into town with his big Russian .44s, eh? He cleaned it up with his iron fists, did Bloody Joe. He allowed it to prosper. He allowed *us* to prosper as you can only amidst lawfulness. Made Del Norte a place good citizens wanted to come and open businesses and help the others grow.

"And what is the thanks he gets after those seven long years? Most of Del Norte turned his back on him."

"Si, si," agree Gomez. "Mannion might be hard, but he's a good man. Not only did he save me from those gringos' necktie party, whenever someone in town needs roof repairs, he sends them to me. Me, I like Senor Mannion. And don't forget those human jackals burned his house and kidnapped his daughter."

The round-faced Mexican, his face carpeted in a short, patchy brown beard, shook his head and made an awful expression. "And what might they do to poor sweet Evangeline?" Again, he shook his head. "It is terrible to think of."

"Ernesto's right," said Bottoms. "I understand Mannion. He comes from an earlier time. Just like most of us excepting the young'uns amongst us. He knows what it takes to keep a lid on a town even in these more modern times, an' he's got the guts to not mind getting crossways with that lawless brute, Whip Helton or his thug of a father. How many years are the Heltons gonna keep stomping with their tails up in these parts before someone finally takes them down?"

"Mannion took him down," put in Gomez. "I just wish he would have taken him *all* the way down, *¿comprender?* What that lobo does to the girls"—again, he gave his head a slow, dark wag —"is just awful! I caught him molesting a little blonde German girl by the creek one day when I was doing a little panning. I objected and..."

He held up his left, black gloved hand missing its last finger. "...he shot off my little finger."

"I'll be damned," said Hennessey. "I always wondered why you wasn't sportin' all ten but was too polite to ask."

"I thought his mother must be a goat," quipped Lyle Kowalski, grinning mockingly back at the Mexican, who made a lewd gesture with one of his remaining fingers.

"All right, me lads." Hennessey reined his mount forward and booted it into a walk. "Nice an' quiet now, keepin' your peepers skinned on the ridges as well as on the trail, onward we go. Easy does it...quiet as church mice..."

Stringbean clucked to his dun and smiled to himself as he headed up the trail behind Hennessey. Truth was, he was feeling mighty good about how the old Irishman had dressed down the Kowalski brothers. Stringbean himself wouldn't have had the spine to do that. He didn't like to argue nor ruffle folks' feathers, because he too much liked being, well, *liked*.

Truth was, though, he secretly idolized Marshal Mannion. He sort of saw Mannion as the father he'd never had and looked up to the man for the way he commanded respect and even anger and hatred. For the way the marshal took that anger and even hatred so even-handedly—steady as a clipper ship cleaving choppy seas, a wind howling and sails full.

Truth was you either loved or hated the marshal.

Stringbean couldn't imagine being a man you either loved or hated, but he admired it. As for himself, he reckoned most folks liked him well enough, when and if they ever really thought about him. Oh, Molly Hurdstrom probably liked him just fine. She was the freighter's daughter he'd been sparking, riding over to her folks' place every Saturday evening just after supper and sitting with her on the wooden glider on the Hurdstrom family's porch, sipping tea or lemonade and eating strawberry shortcake.

Truth was, he wasn't really sure how Molly felt about him, because she'd never said, and he was too shy to ask her. But then, he'd never had the spine to tell her how he felt, either. Molly was friendly enough, and she'd held hands with Stringbean briefly a time or two when her mother hadn't been peering out the kitchen window at her and Stringbean, making sure nothing untoward was happening, like Stringbean sliding a little too close to Molly on the glider or, worse yet, stealing a kiss.

Yessir, what you had here in Stringbean McCallister was a mild-mannered man no one loved or hated. What you had here was an effective deputy who would likely never make a full marshal. Stringbean wasn't afraid of raising his voice, though, when things started getting out of hand, and most rowdies took his orders because he was just such a doggone reasonable guy just trying to do his job that he was hard to get mad at.

"All right, Stringbean," a drunk would say when Stringbean had been summoned to a saloon to break up a fight. "Don't get your drawers in a twist. Go ahead—throw the cuffs on and take me over to Hotel de Mannion. I could use a free meal, anyways."

(That's what Joe's office and jail were locally known as: Hotel de Mannion.)

Most if not all of Del Norte saw Stringbean as an agreeable fellow, just a twenty-four-year-old former stockman working for wages and doing the best he could with the gifts God gave him—which had been a talent for breaking broncs. He'd worked as an itinerant bronc buster on local ranches until one had thrown him a little too hard and dislocated his hip, which hadn't worked right since.

So, once he'd healed after being laid up for over a month in a bunkhouse over by Cimarron, on the Cimarron River, he'd come to Del Norte and applied for the deputy marshal's job and got it because no one else had applied for it, no one else wanting to work with the uncompromising Marshal Mannion, apparently. But Stringbean loved working for the man and secretly wished he himself were such a man you either loved or hated and who could take the hate without so much as batting an eye at it.

Or maybe even liking it a little despite the danger in it.

Stringbean suspected that deep down—and he'd been a keen observer of the marshal ever since he'd started working for the man—that Bloody Joe took a strange sort of pride in being hated. That's just how he was. A singular fellow, indeed. One who never backed water or gave ground for anyone. One, Stringbean suspected, who was a total stranger to fear.

Whereas Stringbean was not. But, oh, how he wished he were!

He had a feeling that if he were a little more like Marshal Mannion he'd know by now how Molly felt about him. Heck, he'd probably have known that a minute after meeting her. As for Stringbean himself, however, he was just going to have to wait and see. Maybe he'd made no impression at all on her. Maybe he never would.

Imagine that—a man who made no impression at all!

He wondered what being a man like Mannion was like —a man who knew within a matter of seconds after meeting a man exactly where he stood in that man's eyes.

Or in that girl's eyes, say...

Stringbean reined his horse in suddenly, having been in such a deeply pensive state he hadn't realized that Mr. Hennessey had reined his horse to a sudden halt before him. The dun rammed into the left hip of Hennessey's roan. Hennessey's mount gave an indignant whinny, and Hennessey turned to give Stringbean an annoyed scowl, his thick red brows furrowed over his deep, Irish-blue eyes.

"Dammit, Deputy!"

"S-sorry, Mister Hennessey. What're you stoppin' for?"

Hennessey lifted his head and loudly sniffed the air. "For God sakes, boyo—don't you smell it?" He sniffed again. "*Wood smoke!*" He turned to look up the forested ridge on their left. "Someone's nigh..."

CHAPTER 10

"'SOMEONE'S NIGH' STRINGBEAN MUTTERED TO himself, trying to make the phrase stick in his head, to understand it. "Oh, someone's near!"

Now, smelling the smoke himself, knowing he should have smelled it before now and would have if he hadn't been imagining a whole new life for himself in the life of Marshal Mannion—as if that could ever happen!—he shucked his Winchester repeater from his saddle boot and stared up the ridge on his left.

"What's the plan, boyo?"

"What?"

"The plan," Hennessey said. "You know—how do you want to play it? You're the one with the badge, Deputy."

Hennessey's eyes burned into Stringbean. They were like glowing brands tattooing his cheeks with shame for being taken so off-guard and for being so slow to respond to the man's question.

He glanced behind him. George Bottoms, the Kowalski Brothers, and Ernesto Gomez were staring at him expectantly, brows raised, eyes anxious, grave, waiting...

Stringbean wished the marshal were here. He'd know what to do right off, without even thinking about it. He'd just start giving orders and men would be moving and the marshal would be moving himself.

Stringbean drew a breath, stared up the ridge that was a steep blanket of blue-green evergreens, looking sort of misty now in the late afternoon light, with the sun tumbling back behind the posse, in the west. His mind was racing way too fast to be much good.

What Stringbean needed was to settle himself down and imagine what the marshal would do. He could do that. He'd ridden with Marshal Mannion enough times in similar situations, coming upon possible outlaws suddenly and unexpectedly, though of course each situation was at least moderately different from the others.

"All right," Stringbean said, nodding, squeezing the carbine with his gloved hands. He turned to Hennessey, the man's blue eyes still burning into him, rife with impatience. He, of course, was the more experienced man here. Stringbean should probably ask him what *he'd* do.

But no. Stringbean was the one in charge.

This was his decision. It had to be up to him. And by God, he was up to it.

"All right—here's what we do." He turned to the four men regarding him skeptically from behind. "You four wait here with the horses." He turned to Hennessey hipped around in his saddle ahead of him, regarding him expectantly. "Mister Hennessey and me—we'll leave our mounts here with you, and we'll check it out. Could only be a couple range riders cookin' some afternoon coffee. We'll steal up the ridge real quiet-like and check it out." He hiked his shoulder. "Could be nothin'. Could be a trap."

Stringbean liked it when Mister Hennessey arched his

brows in mild surprise and pooched out his red-mustached lips in approval.

"If it's a trap," Stringbean said, turning to the four others behind him, "I'll trigger two quick shots. That means you fellas haul your asses up that ridge lickety-split an' help out!"

Gomez nodded first.

The Kowalski brothers glanced at each other before turning to Stringbean and nodded, too.

George Bottoms was a tall, lean, craggy-faced man with thick salt and pepper hair under the tan Stetson he'd worn as a ranch foreman but was rarely seen in anymore other than when he rode with a posse. In town he wore a bowler hat and used a walking stick to help with his game knee. He wore a flannel shirt, suspenders, and broadcloth trousers as well as a long, cream, canvas jacket. Two old Colts bristled on his hips.

He gazed up the ridge edgily, tapping his thumb on his Winchester's hammer.

Finally, he turned his gaze to Stringbean and said, "I reckon it's what Mannion would do. We'll wait here. You check it out, Stringbean, and let us know. We'll watch your flank."

Stringbean felt even better now that he had Bottoms' approval, too. He felt like smiling or cracking some joke but that would only betray his relief. He should not be relieved he hadn't messed up. *Because he hadn't been going to mess up, by God.* He'd been taught by the best.

He'd been taught by Marshal Mannion himself.

"Well, what're we waitin' for, Mister Hennessey?" Stringbean, in a rare moment of aplomb, swung his right boot over his saddle horn and dropped straight down to the ground, landing flat-footed.

He tossed his reins up to Lyle Kowalski who wasn't

ready for them. Kowalski looked chagrined as the reins dropped to the ground. Stringbean, feeling his oats now, gave a little snort of mild reproof then picked up the reins and tossed them to Kowalski again, who was ready for them this time.

Stringbean glanced over to see Ernesto Gomez smiling at him. Feeling his cheeks warm a little with embarrassment, Stringbean turned to where Hennessey had just dismounted his chocolate bay and now shucked his Henry repeating rifle from its saddle boot. He racked a round into the chamber and gestured up canyon.

"After you, Deputy." He smiled as he pinched the brim of his hat at Stringbean.

Stringbean flushed again, this time with pride but, keeping a poker face, set his carbine on his shoulder and began tramping up the canyon, looking for an easy place to climb up out of it.

He found one not far from where he'd left the four other men and the horses. The ridge wasn't so high here, only fifty feet or so, and it leaned back against the mountain with piled rocks and boulders that formed a ladder of sorts. Stringbean scrambled up the rocks, wincing a little at the hitch in his right hip and silently cursing the horse that had thrown him. At a more precarious spot in their climb, he had to toss his rifle up onto a rock above him and use his hands and arms to hoist himself up off the rock six feet below.

When he'd gained the upper rock, he dropped to a knee and extended his hand to Hennessey, who was huffing and puffing and sweating below him, fagged from the exertion. Hennessey was Stringbean's height, about six-foot-one, but he was a good three times heavier.

Hennessey accepted Stringbean's help and, working together and with much grunting from Hennessey and some salty Irish cursing in the bargain, the big man soon gained the rock that Stringbean was on.

"Much obliged, boyo," the Irishman said, still breathing hard, his face above his beard nearly as red as the beard itself.

Stringbean could smell the sweat on the man. It was tinged with the smell of Irish whiskey. Stringbean had seen the man tipping back a hide-covered flask a few times during the ride.

"You all right?" Stringbean asked the older man.

Hennessey held up one finger. He reached into a pocket of the broadcloth coat he wore over a hickory shirt and brown wool vest. He pulled out the flask, unscrewed the cap, and took one pull, then one more, and held the flask out to Stringbean.

"Boyo?"

Stringbean smiled, shook his head.

"More for me, then, lad," Hennessey said and returned the flask to his pocket. "All right—I'm good as new!"

Stringbean swung around and easily climbed the last several rocks to the lip of the ridge. Hennessey followed him and both men squatted on their haunches, peering up the forested slope before them. Stringbean sniffed the air again.

"Where do you think that smoke is coming from exactly?" Stringbean didn't mind asking the more experienced man.

Keeping his voice low, Hennessey said, "I'd say up the slope maybe a hundred yards on the left."

"All right, then." Stringbean rose and, holding his Winchester up high across his chest, began climbing the steep slope, meandering around firs and pines with here and there a shaggy cedar lending its own distinct aroma to the pungent, exhilarating tang of the forest.

Crows cawed intermittently, angrily.

Occasionally, pinecones dropped from boughs with soft thuds as they struck the soft ground.

Hennessey climbed to Stringbean's right, huffing and puffing, his face turning even redder than before, his blue eyes rheumy. Stringbean climbed more easily even on his game hip, but he didn't feel too superior for all of that. Hennessey made have had years on him—years as well as vices that hadn't been kind to his body—but Stringbean knew the years caught up to every man eventually. He was the younger, less experienced man here, and he just hoped he didn't embarrass himself when the chips were down.

"There, there, there," the older man said after another ten minutes of hard climbing.

Stringbean glanced at him. Hennessey had dropped to a squat again and was pointing up the slope and to the left with raised arm and jutting index finger.

Stringbean followed the man's pointing finger. Gray smoke rose from inside a field of scattered rocks that appeared to have spilled down from an outcropping just beyond it, a little higher up the slope. Stringbean couldn't see the flames that made the smoke, but he saw the smoke, all right. It rose straight up from the rock field and then sort of flattened out and turned blue as it drifted down slope through the trees on a gentle breeze.

Stringbean followed a plan in his head. It wasn't that hard, he realized. You just had to slow your mind down, stop worrying about what other men thought of you, and use *logic*. Yeah, that was the word. Logic. He wasn't sure where he'd heard the word before—he'd had damned little schooling outside of a horse corral—but he knew what it meant.

A good word, logic.

He turned to Hennessey. "I'll swing around to the right, get above them rocks, and then come back down. I'll have a better look-see up there. Looks like there might be a little opening on the right rear corner. You swing around to the left, come at it from the other side. Looks like there might be an opening there, too."

Stringbean had chosen the right side because he, being the younger man, still had the steam to climb a little higher on the slope. Made sense to him. It must have made sense to Hennessey, too.

He glanced at Stringbean and gave a knowing wink and a nod.

He rose and, crouching over his Henry repeater, crossed before Stringbean, heading upslope to String-bean's left in his shamble-footed, bull-legged gait. String-bean rose, then, as well and, slanting right, continued climbing the slope.

He steered well wide of the tightly scattered rocks, peering carefully all around him, knowing the smoke could very well be a trap. On the other hand, he and Hennessey might find themselves surprising Whip Helton and his other four gang members, who'd maybe stopped here to have some coffee and a bite of lunch. They might have thought the rocks would disperse their smoke enough that anyone riding through the cut below wouldn't smell it.

Not the best logic but then Whip Helton was known better for his hellion ways than for his thinking ways.

Stringbean's heart increased its beat as he climbed. He was growing anxious. He could feel sweat oozing from his palms inside his gloves. He winced and shook his head against it. Fear was the enemy, he knew. "It stiff-ened your limbs and clouded your thinking, made you slow to react."

That was a direct quote from the marshal himself, muttered at Stringbean when they'd been about to take down a gang of stagecoach thieves who had killed a messenger, stolen a mine payroll, and had been holed up in a little sheep herder's shack near the Taylor River in the Sawatch Range.

That had been two years ago, right after the marshal had hired Stringbean, but Stringbean remembered those words as though he'd heard them only yesterday. He went over them again and again in his head. You had time to do that when, as the junior deputy, you often had to pull night duty and make the rounds every hour or so, checking to make sure doors were locked and that no shadows of would-be robbers lurked beyond the dark windows.

Now he stopped and peered down the slope to his right at the scattered rocks, which formed a ragged circle roughly one quarter the size of your average breaking corral. The smoke still rose from inside it but much more thinly than before. If the gang was in those rocks, they weren't adding anymore fuel to the fire.

Slowly, quietly, Stringbean levered a live round into his Winchester's action. He began moving down the slope, angling right. The rocks grew before him, pale rocks spilling down from more pale rocks piled higher above them, on a large shelf bulging out of the slope.

With each step Stringbean's anxiousness grew.

He slid his gaze across the rocks higher on the slope. Helton's men could be holed up in those rocks. They might bound up at any time and commence flinging lead at Stringbean and Hennessey farther down the slope and on the other side of the scattered rocks. On the other hand, the tough-nuts might be sneaking up behind Stringbean now.

That thought made him swing around suddenly and with a startled grunt.

Movement up the slope beyond him!

He sucked a startled breath and began to draw his finger back against the trigger. He stopped when a crow's angry caw assaulted his ears. He watched in momentary relief as the giant black bird winged up from whatever dead meat it had been feeding on, on the ground, and angled up through the pine boughs, followed by one more, also angrily cawing, and then one more.

The cawing continued to rattle Stringbean's eardrums.

He swung back around quickly, looked around again thoroughly, then continued his descent of the slope. He moved through the rocks, weaving around them, until he saw an opening beyond which a slight clearing appeared to lay. Taking one slow step at a time, aiming the Winchester straight out from his right shoulder, finger tight against the trigger, Stringbean stepped into the clearing in the rocks.

As he did, Hennessey, his rifle's butt snugged up against his thick right shoulder, also stepped into the clearing. The fire ring lay just ahead of Stringbean. The fuel was mostly a large pile of gray ashes in which only a few feeble, orange flames shimmered.

There were no men here. There were no horses here.

No tack piled around the fire, which had obviously been much larger than that needed to boil coffee and maybe heat a pan of beans.

It had been a bonfire.

Hennessey must have realized that at the same time

Stringbean did—that the fire had been built only to lure them toward it—because he swung around sharply just as Stringbean did, expecting one of the marauders to be coming up behind him. When none did, Stringbean turned forward once more.

He looked at Hennessey, both men aiming their rifles at each other. Realizing this, both men lowered their long guns quickly. Hennessey stared down at the ground before the fire as he quartered around to the downslope side of it. Stringbean swung around the fire's left side and moved up to within eight feet of where Hennessey stood staring down at rocks laid out unnaturally upon the ground.

Yeah, unnaturally. Someone had arranged them in a certain way.

And then he realized what that way was.

He'd had damned little schooling outside of a breaking corral, but he could cypher a little and had learned his letters well enough to read the three words the rocks formed:

YOU ARE DEAD

Stringbean looked up at Hennessey, whose own eyes widened as he, too, read the message formed by the rocks. Hennessey's eyes met Stringbean's and then widened even more, in shock, just as blood and gore suddenly shot out of the stout Irishman's broad chest. Bits of bone and shredded heart splattered across the ground between him and Stringbean. Stringbean heard the buzz of a bullet pass over his left shoulder, its course altered by Hennessey's breastbone and ribs, most likely, before the thunder of the rifle that had fired it assaulted

Stringbean's ears and shattered the former near silence of the forested slope.

The echoing report was followed by a man's raucous, victorious, coyote-like howl.

Stringbean stared in horror as Hennessey dropped his Winchester and staggered toward him, eyes wide, blood quickly spreading around the fist-sized hole in his chest. Hennessey moved as though drunk, reaching out with his right hand toward Stringbean, as though pleading for help. He took only three heavy steps before he gave a rattling grunt and dropped in a heap at Stringbean's feet.

Stringbean froze, staring down at the quivering figure of Hennessey lying belly down before him. In the distance, from the direction of the cut in which he and Hennessey had left the four other posse riders, came the loud blasts of several rifles. Beneath those echoing blasts and the coyote-like yells of the ambushers, men shouted and screamed, and horses whinnied shrilly.

A bullet sang past Stringbean's left ear so close he could feel the warm curl of air against his flesh. He jerked with a start and looked past where Hennessey had been standing seconds before to see the silhouette of a man down on one knee maybe fifty yards away lowering a rifle from his shoulder to pump a fresh round into the action.

"*Ambush!*" Stringbean cried.

Panic like none he'd known before overwhelmed him. He dropped his rifle, twisted around, and ran back the way he'd come. At least, he thought it was the way he'd come. His brains were scrambled so that all he knew was the overwhelming compulsion to escape certain death.

When he'd left the rocks behind him, he ran up the slope and into more rocks, screaming, "*Ambush! Ambush!*" at the tops of his lungs, hearing the growing din of several horses galloping toward him.

Behind him, men howled and whooped and yelled.

One shouted, "Look—it's Stringbean!"

"Got him on the run!" another yelled above the thunder of galloping hooves and blowing horses.

The others laughed.

Mindlessly, his mind knowing only fear and the need to escape, Stringbean ran straight up the ridge and then down the other side until the ground suddenly dropped away beneath him.

He screamed as the earth swallowed him.

Too late had he seen the gaping hole in the ground before him, the mine tailings piled on the other side of it and dropping down the rocky slope beyond. He screamed again as he dropped down the slanting, rocky wall of the mineshaft, daylight sliding back away from him and darkness wrapping itself around him like a large black hand.

CHAPTER 11

ROUGHLY TWENTY-FOUR HOURS LATER, MANNION reined Red to a halt in the dry streambed rising into the first front of the San Juan Mountains—a road of sorts that prospectors occasionally followed during dry times of the year to placer deposits that spotted this neck of the vast range. He knew that game also used the road, for every time he'd ridden up here, hunting either outlaws who also often followed the road deep into the mountains, or wild game to fill his larder for the long mountain winter, he'd always come upon plenty of elk, deer, bear, and even mountain goat scat.

Ahead, Stringbean's zebra dun stood munching needle grass growing up around the base of a boulder that resembled a badly listing table. Mannion's heart kicked the same way it had when, only a few minutes ago, he'd come upon Brian Hennessey's chocolate bay and a coyote dun he recognized as that belonging to George Bottoms, the former New Mexico ranch foreman turned Del Norte shoe salesman.

Mannion booted Red slowly up toward the dun, which lifted its head suddenly with a start and turned to see the Del Norte Town Marshal approaching on the bay. The dun switched its tail, shook its head, and whickered a greeting. It recognized the newcomers, looked almost happy to see them.

Maybe relieved.

"Easy, hoss, easy," Mannion said, holding up a placating hand in case the horse should bolt.

But it did not bolt. It stayed its ground and lowered its head to continue cropping the dry grass growing up along the side of the boulder.

"What the hell happened here, boy?" the lawman said, stopping Red then swinging a little gingerly down from the saddle. His head still ached miserably though a few hours of shuteye last night had helped. What also helped was that he'd managed to turn suppressing the pain into a fine art, concentrating instead on Evangeline, who must be as terrified as she'd ever been in her life; than she had ever been in even any nightmare, most likely.

She was damn sure living a nightmare right now. If she was still alive.

Mannion winced at the possibility she might be dead. Used and killed. That stopped him cold, and he could not afford to stop or to even slow down. Not until he had her back in whatever condition she was in.

The dun jerked its head up as Mannion approached, eyes growing suddenly suspicious.

"Easy, easy..."

He grabbed the reins. The horse's saddle hung down its far side, which meant it must have bolted violently at some scare. Mannion had a feeling he knew what that scare had been, but he didn't want to believe it. He did, however, see a notch across the top of the horse's hindquarters—a three-inch furrow crusted with dried blood.

"Bullet burn."

What he feared was likely true. The posse led by Stringbean and Brian Hennessey had run into trouble. Probably a bushwhack. The men must have been shot off their horses. Mannion would likely find them farther up the streambed.

He cursed quietly but passionately, his reignited fury at Whip Helton and the four other devils kicking up the burning throb in his head.

He walked back over to Red, grabbed the bay's reins, swung into the leather, and booted the horse on up the deep, rocky cut. Ten minutes later, he reined to another halt.

Again, his heart kicked. Harder this time.

Ahead, just before the gradually climbing streambed followed a leftward curve, bodies lay piled up in the cut.

Feeling sick to his loins, Mannion clucked the bay ahead until he sat the saddle staring down at the bloody, twisted bodies of George Bottoms, the Kowalski twins, and the Mexican roofer and all-around good hombre, Ernesto Gomez. They'd all been shot out of their saddles, all right. Over the past twenty-four hours, the carrion-eaters, mostly birds, it appeared, had started working on them, but Mannion could still identify each man.

Gomez lay on his back, lips stretched back from his teeth as though he were still in agony from the bullet that had blown the top of his head off. Bottoms lay on his belly, one arm beneath him, the other arm stretched straight out to one side, that hand lying palm up, the fingers curled partly inward. The barrel of his rifle poked out from beneath his chest.

Steve Kowalski had likely taken the bullet in his right

thigh first. He'd crawled to a rock and sat up against it.
That was likely when he'd taken the second bullet to his
brisket. He lay slumped to one side, head hanging down
over his shoulder.

The other Kowalski twin, Lyle, had likely also been
shot off his horse and then had crawled toward the
Spencer carbine that lay just beyond him now as he lay
belly down in the loose rocks and gravel, his right arm
stretched up above his head, the fingers of that hand only
two inches away from the rifle's rear stock.

Mannion felt the burn of rage deep in his soul.

This had been a savage, cold-blooded ambush.

It had likely come from the bank on the right side of
the streambed, for all four riders had been thrown
toward the left bank.

The only two of the posse who weren't here were
Stringbean and Hennessey.

Where were they?

Mannion looked around. He'd just booted Red ahead
along the streambed, believing he might find their bodies
a little farther along, maybe on the other side of the cut's
leftward curve, when he reined in. He stared down at the
indentation of a boot heel. Part of an 'I' shown against
the heel.

Stringbean wore Imperial Boots sold by the mercantiler, Wilfred Drake. Mannion remembered Stringbean
complaining that his old boots were wearing out so that
he had holes in his soles, so he could feel every rock and
goathead he stepped on. The lawman had convinced the
kid that a deputy town marshal, especially one who made
the nightly rounds as many times as Stringbean did,
needed good boots. Mannion had lent the kid twenty
dollars PWP, payable when possible.

He'd be damned if the kid hadn't paid him back in full

the first of the very next month, right after Mannion had paid him his wages. That told Mannion the kid had laid in a stake for himself, which was good. It meant he was thinking about the future and possibly asking for the hand of the daughter of a large freighting company he'd been sparking, though Mannion didn't think he had much of a shot while knowing that Molly Hurdstrom could do a whole lot worse than Stringbean McCallister.

That impression had been made by Stringbean's boot, all right.

Closely scrutinizing the ground, he saw what appeared part of one more track and then a couple more that didn't appear to have been made by Stringbean. They were slightly larger boots. Hennessey's, most likely. The tracks appeared to be heading toward the cut's left bank, where a jumble of rocks would make for a relatively easy climb up out of the cut.

Mannion swung down from the saddle and ground-reined Red.

He shucked his Winchester Yellowboy from his saddle-boot. The 1866 was an old gun that as a young deputy town marshal in Kansas he'd purchased with Wells Fargo reward money from a gun shop in Abilene. Mannion had stuck with the gun over the years because he'd never found another as ruggedly built, dependable, and with a faster shooting action. The handsome piece despite the scars it had accrued from hard use was called a "Yellowboy" because of its bronze/brass alloy receiver, which made it stand out from most other Winchesters on the market.

Of course, it marked its owner as a tad old-fashioned, but Mannion had been called worse.

He walked over and considered the rocks that formed a stairway of sorts to the bank above. Stringbean had probably scurried up the rocks like they were nothing despite his game hip, but Mannion had a feeling Hennessey hadn't had quite the easy time of it. Mannion wouldn't either. Not with his throbbing noggin.

He didn't see an easier way up the bank, however, so he started climbing, moving from rock to rock with ease until he found a more formidable gap from one rock to another one six feet above it. He reached up and set the rifle on the rock above then grabbed the edge of the above rock and, grunting and cursing every word in his vocabulary and making up a few more, he finally gained the upper rock and stayed down on one knee, taking deep slow breaths, eyes closed, until the Mexican bottle rockets ceased exploding behind his retinas.

When he'd regained his composure, Mannion scrutinized the soft forest duff that carpeted the pine- and fir-clad ridge rising in the north and easily found the tracks of two men—Stringbean's and Brian Hennessey's. He followed them up the ridge, not enjoying the climb because it only reawakened the nasty little man in his head smashing a ballpeen hammer against his tender brain plate but follow it he did.

He was taking precious time away from his tracking of the devils who had his girl, but it couldn't be helped. He had to find out what had happened to his deputy and Hennessey, an old army man and ace tracker. Had they climbed the ridge before or after the deadly ambush in the riverbed?

Likely before. Something, possibly a diversion, had led them up here.

If so, what had become of them?

Mannion had a feeling he knew the answer to that, but he had to see for himself.

He found Hennessey roughly twenty minutes later,

after a hard climb that left the lawman sweating even in the cool mountain air—most of it pain sweat. Old Brian had been shot in the back, his heart blown out in ribbons upon the ground before him. Stringbean's rifle lay just beyond Hennessey whom, like the others in the streambed, the predators had not been kind to. His back and the back of his head had been well-pecked, making the body look as though it had been peppered with buckshot.

Mannion stared down at the rifle.

Just beyond it, he picked up Stringbean's tracks as the young deputy had run through the rocks that formed a ragged circle around the long-dead bonfire that had apparently lured him and Hennessey up here. Yes, the kid had been running.

Had he been wounded?

Mannion didn't see any blood on the ground around the young man's boot prints. But the deputy had run, all right, taking long quick strides judging by the half-formed, widely spaced tracks. Mannion followed the spoor to the top of the ridge and stopped, leaning forward and placing one hand on his knee, taking long draughts of air into his lungs while that nasty little man worked on his tender brain with a vengeance.

Catching his breath, Mannion spied what appeared a mineshaft opening roughly twenty feet down from the crest of the ridge. Tailings were strewn along the downs-lope side of the shaft. Likely an exploratory hole pick-and-shoveled by some wandering prospector. The shaft angled into the ground to the right of the hole.

Mannion frowned, a thought occurring to him.

He straightened, sucked another breath into his lungs, and called, "Stringbean?"

No response.

He stepped forward carefully, for this side of the mountain was all rocks, gravel and boulders, and its drop was steeper here than on the other side.

"Stringbean—you down there?"

He gained the shaft and bent forward again, staring into the shaft that dropped steeply to the right. He called louder, "Stringbean? Henry?"

Down in the murky depths he thought he saw a shadow move. "Leave me here, Marshal," came Stringbean's oddly quiet voice. "Just leave me here."

Mannion gave a caustic chuff. "I'll be damned if I'm gonna leave you here, Deputy. You all right?"

A stretched silence and then: "Just bruised some. Think I caught a bullet graze when they fired into the shaft at me."

"How bad you hit?"

"Just a graze."

"I'm gonna fetch my horse and then I'm gonna throw you a rope."

Again, the shadow moved maybe thirty, forty feet down the shaft. "Please, just leave me here, Marshal. I don't wanna see the light of day ever again."

"You'll starve down there, kid."

"I wanna starve down here, Marshal."

"I saw what happened to Hennessey. It's all right that you ran. It's a thing to see—a man getting killed right in front of you."

"Please, just leave me here!" came Stringbean's voice, shrill and quavering and teeming with misery.

"I'll be back in a half hour."

No response.

Mannion swung around and headed back in the direction from which he'd come.

He clambered his way back into the riverbed,

mounted Red, and rode ahead along the cut until the northern wall dropped low enough that it made for a relatively easy climb for the horse. He'd had to ride a good quarter mile to find that low place in the wall, however, so shadows were stretching long when he finally rode Red up and over the crest of the ridge and stopped the horse beside the mineshaft.

He'd just started to dismount when he stopped, frowned and sniffed the air.

Wood smoke...

It seemed to be coming from the direction of Crow Ridge.

CHAPTER 12

MANNION REMEMBERED THERE WAS AN OLD TRAPPER'S cabin in a little clearing under Crow Ridge. That area of the range was on open range that Garth Helton considered his own. So, Whip Helton was likely familiar with the cabin. It might even be where he and the others holed up from time to time after one of their depredations.

Helton was known to disappear for long stretches between jobs, none of which anyone had been able to pin on him—mostly because of who his father was.

Crow Ridge was about four miles, as the crow flies, away from here.

Mannion felt his heart increase its pace. Maybe he was closer to Helton...and Vangie...than he'd thought. Odd to ambush a posse so close to where you were holed up but then Whip had never had to answer to anything he'd ever done in the past so why would he think he'd have to answer to what he'd done now?

"Hold on, kid," Mannion called into the shaft. "I'm gonna get you out of there!"

"I told you to leave me, Marshal," Stringbean called weakly from the bottom of the hole.

Mannion grabbed his lariat off his saddle and stepped up to the shaft. "You know I'm not gonna do that, so don't waste my time. I gotta catch up to Helton and Vangie, so when I drop this rope, dammit, you grab it and wrap it around your waist!"

He took one end of the rope in his right hand and drop the rest of it into the hole and watched it quickly pay out into the murky dimness below.

He heard Stringbean sigh, felt the rope grow taut.

"All right," Stringbean called in the same defeated tone as before. "I have it wrapped around my waist, Marshal."

"Slip-knotted?"

"Slip-knotted."

"All right. Hold on."

Mannion climbed up onto Red's back, dallied the end of the lariat around the horn, turned the bay, and clucked the horse ahead slow. He kept moving one halting step at a time until he heard Stringbean grunting and sighing and spitting grit from his lips behind him. He stopped Red and turned to see his young deputy lying half in and half out of the shaft, arms thrown forward, cheek against the ground.

Mannion booted Red ahead again—three quick steps, evoking an indignant yowl behind him. "You're draggin' me, Marshal!"

Mannion stopped Red and turned to see Stringbean lying on the ground, his boots three feet from the shaft, head lifted to scowl befuddledly at the lawman. "Stop feeling sorry for yourself. All right, you ran! If you hadn't run, you'd probably be dead, so maybe your instincts were telling you to do the right thing."

"I was just plain scared!"

"We all get scared!"

"You don't!"

"Don't let me fool you, kid. And don't put so goddamn much stock in me. I can't live up to it. I bleed same as everybody else, and I make fool mistakes more than most!"

"But...but...you're Bloody Joe..."

"Bloody Joe's a damn fool!" Mannion shot back at the kid. He paused, softened his tone. "You all right?" The kid's lips and cheeks were scraped and both sleeves of his tan shirt were torn. One ear was bloody, as well.

Stringbean rose to his knees and brushed his fist across his ear, probably a burn from one of the bullets the gang had hurled into the shaft, trying to make sure he'd bought the farm. Fortunately, the young deputy must have been hunkered down behind some cover that had saved him. His hat was dirty and badly battered, part of the crown smashed in.

"I reckon I'll live," was all he said, as though not all that pleased at the prospect. He angrily picked up a stone and hurled it sidearm.

"Like I said, stop feeling sorry for yourself." Mannion extended his left hand. "Climb up here. We're gonna ride back and get your horse and then you're gonna help me take down Whip Helton and get my girl back."

Stringbean just stared up at him, lower jaw hanging in shock.

"Did you hear me, boy? Untie that rope and get up here before I lose my temper, which I am prone to do. Now, first we're gonna have to retrieve your rifle, so *get a move on*!"

Stringbean snapped to life, grabbing the loop and throwing it up and over his head. Quickly, Mannion coiled it and hung it over his saddle horn. Then he pulled his left boot from the stirrup and extended his hand to Stringbean, who took it, toed the stirrup, and Mannion swung him up behind him.

"Hold on, tight!" Mannion said. "*Hy-yahh, Red—I'm fixin' to draw Helton blood by sundown!*"

———

MANNION DIDN'T DRAW HELTON BLOOD BY SUNDOWN.

But by sundown, he and Stringbean were hunkered atop a low ridge and peering down at the old trapper's cabin under the anvil-like crag of Crow Ridge, at the base of a pine-carpeted mountain touched with the dull pinks and salmons of the last light filtering over the inky-black western ridges.

Mannion held his old, army-issue field glasses to his eyes, adjusting the focus until the cabin swam into sharper focus. It was a low, square, log building with a slightly peaked, shake-shingled roof. Smoke, dark-gray against the dwindling light, issued from a tin chimney pipe angling up out of the roof in roughly the center of the structure. Wan lamplight issued through the cracks in the shutters that were closed over the windows on the near side of the shack. The two front windows were not shuttered, and the light could be seen more clearly through these, behind a narrow front stoop that ran the width of the shack.

The cabin was larger than most of its kind. Mannion had heard it had been built by four Scandinavian brothers who'd lived here and plied their fur-trapping trade until beaver hats had gone out of style back East. Since then, the cabin had been occupied intermittently by nesters, rustlers, and other men on the run. Ancient hides hung in tatters from spikes in the outside walls and a large, sun-bleached elk head complete with massive horns was mounted over the steps running up to the dilapidated stoop. At the moment, a large crow was perched on one of the horns, lifting one large wing to preen while several others were lined up along the peak of the roof above it, black blobs against the forested, salmon-lit mountain rising beyond them, occasionally giving their raucous cries.

They seemed to be waiting for something.

Just as the thought drifted through Mannion's aching head, the front door opened, bleeding more wan, amber light out onto the stoop. The silhouetted figure of a hatted man appeared, stepping out of the cabin and walking a little uncertainly across the porch. He stopped atop the front steps and tossed something out into the yard, "Here ya go, carrion-eaters!"

He whooped a laugh then turned and strode back into the cabin, boots thudding dully on the stoop's worn wooden floor, and closed the door behind him. The crows lighted from their perches, cawing loudly, and descended as one upon the morsel—meat or bone, prob-ably—that the Helton gang member had thrown. There was a brief but raucous row on the ground where the food had been thrown and then one crow rose, appar-ently victorious, to wing off into the growing dusk toward the forest-clad mountain behind the lodge, the others following, giving their indignant cries.

The cries echoed in the otherwise silent evening, dwindling gradually.

Mannion shifted his magnified gaze to a lean-to stable and pole corral behind the cabin. Five horses milled there, two running in small circles, tails arched, dust lit by the salmon hues lingering after the sunset rising around them. They'd been stirred into motion by the crows.

Mannion drew his field of vision nearer, to where a shallow stream ran along the base of the rise he and Stringbean were on. It came in from Mannion's left and continued to his right before swinging out from the rise and heading east, straight out away from the rise, paralleling itself with the front wall of the cabin. The water in the narrow creek glinted green in the last green light remaining in the sky.

Mannion lowered the binoculars and turned to Stringbean lying belly down to his right.

Stringbean turned to him, eyes wide with expectation, rifle in his hands. His hands shook slightly, Mannion noticed.

"You clear?" he asked.

"Huh?"

Mannion closed a gloved hand over the breech of the quivering rifle in the young man's hands. "About earlier—forget it. It's ancient history."

"I got that whole damn posse killed, Marshal."

"No, you didn't. Helton did. Hennessey walked into that trap, same as you. Could have happened to anyone." *If anyone got them killed,* Mannion thought, *I did. But I can't think about that now. I have to keep my mind on the task at hand, on killing Helton and getting my girl back. There will be plenty of time to go over my own transgressions, not the least of which being I was soused when Helton attacked.*

Plenty of time...

"But I ran."

"That's why you're here. You ready to get back on the horse that threw you? If not, I'll leave you here."

Stringbean ran his tongue across his lips, drew a breath, and nodded. "I'm ready."

"You sure?"

"I'm ready."

"You certain-sure?"

Stringbean smiled with one half of his mouth. The rifle stopped quivering. "Certain-sure."

Mannion smiled. "What we're gonna do is head down there together. Once we reach the stream, I want you to follow it until you can see the cabin's back door."

Mannion had been out here before, had holed up in the shack himself while chasing outlaws, so he knew the place had a rear door.

"You hunker down there. Stay out of sight. If those horses see you or wind you, they'll whinny. If any of those devils run out the back, shoot 'em. But be good and careful you don't shoot Vangie. There's enough light, you'll be able to make her out. I'm betting that if she's in there, she'll stay in there. She's probably in no condition to leave on her own."

Stringbean looked at him uncertainly. "*If* she's in there...?"

Coldly, Mannion said, "They might've already had what they wanted from her and killed her." There it was. The facts. On the surface, he was a stone. Inside, his heart was breaking. But he had to face facts. If he was anything at all—and over the past day or so Bloody Joe had been doubting nearly everything he'd thought he was except one thing.

He was still a man who faced facts.

At least he still had that. He didn't want to face the fact of Vangie's death, but if he had to, he would.

It might very well kill him, but he would.

"You'll hear me go in," Mannion said. "It won't be quiet. Watch the back door." He squeezed Stringbean's right shoulder reassuringly then rose. "Let's go."

Staying low, closing his right hand over the Yellow-boy's brass receiver so that the last rays of sunlight wouldn't reflect off it, Mannion started moving down the ridge, weaving between rocks and cedars, keeping an eye on the front door and the two front windows, which still had glass panes in them despite the amount of time the place had been abandoned. He hoped his and String-bean's silhouetted figures merged with the silhouette of the ridge, so they wouldn't be seen if one of the kidnapping devils was watching through a window.

He doubted they would be. They thought he was dead. They probably thought Stringbean was dead, as well.

He and Stringbean gained the base of the ridge and stepped into the cut the stream ran through, pushing through shagbark and willow. They each easily leaped the four-foot-wide ribbon of faintly glinting brown water. It smelled gamey this late in the year. Mannion had just planted both feet on the opposite side of the stream when he heard the scape of the cabin's front door being opened.

Ancient hinges squawked.

Mannion glanced at Stringbean, whispered, "Down!"

They threw themselves down against the stream's embankment, which rose maybe five feet above the water. Mannion doffed his hat and slowly edged a look over the lip of the cut toward the cabin, which lay roughly sixty yards away. The cabin door was open, bleeding wan amber light onto the stoop where a man was just then walking uncertainly away from the door and over to the three front steps dropping to the yard bristling with short, brown grass and mountain sage.

He was tall and thin, and he wore a red shirt and black pants. Even in the murky light, Mannion could see the long, girl-like hair hanging down over Whip Helton's shoulders, see the glint of the gold spike in his left ear. A six-shooter bristled low on his right thigh. The bandage on his nose glowed whitely; so did the one wrapped around his left hand.

Helton laughed and turned his head to call over his shoulder in a distinctly nasal tone, "I told ya she might be Bloody Joe's daughter, but she'd still be a good time. Didn't I tell you, fellas? Was I *right*?"

Inside came chuckles and laughter. One man whooped; he or someone else pounded a fist down on a table. Bottles rattled together.

A dragon's breath of unbridled fury rose in Mannion.

"Why, you..." he muttered, unable to keep himself from lifting his Yellowboy over the top of the cut, resting it on the ground before him and aiming down the barrel at where Whip Helton had just opened his pants and was making water in the yard from the top of the porch steps. The arcing urine glinted in the fast-fading light.

Mannion lined up his sights on Helton's head, which jerked up and down as he continued laughing at what one of the other men was saying behind his back in the cabin too softly for Mannion to hear from this distance.

Mannion thumbed back the Yellowboy's hammer and couldn't help but draw his right finger back against the trigger. His heart was an untethered mustang, his ears twin lumps of molten iron.

To his left, Stringbean squeezed his arm, whispered in his ear, "Not yet, Marshal."

Mannion jerked his arm back. "Leave go of me, damn you!"

Again, Stringbean squeezed his arm. "Joe...not yet."

Mannion eased the tension in his trigger finger. He wasn't sure what had stopped him. The unfamiliarity of the kid addressing him by his first name for the first time in their relationship?

Whatever it had been, it had likely saved his daughter's life.

Mannion glanced at Stringbean. Feeling his cheeks warm with chagrin, he pulled the Yellowboy back into the cut, pulled his head down, as well. He turned to Stringbean.

"Thanks, Henry."

Stringbean gave a lopsided grin.

From the cabin came the scraping thump of the front door closing.

Mannion edged another look up over the lip of the cut. Helton had gone back into the cabin.

Mannion turned to Stringbean, jerked his chin to indicate the cabin's rear. Stringbean nodded then rose to a crouch and, keeping his head down beneath the lip of the cut, began walking quickly upstream, holding his rifle in one hand straight down by his side. He and Mannion had removed their spurs and dropped them into their saddlebags, so his passage was a relatively silent one save for the soft crunch of grass and the squishing sound of mud.

Mannion took one more careful gander at the cabin then set his hat on his head, rose, and climbed up out of the cut. Holding the Yellowboy low, he strode toward the cabin door. He did not walk slowly but took long, even strides, his free hand clenched into a fist beside him, his right index finger tapping eagerly against the trigger.

His jaws were hard, green eyes beneath the brim of his black Stetson ablaze with an inner conflagration that if an actual fire would have taken out two good-sized city blocks. He leaped up onto the porch, avoiding the steps. He was across the porch in two strides. He raised his right foot, drew the knee back nearly to his chest, and rammed it forward, slamming the flat sole of his boot against the door just left of the iron handle

The door exploded inward, latching nail and slivers from the frame flying inward, as well, the nail clattering tinnily onto the rotting floorboards. Mannion took one step inside, drew the Yellowboy's hammer back, and pressed his cheek up taut against the stock, aiming down the barrel.

There they were—all five of the devils.

Four, including Helton himself, sat at the square pine table eight feet in front of the door, beneath a rusty railroad lamp hanging from a nail in the four-by-four-foot ceiling support post and casting a watery light but mainly shadows throughout the nearly empty cabin. The fifth man was the man who'd grabbed Vangie. Tall, long-haired, wearing a ratty bowler hat and wash-worn long-handles, had just turned from the sheet-iron stove to the right of the table and a little beyond it. He held a spoon to his mouth, his other hand cupped beneath the spoon to catch any drips.

In the corner of Mannion's right eye, Mannion saw a naked female figure lying on a cot against the wall over there, beneath a shuttered window. She lay on her side, chin dipped to her chest, arms crossed on her breasts, knees drawn to her belly. Evangeline's tender skin shown pink in the flickering light of the lamp. It was a shocking spectacle—seeing your daughter naked and in the full flower of young womanhood you hadn't even realized she was in till now. Even more shocking under the circumstances of her having been deflowered by savages.

They hadn't even covered her with a blanket.

"What's the matter, you sons of bitches?" Mannion smiled coldly. "See a ghost?"

CHAPTER 13

MANNION COMMENCED FIRING, THE YELLOWBOY bucking and roaring.

He shot the bowler-hatted SOB who'd first taken and pawed Vangie first and then he shot the red-shirted Whip Helton just as he leaped to his feet and clawed for his revolver.

He didn't give the savages a chance. Not even one-half of a goddamn chance. He just fired until all four, who'd just begun leaping to their feet and reaching for iron when the Yellowboy had begun roaring, were screaming and dropping, one flying up onto the table, scattering bottles, glasses, coins, greenbacks, and pasteboards.

The others jerked and danced bizarrely around the table, and dropped with resolute, slapping thuds.

Mannion fired, smiling through gritted teeth, until the Winchester's hammer dropped with a benign ping, empty. Smoke wafted so thickly in front of Mannion that he saw murkily one of the fallen leap suddenly to his feet, shoving one of the others aside who'd fallen partway over him. A gun flashed from just above the table and on the other side of it. The bullet burned angrily across the outside Mannion's right arm, just above the elbow.

Mannion cursed and staggered backward, dropping the Yellowboy. As he did, the shooter yelled, "You go to hell, Mannion, you bloody bastard!"

The gun flashed and popped again.

That bullet tore into the doorframe to Mannion's left.

Mannion had just reached for the top-break Russian holstered on his left side when the shooter gave an agonized wail and took off running to Mannion's right, long, brown hair flying back behind him. Mannion got the Russian raised and aimed and thumbed the hammer back and managed to squeeze off two shots, the Russian roaring and adding to the thickness of the smoke murk before him, before the shooter threw himself into a long dive, head down, arms and hands thrust straight out before him.

Mannion fired one more shot. The bullet hammered into the wall just behind and beyond the flying man a half-second before the man smashed into the shuttered window before him, shattering the rotten wood, and disappeared outside. There was a hard thud and a groan as the man, none other than Whip Helton himself—Mannion had recognized the voice as well as the long hair and the Spanish-style red shirt—struck the ground.

Helton groaned and then there was the sound of running feet and deep grunts as the wounded man fled.

"Dammit!"

Mannion was about to swing around and run out the front door to throw more lead at Helton but then he saw Vangie lying there against the far wall. She was staring at him through the smoke haze, but it was almost as though she didn't recognize him. Her eyes were glassy, her face expressionless. She shivered as though deeply chilled.

Outside, running foot thuds sounded again, these coming from the rear of the cabin. The foot thuds stopped. Stringbean yelled, "Stop, damn ya!"

Three quick rifle reports then Stringbean took off running again, breathing hard.

Mannion lowered the smoking Russian and walked, stumbling as though drunk, toward his daughter. As he did, he shuddered. Her eyes reminded him of the hopeless eyes of the woman who'd tricked him into killing her.

"Oh, my dear, poor girl," Mannion practically wailed.

He shoved the Russian into its holster and dropped to a knee before the cot. He placed his hand on Vangie's head.

"No!" she cried, jerking her head back and staring up in terror at her father.

"Oh, no, my poor girl. It's your father. Don't you recognize me?"

Then she seemed to. The terror left her eyes, and she lowered her head back down to the cot and crossed her arms over her bare, chafed breasts once more. She continued shivering as though deeply chilled.

"Sure, sure—you know it's me," Mannion said, rising and easing one hip onto the cot beside his daughter, the dry wood creaking beneath his weight. "Sure, sure—you're all right now, dear girl." He placed his hand on her shoulder, squeezed, and sobbed. "Good Lord, what did those savages do to you?"

He sobbed again squeezed her arm then remembered that she was naked and fetched a bedroll from one of the other cots arranged haphazardly around the room and covered her with it. Then he gently lifted her up into his arms, hugged her close against him. She did not hug him back but just sagged limp against him, face against his shoulder, her arms hanging straight down at her sides.

"Those savages!" Mannion wailed at the ceiling. "What did they do to my poor, dear girl?"

But he knew.

He held his daughter and sobbed for a long time.

When he heard footsteps rising in the distance, he eased Vangie back down on the cot and covered her again with the blanket. She lay as before, shivering and staring, her mind seemingly blank of anything except the horror she'd endured.

Mannion scrubbed tears from his face with his shirt-sleeve. He doffed his hat and leaned down to plant a tender kiss on Vangie's cheek.

"Get you home tomorrow, girl. Get you to the doctor."

He set his hat on his head, rose, and crossed the room to the open front door.

Stringbean was just then walking around the corner of the cabin to Mannion's left.

"Did you get him?" Mannion asked.

"That was Helton?"

Mannion nodded.

Stringbean stopped, slouched, and shook his head. "He got away in the brush. I'm afraid I'm not much good at anything tonight, Marshal."

"Like I said, stop feeling sorry for yourself or you're fired." Mannion paused and stared off into the night, his eyes hard as granite. "If he doesn't die from that bullet I gave him, he'll die later. He'll die hard."

"What about his pa, Marshal?"

"Garth Helton will die, too, if he tries to stop me."

Stringbean knew if not by his employer's bloody reputation, then by the look in the marshal's eyes that what he'd just promised was every bit as good as an oath written in blood.

———

GARTH HELTON TOOK A DEEP DRAG OFF THE LONG, slender cigar and blew three smoke rings into the murky morning shadows that hovered over his desk in the second-floor office of his Spur headquarters ranch house.

He gazed broodingly at the rings quickly dissolving into the shadows on the other side of the large desk nearly buried under account ledgers and stockmen's manuals and various coffee-stained, age-yellowed bills of lading and supply receipts that had been lying there for years. Helton never let his cleaning lady, a middle-aged, half-breed Arapaho named Wynona Frost—or anyone else, for that matter—clean or straighten his office.

Not that there was anyone else to do it. His wife, Berenice, hadn't cleaned a thing in years. All Berenice ever did was sit around and drink brandy and read old books or sit staring out the windows in sullen contemplation—of what, only God and Berenice herself knew.

Maybe she didn't even know, so pickled was her brain.

The fact was she hated Garth. Always had. Theirs had been an arranged marriage. Oh, they'd tried to make a good show of it for the first two or three years, but then Berenice's revulsion of her husband had become so great that, unable to divorce him lest her father cut her out of his will, she'd moved out of their bedroom and turned to drink.

She'd once been a beautiful woman, twenty years his junior. But the drink and depression as well as the isolation of the ranch had turned her into an old woman in just a few years.

The fact was Garth had never thought much of Berenice, either. Beyond her once unsullied appearance, that was. He'd seen her as shallow and a bit frivolous, having been raised by an Eastern shipping and railroad magnate named Malcolm O'Leary who'd been business partners with Garth's father. O'Leary had made Garth's father as well as Garth himself rich men.

He'd sent Garth and his daughter out West to diversify their business interests though until he'd moved out here, Garth had had no interest nor experience in the cattle trade. He'd school himself tirelessly and relentlessly, however, and, with his father-in-law's financial backing and his own innate pugnacious nature had turned the Spur brand, once a much smaller spread owned by a homesteader from Missouri, into one of the largest and most prosperous ranches in southern Colorado.

And he damned sure intended to keep it that way despite his loco son who was liable to ruin his name as well as his reputation if Garth didn't get a halter on that boy fast...

The problem was Whip was as crazy and as frivolous as his mother. It ran in the O'Leary blood, he'd heard, though Berenice's father had managed to harness that energy and use it for practical, unwavering drive and financial profit.

His thoughts had only just turned to his firebrand son when he spied movement out the window to his right. He turned to see a horseback rider just then ride through the high, wooden portal and open gate and into the yard, angling up the hill toward the house. Right away Garth recognized his forty-two-year-old foreman, Quint Wayne, a big, capable man in a tall, black Stetson, red neckerchief, thick, dark-brown mustache, and brown leather chaps. He rode a black-speckled gray and was pulling what appeared to be a travois.

Garth narrowed his eyes, scrutinizing the contraption

that Wayne was pulling. A travois, sure enough. A man lay on it, black hat pulled down over his eyes. A blanket had been pulled up to the obviously injured man's shoulders, but Garth could still make out the red shirt the man was clad in.

It was then that, despite the low-tipped hat, that Garth knew the man being carried toward the house on the travois was none other than his son.

Garth's heart kicked in his chest.

Now what kind of a mess has that young fool gotten himself into?

The fact was while Garth suspected the kid was a lost cause, he would not...could not...write him off. He was the only son he had, and he was bound and determined to hammer Whip into good enough shape to take over the ranch in a few years, so Garth and Berenice could move into Del Norte and concentrate more on his mining and railroad interests. He was certain that with his wherewithal, he could turn Del Norte into the next Leadville complete with fancy saloons and opera houses —a financial and cultural hub of sorts.

Change the name to Heltonville!

Despite having just seen his son pulled into the yard on a stretcher, Garth almost smiled at the notion. But then the bulk of his attention returned to Whip, and worry weighed heavy inside him once more. He set the cheroot in an ashtray, rose from his high-backed leather chair, and stepped out from behind his desk, cursing as he tripped over the books and folders bleeding papers piled willy-nilly throughout the room that smelled of ancient cigar smoke, good bourbon, wood varnish, leather, and smoke from the pine and cedar he burned during the cold months in the large fieldstone hearth behind his chair.

Helton was a big man, and his high-topped stockman's boots into which the cuffs of his corduroy trousers were tucked thundered on the carpeted stairs as he moved quickly down the steps. When he reached the bottom, a gravelly female voice said, "That's your son just now being dragged into the yard, Garth! Take a good look!"

Helton turned to see Berenice standing at a parlor window, holding the heavy green felt curtain aside with one hand, holding her ubiquitous brandy mixed with a spoonful of branch water in the other hand. Her long, dark-brown hair liberally streaked with silver hung down over her shoulders. It didn't appear to have been brushed in days and lent a wild air to her wild, sky-blue eyes set in the crags of her narrow, once-beautiful face.

None of that beauty remained. It might have if the eyes had not been cast with a glistening, perpetual lunacy.

"You've done this to him, Garth!" she continued her rant, usually pale face now flushed with fury. "Take a good look. It's your ham-handed, hard-headed ways that turned him bad!"

"Go to hell, woman!" Garth stomped across the parlor and through the foyer before pushing out the heavy oak door and crossing the broad porch to stand atop the steps, staring down at Quint Wayne just now drawing his horse up to one of the hitch racks.

"What the hell happened?" Garth barked, clenching his fists at his sides.

Wayne glanced up his employer, glowering and narrowing one flinty eye shaded by the brim of his tall Stetson. "Mannion ran Whip and his pards down at that abandoned cabin under Crow Ridge. Whip took a bullet in the belly. One of the night riders found him and was bringing him in as I was riding out. He's unconscious now, Whip is, but Chip Stockton said he was about halfways conscious when he found him, and that's what Whip told him, all right."

Rage burned in Garth's belly. It fanned upward to spread throughout his chest. "That bloody bastard oughta be dead! I paid for him to be dead!"

"Shrake?" Wayne said as he swung down from the saddle.

"Yeah, Shrake."

"Last I heard he was at that hog pen near Yellow Butte."

"Don't doubt it a bit. With that half-breed whore he so fancies." Garth glanced behind the foreman's horse at his unconscious son on the travois and said, "Bring him in then send for the doctor from Del Norte. Then saddle me a horse and bring him up here pronto. You and I are taking a ride to Yellow Butte."

"You got it, Mister Helton."

When Wayne had pulled Whip up off the travois and had him in his arms, Garth said, "Any life in that loco shoat?"

"He's still breathin', sir."

"He'd better be. Get him inside!"

"You got it, Mister Helton," the big foreman said as he climbed the porch steps.

Garth stepped aside to let him pass. As he did, he saw his daughter, Landry, skulking around by the hawthorn hedge at the corner of the house. She was barefoot and she held a rumpled bouquet of wildflowers in her dirty left fist. She stared up at her father, a perpetually befuddled cast to her gaze. It was as though she never quite understood what she was seeing.

Loco. Just like her mother. O'Leary blood.

"What the hell are you doing out here, young lady? And barefoot again, no less!"

"I was picking wildflowers for Mama." Landry smiled and held up the flowers. "These are her favorite." She frowned suddenly. "What happened to Whip? Did he get into trouble again?"

"Never you mind!" Helton barked and hooked his arm to indicate the door behind him. "Get inside and help your mother with your brother. And get some shoes on. If I told you once, I told you a thousand times I didn't want you traipsing around the headquarters barefoot!"

As Landry ran up the steps, bare feet slapping the wooden risers, giggling under her breath, Garth sighed and shook his head. "Good Lord," he complained. "Why couldn't *one* of you have taken after me?"

CHAPTER 14

IT WAS LATE MORNING ON A WEEKDAY, ALMOST lunchtime, but the main drinking hall in the San Juan Hotel & Saloon was as quiet as it was on a Sunday morning.

Its only customer sat at a table in the middle of the long, broad room striped with morning sunlight and shadows flooding in through the two, large, plate glass windows. The place had cleaned out after Mannion had taken Evangeline upstairs to Jane's room and waited for the doctor whom Stringbean had summoned as soon as they'd ridden into town, Vangie riding on Mannion's lap, wrapped in a blanket and cradled in his arms.

When Mannion had come downstairs, leaving his daughter in the care of Jane and Doc Bohannon, Del Norte's primary medico, his disposition had been so bleak and severe that not long after he'd ordered a bottle at the bar and had taken the bottle and a glass to the table, the conversational hum in the room had dwindled steadily to whispers. Heads turned toward Mannion, the other customers casting wary gazes at him. The Del Norte Town Marshal had seemed so down and depressed and broodingly enraged that many thought he was liable to pull his two big Russian .44s and start shooting up the place.

Not that he'd ever done that before. But knowing his reputation for sudden violence, Del Norte's citizenry wouldn't put it past him. Nor did they care to take a bullet meant for the chandeliers or the big, leaded glass mirror behind the bar. By ones and twos and then threes and fours, the other customers had polished off their drinks, downed the last of their sandwiches from the free lunch layout, donned their hats, slid back their chairs, and fled through the batwings, casting wary looks back over their shoulders.

The last of the fleers had been Del Norte Mayor, Charlie McQueen.

McQueen had pushed away from the bar and, donning his crisp bowler, had made his way to the batwings. He'd steered wide of the brooding lawman while keeping his own dark eyes on Mannion, reprovingly shaking his head.

He paused, stared at Mannion for another stretched second, then pushed through the batwings and was gone.

Now the only other man in the room was the stout morning apron, Mort Crawley, who stood drying a dimpled beer schooner behind the bar, casting frequent, cautious gazes toward Mannion. Not that Mannion noticed. He'd been only vaguely aware of the saloon clearing out around him. His mind was turned in on itself, brooding over the tragic fate of his beloved daughter at the hands of the known rapist and general all-around no-account scoundrel, Whip Helton and Helton's demon pards.

He was only vaguely aware of the whiskey he was sipping, as well, so that when he lifted the glass to his lips, he was surprised to find it empty. He held the glass out in front of him and stared at it. He no longer saw the glass. What he saw instead of the glass was the sneering face of Whip Helton and then the blank eyes of his daughter as Vangie had lain on the cot at the abandoned cabin, shivering at the horror that Helton and his ilk had inflicted on her.

Mannion's eyes turned even harder than before. The lids twitched. His face turned a deep purple. His fingers tightened around the glass until they turned first scarlet then white. The glass broke with a grinding screech and the shards rained down onto the table.

"Mannion!"

He jumped with a start, his right hand automatically angling across his belly for the Russian holstered for the cross-draw on his left hip. He closed his hand around the handles but left the piece in the leather. Doc Bohannon stood at the bottom of the stairs—a short, squat man with a big, round belly and longish silver hair hanging down from his bullet-crowned black hat. He held his medical kit in his right hand, and he was regarding Mannion with a shocked scowl.

He walked quickly toward Mannion, the scowl remaining on his soft, pale, blue-eyed face. "Good God, man—what're you trying to do to yourself?"

Mannion just felt a burning sting in the palm of his right hand, which he'd closed over the Russian's grips. He raised the hand and saw the long glass shard embedded in the flesh. Dark red blood oozed out around it. Bohannon set his kit on the table and produced a powder blue handkerchief from a back pocket.

"Never mind me, Doc," Mannion said, giving the hand a disregarding flick. "How's Vangie?"

"Just wait a damn minute." Bohannon brushed his

fingers across Mannion's bullet-burned right temple. "I should check those sutures, too. You're damned lucky to be alive, Mannion. I don't know another man who could have endured what you've endured and still be alive."

"I don't feel all that alive, Doc." Mannion had been suppressing the agony in his head for so long he'd made a habit of it. Now that his mind had been directed to the wound, however, he endured the crushing pain until he was able to suppress it again.

"Well, be that as it may..." Bohannon dropped the hanky on the table, brusquely grabbed Mannion's right hand, and plucked the shard from the palm. "You're not gonna bleed to death in my presence, for chrissakes."

He wrapped the cloth tightly around the hand and knotted it.

Mannion stared up at the man, waiting, not sure he was going to want to hear what the doctor had to tell him.

Bohannon sighed and snapped his brown wool vest down over his considerable belly. "Now, then, the girl. They treated her poorly. Awfully poorly. However, physically, I believe she'll recover."

"Mentally...?"

"That's hard to say."

"She still hasn't said anything?"

Bohannon shook his head and pulled his mouth corners down beneath his long, drooping, silver mustache. "No. I'm not entirely sure she was even aware of my and Jane's presence. Jane and I bathed her, and she just stared off into space."

Mannion remembered the look in her eyes. *Those eyes...*

"Jane is still with her," Bohannon continued. "I don't

think she should be left alone for a while. Best to keep an eye on her."

"Dear God." Mannion raked a hand down his face, digging the fingers into his unshaven flesh. He turned to Bohannon. "Can I see her?"

"Sure. Keep it short, though, Joe." Bohannon placed a comforting hand on Mannion's left shoulder, squeezed. "She needs her rest."

The thuds of a galloping horse rose in the street beyond the batwings. They rose in volume until they were louder than the various other sounds issuing from the street. Mannion turned his head to the front window left of the batwings as a rider pulled a clay bank gelding up to one of the hitchracks fronting the saloon.

The rider swung quickly down from the saddle, his dust rising to engulf him and the sweat-lathered mount. A tall, slender man in a funnel-brimmed cream hat and checked shirt and suspenders as well as batwing chaps and two holstered six-shooters, he quickly looped the reins over the tie rail. As he did, Mannion's eyes automatically slid to the horse's sweat-silvered right wither.

It wore the blaze of Garth Helton's Spur brand.

The man ran up the porch steps two steps at a time, spurs jingling. He crossed the porch, pushed through the batwings, and started striding toward the staircase at the rear of the room. When he saw the doctor standing at Mannion's table, he stopped abruptly and said, "Doc, I was told I'd find you here. Mister Helton needs you out to the—"

He stopped when he saw Mannion.

"Out to the...out to the..."

"Out to the Spur is what you're probably trying to say, Yates," Mannion said, glowering at the man. He knew most of the Spur riders on sight. They were a nasty lot, but he'd locked each of them up at one time or another over the years. They were tough men, but, while he had only two others to back his play, he was tougher. And so far, none had wanted to deal with killing a town marshal. Their boss had likely warned them not to and get Helton crossways with the town.

Now that's likely changed. Garth Helton would send someone to kill him now for sure, the town be damned though Mannion had a pretty good feeling that most of the town was turning against him along with the mayor and several other wealthy mucky mucks who thought Mannion had outstayed his welcome here in Del Norte.

Ungrateful bastards.

Yates switched his nervous gaze to the doctor. "Yeah...that's...uh..."

Mannion kept his eyes on the Spur rider as he said to the sawbones, "I gave Whip a pill he's having a hard time digesting, looks like. His old man wants you to go dig it out." He glanced up at Bohannon. "You're wasting your time, Doc. He's going to die one way or the other. But make it hurt, will ya?" Mannion smiled coldly. "Make it hurt really good."

He turned back to the Spur rider and added, "And tell him I'll be coming for him."

Looking at Mannion now, Yates flinched.

The doctor sighed and hiked his heavy shoulders then started walking toward the batwings. "I'll fetch my buggy from the livery."

When the doctor and Yates were gone, Mannion set his hat on his head, rose, crossed to the stairs, and climbed them heavily. He wasn't eager to see Vangie again in the state she was in. Those eyes haunted him.

What was with all the sad eyes?

He suspected he might be acquiring that haunted

look himself after all his travails of late. At the moment, he could kind of understand why Sarah had done what she'd done, though he'd never do it himself and leave his daughter alone.

He climbed to the third floor and knocked on the door to Jane's suite.

"Come in, Joe," came the deep, slightly raspy as well as sad voice on the other side of the door.

Mannion twisted the knob, stepped inside, and removed his hat.

Jane's office lay before him. She sat at her big desk that abutted the wall to the right. The desk was built of cherry and adorned with brass handles and two large, brass candelabras and a pink-shaded Tiffany lamp. Otherwise, the desk had almost nothing on it save for a cut glass goblet half-filled with amber liquid she'd been slouched over, elbows on the desk, fingers kneading her temples, as Mannion had stepped through the door.

She turned to him now, sweeping her thick, curly red hair back from her face with a customarily beguiling shake of her head. Her voice had been sad. Her brown eyes were sadder. They glistened with emotion as she sat back in the chair and, fingering the string of pearls hanging down over her low-cut corset, said, "I'm sorry, Joe."

"I'd like to see her."

Jane canted her head to indicate the door in the wall to Mannion's left, which lay beyond a small parlor area complete with a small, brick fireplace outfitted with red leather chairs, small cherry tables, and a scrolled-back, red velvet fainting couch as well as a piano. A harp was mounted on the wall above the piano.

A cultured lady, Jane Ford. Mannion had no idea what she saw in him. He knew what he saw in her—a tender heart that maybe someday might temper the hot-running passions of his own, a keen intelligence, and a magical lover. After Sarah's death, before Jane had come along and they'd inexplicably gotten together, he'd never once associated with another woman. Not even percentage girls. Sarah's suicide had robbed him of that sort of passion. All he'd had left was anger.

Maybe it's all he still had left.

He pegged his hat and walked past the large liquor cabinet abutting the wall on his left, as he headed for the bedroom. At the door, he stopped, hesitating, his heart chugging painfully, blood rushing in his ears. His daughter might have been taken from him for good.

Rage kicked up the pain in his temple.

What tempered it, though, was hoping that Doc Bohannon would pull Whip Helton through so Mannion could hunt him down all over again and kill him for keeps this time.

Yeah, maybe all he had left was rage.

He twisted the knob, opened the door, stepped through it, and gently latched it behind him. The last thing he saw before he heard the click was Jane gazing at him, the skin above the bridge of her own sad, beautiful eyes ridged with worry for both him and Vangie, he knew.

Like the rest of the town, she wondered how this would affect him.

How he might lash out. Of course, lash out he would. Every soul in town knew him well enough to know that much. They were likely bracing for it.

Mannion walked slowly to the bed. Vangie lay hidden beneath the covers, turned to face the wall on Mannion's right. He could tell she lay much as she'd lain on the cot when he'd first seen her in that devil's lair.

He was glad she wasn't facing him.

He didn't want to see her eyes.

He sat gently down on the edge of the bed, placed his hand on her shoulder over the covers, and silently promised her that she would be avenged, or her father, Bloody Joe Mannion, would die trying.

CHAPTER 15

GARTH HELTON LOPED TO THE TOP OF A LOW RISE northeast of Del Norte and checked down his buckskin stallion. His ramrod, Quint Wayne, reined in his own mount beside his boss.

"Miserable damn place," Helton groused as he stared down the rise at the old Yellow Butte Stage Station that sat along the road between Christo and Cimarron. The Cimmaron River angled around behind the place, the river itself flanked by an aspen forest. The aspens were just starting to change now in late August, and there was a coolness to the breeze that ruffled the sunlit water, making the stream glint like a long, slender gown of gold sequins.

The stage had been abandoned years ago when the Sangre de Christo Stage Line had gone bankrupt mostly because its coaches kept getting held up, so no one wanted to ride the damn things or ship valuables in their strong boxes. That was before Mannion had come to Del Norte. Now things had calmed down considerably in his part of the county, but the stage line had not resumed service.

The place had been bought from the stage line by an old rancher's widow named Alma Larson whose dead husband had left her the all-but bankrupt Black Bird Ranch just up the creek from the stage station. Mrs. Larson had erected four small plankboard, tin-roofed shacks behind the main cabin, and that's where her percentage gals tendered their services mostly to local cow punchers as well as to, it seemed, Helton's hired gun, Cole Shrake. Seemed that Shrake had taken a fancy to one of the girls who plied the old trade here for Mrs. Larson.

The main cabin slouched under its brush roof, the right side of its front stoop listing precariously. Elk Antlers with one end broken off were mounted above the front door and several rusty wash tubs hung from nails in the stoop's low front wall. A little blonde clad in a very short and low-cut pink dress sat on the top step of the porch, one nearly bare leg crossed on the other as she picked at her foot.

Two saddled horses stood at the hitchrack to the left of the girl, hanging their heads and desultorily switching their tails. A wheelless coach sat in the tall brush along-side of the moldering, gray log barn to the left of the cabin and its flanking hog pens, an equally moldering corral trailing off the barn's opposite side, several of its fallen rails nearly hidden in the brush growing up around it.

Mrs. Larson was out to the right of the cabin—a gray-haired, short, rotund little woman in a shapeless gray sack dress and with a flowered scarf around her head. She had several rugs hung up on a sagging wash line, and she'd been beating them with a stick, making dust waft, until she'd spied Helton and Wayne sitting the rise to the west of her place.

Now she stood holding the stick in one hand, holding her other hand up to shade her eyes as she scrutinized the newcomers.

Helton turned to Wayne and jerked his chin at the road ranch. "*Hy-ahh!*"

He spurred the buckskin on down the slope, Wayne following suit and catching up to ride beside him. Together they loped across the stage trail and into the yard where they checked their mounts down to trots before reining up in front of the old woman standing at the wash line. She shook her head and waved her hand distastefully at the wafting dust.

"Mrs. Larson," Helton said by way of greeting.

She just scowled at him, her face lumpy and deeply lined, eyes set deep in doughy sockets. She slid her fishy gaze between him and Wayne as though she suspected they were up to no good.

"I'm told you got a man holed up here with one of your girls. Cole Shrake," Helton said.

"I don't know names," the little bird croaked out.

"Which cabin belongs to the half-breed?" Wayne asked her.

She held up three spidery fingers poking up out of black, half-fingered gloves.

Helton and Wayne shared a look then swung their horses around and booted them down along the side of the cabin. At the rear of the place, Helton stopped the buckskin and swung down from the saddle. An unsaddled horse was grazing a ways off in the brush. Helton recognized the mount as Shrake's coyote dun.

He glanced up at his foreman. "He's here, all right. Come on."

"You got it, boss."

Wayne swung down, dropped his reins so both horses

stood ground-reined side-by-side. Wayne, a little taller than Helton but not by much, followed the older man past the door of the first cabin on the right. A number four had been sloppily written in black paint on the cracked and splintering pine boards. The door of the next cabin wore number three.

Helton stepped up to the door, slightly to the left of it, and drew the big Colt .45 he carried high on his right hip. He clicked the hammer back then glanced at Wayne and jerked his head to indicate the door.

Wayne nodded, stepped up to the door, and threw his arms up as he raised his right knee high and slammed the bottom of that boot against the door with a heavy grunt. The door burst inward to slam against the wall. Before it could bounce back, Helton stepped inside and caught it with his left foot. Straight before him lay the bed on which both Shrake and a plump, black-haired, copper-skinned, young woman were just now sitting up, startled, the girl giving a panicked cry and lifting a grimy white sheet to cover her breasts.

Helton raised his forty-five and extended it straight out from his right shoulder.

The bare-chested Shrake raised his hands as though to shield his face, yelling, "Hey, what in the *hell*—"

Helton's Colt roared.

The girl screamed and flopped straight back against the badly rumpled bed, a forty-five-caliber-sized hole in the dead center of her forehead.

Shrake had squeezed his eyes shut and turned his head to one side.

Now he opened his eyes, slowly lowered his hands, and cast his terrified look at the big man standing in the smoky doorway. He turned to the girl and widened his eyes and hung his lower jaw.

"*Holy Christ, Helton!*"

Helton slid the still-smoking Colt toward him and yelled, "Do your damn job!"

Shrake looked at the girl before turning his horrified gaze to the rancher once more, scowling angrily now. "I done told you—he's laid up in his lady friend's hotel!"

"No, he's not. Fast healer is Bloody Joe. He put a bullet in my boy while you were whore mongering." Helton narrowed one eye as he aimed down the barrel at the regulator. "Do your job, Shrake, or the next one's for you!"

He lowered the gun, shoved it into its holster, turned around, glanced at Wayne, and strode back toward the horses.

SHRAKE BURIED THE DEAD INDIAN WHORE WHILE THE old biddy who ran the road ranch, Mrs. Larson, castigated him up one side and down the other, as though *he* were the one who'd killed the girl! She'd even swatted him a few times about the head and shoulders with the stick she'd been using to beat the rugs with.

Hell, Shrake hadn't killed Mouse. (That had been her name—Mouse.) Helton had drilled her that third eye. Still, the old woman blamed Shrake for the death of her best money maker.

The regulator supposed Mouse's death was his fault. He'd gotten soft and lackadaisical in these later years. Overconfident in his abilities, maybe. And lazy. Instead of frolicking with the half-breed girl and getting her killed—he just could not resist a plump half-breed, for some reason!—he should have been keeping tabs on Bloody Joe. He should have stayed in town and then followed Mannion when he'd ridden out after Helton's kid and those jaspers Whip rode with and blown the uncompromising lawman out of his saddle.

No, instead, Shrake had convinced himself that it would take a good week for a man of Mannion's age, late-forties, to get over a head wound like that. If he ever did.

Well, Mannion had, obviously. And he'd left Shrake with a dead whore and looking like a damn fool.

Shrake felt bad about the girl. Not heartbroken. It wasn't as though he'd had any real feelings for her. He'd just enjoyed her company in the mattress sack. Right talented, she'd been. More than feeling bad about the whore, Shrake was embarrassed. Not only had he under-estimated Bloody Joe Mannion, but he'd let himself get tracked down and surprised by a man nearly twice his age.

Cole Shrake was not a man without his enemies. He could not afford to let his guard down like he'd done with Mouse. He could not afford to let himself get tracked down and surprised while he was playing slap 'n' tickle—actually, more tickle than slap—with a half-breed whore.

It could very easily be him lying in that grave instead of the girl. It would serve him right, too.

Cole Shrake, you are a professional killer. Start acting like it! he reprimanded himself now as he trotted his coyote dun along the trail to Del Norte. He'd camped along the trail last night and had gotten up early to ride the rest of the way into town and get the job done. He had a reputation to maintain, and he'd done some critical damage to it out here today. He was going to have to make up for it.

What better way than to kill Bloody Joe Mannion?

So many men had tried. Shrake alone would succeed.

He smiled to himself and kicked the dun into a lope,

fifteen minutes later following the trail into a bustling Del Norte, which was fairly overrun with ranch, mine, and lumber wagons with still here and there an old mountain man complete with buckskins and coonskin cap in town to fill the larder of his remote cabin, still stubbornly clinging to the old mountain ways. The mountains surrounding Del Norte—the San Juans, the Sawatch, and the Sangre de Christos—still teemed with such old salts living alone or with Indian wives in cabins they'd likely built with their own hands damn near fifty years ago, long before silk had replaced beaver for men's favorite hats.

Out front of a grocery store, a man in a bowler hat, a bloody green apron, and with a cigarette dangling out of his mouth was skinning a big mule deer buck.

As Shrake passed, the man glanced up at him, glanced away, then turned back for a closer look. Shrake turned his head forward. He didn't like being looked at too closely. He prided himself on his anonymity, or relative anonymity, anyway. Most regulators were braggarts especially when drunk. Shrake rarely got drunk and when he did, he was usually alone out on the stalking trail and even if he wasn't alone, he didn't go shooting his mouth off about what a great killer he was.

That was a great way to get yourself turned toe down, a feast for the coyotes and crows.

He didn't like towns. That's why he'd been out at Yellow Butte. He didn't want anyone to see this stranger lurking around the hurdy gurdy houses and saloons too long and become suspicious of his intentions. Especially Bloody Joe.

While Shrake had a reputation for efficient killing, a man who could always be called on to get the job done when others could not, he was not widely recognized. He doubted Joe Mannion would have recognized him. But he was a stranger here in town, and strangers stood out especially for lawmen of Bloody Joe Mannion's ilk.

Shrake rode the length of Del Norte's main drag without seeing hide nor hair of Bloody Joe. That was strange. Shrake had investigated Mannion thoroughly, and he knew Mannion to be a lawman who didn't hide in his office. He was usually out walking the boardwalks and mixing with the crowds in saloons, knowing his presence alone would cut down on trouble, and knowing a lawman couldn't stop trouble if he was sitting behind a desk.

Shrake rode past Mannion's office twice and saw only an older, heavier man wearing a deputy's star sitting on the stoop sipping coffee, a double-barrel Greener leaning against the wall behind him. That would be Rio Waite. Shrake had seen the other deputy, a tall, slender lad named Henry "Stringbean" McCallister, making the rounds as Shrake had been perusing Del Norte's main drag, staying within traffic tangles and trying not to look overly suspicious.

Finally, Shrake pulled his horse up to a saloon and tied it at the hitchrack. He'd go in and have a beer and keep an eye on the street.

He'd just stepped up onto the boardwalk when a tow-headed boy of maybe nine or ten appeared, stepping up onto the boardwalk to Shrake's left. The kid wore sack trousers, a striped shirt, suspenders, and a wool watch cap. He had a lumpy burlap sack of what was probably parcels headed for the post office slung over one shoulder, and he was slouched beneath the bag's weight.

An errand runner for local businesses, this kid. Probably cost them dimes and nickels. A real steal.

Shrake waited for the kid to approach then smiled

and pinched his hat brim as he stepped into his path. "Hello, there, young man."

The boy started to walk around Shrake with a muttered and none too friendly, "Hello."

Shrake grabbed his arm then looked around to make sure no one was close enough to overhear and said, "You haven't seen the town marshal lately, have you, son?"

The boy looked indignantly at the hand on his arm and then scowled up at the man it belonged to. "Bloody Joe?"

"That's right," Shrake chuckled.

The kid's frown deepened as he turned his head to one side and narrowed a suspicious eye. "Who wants to know?"

"Just an old friend from long ago. Thought I'd pay Joe a visit after all these years."

"If the marshal ain't in his office, he's probably up in the San Juan Hotel with his daughter. She's been feeling poorly, Miss Vangie has."

The boy started to move around Shrake again when Shrake again grabbed his arm, turned him to face him. "Say, uh, if you see the marshal, don't tell him I inquired, all right, boy?" Shrake gave an oily smile. "Want it to be a surprise." He winked.

The boy rolled his eyes, gave a weary sigh, and continued up the boardwalk, slouched beneath the mail bag.

Shrake raked a pensive hand across his mouth as he turned to face the busy street. The San Juan Hotel and Saloon, easily the largest building Shrake had seen in Del Norte, lay just up the street to Shrake's left. He could keep an eye on it from here.

He'd varnish his tonsils and wait for Bloody Joe and shoot the son of a bitch right out here on the street. It was busy enough that Shrake thought he could get lost in the crowd before returning to his horse and riding away, leaving Mannion in a bloody pile behind him.

Shrake gave a thin, self-satisfied smile as he turned and pushed through the batwings.

CHAPTER 16

STRINGBEAN MCCALLISTER STEPPED AWAY FROM THE front wall of Mortimer's Drygoods and into the path of young Harmon Hauffenthistle. "Say, there, Harmon—workin' hard or hardly workin'?"

The young towheaded oddjobber, only nine years but who worked nearly as hard as any full-grown man in Del Norte, stopped and looked up at Stringbean with an impatient sigh. "I swear, if one more person gets in my way... If I don't have these parcels to the post office by the time the afternoon stage pulls out, Mister Ambrose is gonna have my—"

"What'd that stranger want with you, Harmon?"

Deep scowl lines stretched across young Harmon's deeply tanned face that looked even darker in contrast to his close-cropped, pale blond hair. "Huh?"

"The stranger who stopped you back yonder in front of the Three-Legged Dog?"

Harmon glanced over his shoulder. "Oh, you mean the tall drink of water with the big 'stache?"

"Yeah."

Harmon shrugged a shoulder. "Said he was a friend of

Marshal Mannion's. Wanted to know if I seen him today. I hadn't so..."

The boy started to walk around Stringbean, who grabbed his arm, stopping him.

"Hey, Stringbean, hangit, anyways, I gotta—"

"He said he was a friend of Marshal Mannion?"

"Yeah, that's right." Harmon jerked his arm free of Stringbean's grip and continued up the boardwalk. As he did, he glanced back over his shoulder. "Hey, Stringbean, if you see the marshal, don't tell him the fella asked about him. He said he wanted it to be a surprise." He turned his head forward and continued walking. "Gotta run. Some of us *work* for a livin'!"

He gave an amused little snort then stepped down off the boardwalk and hustled across the cross street, bellowing loudly at a dog that ran out from beneath a boardwalk to nip at the boy's ankles.

"Very funny, Harmon," Stringbean groused under his breath.

"Henry!"

Stringbean swung his head to see the girl he'd been sparking, the freighter's daughter, Molly Hurdstrom, just then stepping out the door of the grocery store, a box heaped with airtight tins, jars, and small burlap pouches, one marked ARBUCKLES, in her arms. She wore a blue-and-white checked gingham dress and a little straw hat trimmed with faux blueberries atop her lovely head. Stringbean always felt his insides twist when he saw her with her sparkling gray eyes and heart-shaped face with pretty, pert nose and thick, chestnut hair piled up on top of her head. Some of those lovely locks dangled down against her cheeks in sausage curls.

"Molly!" he said.

"How are you, Henry? I haven't seen you in a while."

Molly was the only person in town who regularly called him by his given name. Stringbean appreciated that she did, too. Privately, he wished the other town folks would stop calling him Stringbean now that he was darn near in his mid-twenties. Besides, the nickname didn't seem fitting for a man of the law—though, also privately, Stringbean hadn't been feeling like much of a lawman after the other day when his posse was ambushed and he lit out like a fawn with a forest on fire behind him.

Stringbean hemmed and hawed. "I, uh...well, I..."

"Could you help me with this, Henry? It's getting rather heavy," Molly said as, wincing, she hefted the box in her arms.

"Oh, fer Pete's sake! Look at me standin' here with my tongue in my throat while you..." Stringbean took the parcel out of the girl's arms.

"My buggy's right there," she said, pointing at the fancy, red-wheeled, leather-seat chaise sitting in the street at the south end of the boardwalk fronting the store.

"I'll set it in there for you—don't you worry about that!"

"Thank you so much, Henry," she said, following him and giving the beaded cloth reticule hanging from her right wrist a pensive little toss.

When Stringbean had set the box on the chaise's rear seat, he turned to see Molly frowning up at him. "How come you haven't stopped by the house lately, Henry? You usually come for at least a short visit a few times a week."

Stringbean frowned back at her. If he didn't know better, he'd have sworn the girl had actually missed his visits. That didn't seem possible. She'd never let on how she felt about him one way or the other. She'd always acted rather cool in his presence, and that, since he was heartsick for her, had made him even shyer and more awkward than he usually was around pretty girls.

"Uh...well," Stringbean said, "I, uh...I guess I wasn't sure you really *wanted* me to stop by, Miss Molly. And, uh...well, to tell you the truth I've been feelin' a little off my feed of late."

"You have? How come? Are you sick?" She stepped forward and placed her hand on his forehead. "You don't seem to have a temp—"

"Nah, nah, not like that," Stringbean said, feeling a little better in general about everything just by the feel of the girl's tender flesh against his. But only marginally so. His act of cowardice still haunted him despite the marshal having told him to forget about it. "Not so much physical as I just been...well, I ain't been—I mean, *haven't* —been sleepin' well."

"Oh, no!"

"Yeah."

"What's wrong, Henry? You don't look like yourself."

He studied her closely. There was a deep seriousness in those pretty gray eyes. Rungs of genuine concern were cut across her forehead. He was beginning to think that she felt more for him than he'd thought. Here, he'd almost made up his mind that he'd been wasting his time sparking the girl, that maybe she'd set her hat for someone else—a young man with a little more education, money, and a brighter future. Maybe she, like Stringbean himself, was just shy and found it hard to express her true feelings.

Now, however, considering what had happened the other day, his proving himself a coward, he was beginning to believe that if she truly did feel something deeper for him than what he'd thought, he didn't deserve those feelings. That was another reason why he hadn't visited her lately. He preferred to stay in his room at Mavis Branch's Rooming House when he wasn't on duty for Marshal Mannion, stewing in his own cowardly juices.

He couldn't tell Molly about his turning tail and running from trouble. He couldn't ever tell anyone for the whole rest of his life. It was bad enough that the man he admired and respected most in this world knew about it. It was so humiliating that he sometimes wasn't sure he could bear the weight of that awful load—the load of his cowardice—on his shoulders.

Suddenly, he became aware of himself just staring at the girl, a pained look on his face, mouth opened to speak but with no words getting out.

"Oh, Henry," Molly said, reaching up to place a hand on his cheek. "Something's not right with you."

"I...I...uh..."

She pulled her hand down and gave him a direct, commanding look. "You come up to the house tomorrow night. For supper this time. My parents have been wanting to get to know you better, anyway, since they know how I feel about you. Leastways"—now it was her turn to twist a pained, puzzled look— "if you feel the same about me."

"Oh, I do!" Suddenly, he found himself reaching over and squeezing her hand in his. He was surprised by the swiftness of the action. Before it had taken him a good half hour to forty-five minutes to work up the gumption to do something like that. And he guessed now that that was why she was as puzzled about how he felt about her as he was about how she felt about him. "And I'd...I'd...well, I guess I'd love to, Molly."

He realized, however, he had not put much passion in

his voice. He was torn. On one hand, he was thrilled to know that she cared about him maybe even as much as he cared about her. On the other hand, he didn't deserve her. If he were to say, marry her, he'd owe it to her to tell her what he'd done.

And he just couldn't.

He couldn't tell anyone. Not ever. Not if he lived a thousand years.

Which meant he couldn't, in the end, have her. But having supper with Molly and her parents would likely cheer him up and distract him from his miseries.

"It's a date, then." She smiled brighter than he'd ever seen her smile before. She even glanced around guiltily then stepped forward, rose onto her tiptoes, and placed a gentle kiss on his cheek. "See you tomorrow night, Henry!"

Stringbean stood in shock, his cheek fairly tingling where she'd kissed it.

He stood numbly staring at her sitting in the driver's seat of the chaise, waiting for a break in the wagon and horse traffic before she pulled the chaise out into the street, swung around, flicked the reins over the back of the fine Morgan in the traces, and headed back in the direction of the neat, two-story, white frame house she shared with her parents by the creek.

He followed her with his gaze as she retreated down the dusty street then remembered with a shock the tall stranger who'd asked Harmon Hauffenthistle about the marshal. He turned his attention ahead toward the Three-Legged Dog Saloon just in time to see the man step out of the batwings and into the street on the right side of his horse. He was moving with a furtive air. He was moving around on the other side of the horse, so Stringbean couldn't see what he was doing exactly, but he did see the man turn his head and gaze toward the street's other side.

Stringbean followed the man's gaze.

The marshal was walking along one of the boardwalks there, heading back in the direction of the jailhouse. He must have just left the San Juan Hotel, where he'd been spending an hour with his daughter every morning since the marshal and Stringbean had brought the poor girl back to town. The tall, mustached gent ahead of Stringbean turned his head away from the marshal suddenly, as though not wanting to be seen watching him.

But Stringbean had seen him, all right. He'd seen him when he'd ridden into town earlier, and he'd been keeping an eye on him because Marshal Mannion had always told Stringbean and Rio Waite to keep an eye out for strangers. Del Norte was really bustling these days, with more and more folks pouring in to take advantage of the ranching and mining boom, so it was sometimes hard to identify the most recent strangers.

But Stringbean had spied this tall, sort of good-looking fellow riding a tall, handsome coyote dun right off. Stringbean wasn't sure why, but the man had the air of trouble about him. He also had a pretty Henry repeating rifle jutting up from his saddle sheath. That and the general, furtive air of the man, riding in traffic as though trying to be inconspicuous, and the way he'd looked around, turning his head from left to right and back again, as though trying to pick someone out of the crowd, and keeping his hat pulled low over his eyes, had caught Stringbean's attention.

Stringbean's pulse quickened as the man, carrying the rifle now down low by his right leg, mounted the board-walk on Stringbean's side of the street and began walking quickly in the direction the marshal was heading. Stringbean followed him, his pulse quickening even more. The man turned his head often to keep track of the marshal and quickened his pace.

He was following Marshal Mannion, all right. Of that, Stringbean was certain.

Stringbean quickened his pace to keep pace with the stranger, doubt nipping his heels like a rabid cur. Doubt in his own abilities. Doubt about his being able to make the right decision about just what he should do.

Should he run across the street and try to catch up to the marshal and warn him?

Or should he stay on the heels of the stranger and wait for him to make a move?

What if he made a move? Would Stringbean be able to make a move, then, too, or would he freeze and run the way he'd done the other night?

Stringbean had just crossed the next cross street and mounted the boardwalk fronting a ladies' dress shop when the stranger stopped suddenly and glanced behind him. Stringbean froze in his tracks then quickly stepped into the recessed doorway of Mrs. Baumgartner's House of a Thousand Delights—a hurdy gurdy house complete with a red lantern in the window.

He winced and closed his eyes. Had the man seen him?

Stringbean removed his hat and edged a look out around the corner of the entranceway, casting his gaze up the street. If the stranger had seen him, he wasn't letting on. He stood at the edge of the boardwalk, peering over a parked freight wagon toward the street's opposite side.

Stringbean cast his own gaze in that direction.

The marshal had stopped to chin with a local barman taking a break to smoke a big cigar on the boardwalk fronting his saloon. Meanwhile, on Stringbean's side of the street, the stranger was watching him. Then, suddenly, pulling his hat brim down lower over his eyes, the man continued walking up the street. A few seconds later, he turned into a break between a feed store and Mr. Dunham's tonsorial parlor, disappearing from Stringbean's view.

Stringbean quickened his pace, weaving through the pedestrian traffic before getting held up momentarily by two big Chinese miners arguing out front of the feed-store in their unintelligible tongue. Stringbean slipped around them, avoiding their gesticulating arms and the lit cigar one was wielding like a saber. He stopped at the far corner of the feed store to peer down the break between the feed store and the barber shop.

The man wasn't there—only tufts of sage, some rotting lumber, and trash. A squirrel was sitting in a gap between a barrel and a lumber pile, munching some morsel it had found among the trash.

Stringbean stepped forward and stopped at the near corner of the barber shop.

His heart kicked fiercely.

Shipping crates were stacked at the mouth of the small gap between the barber shop and the little cigar shop beyond it. The stranger was down on one knee in the break, resting his Henry rifle over the top of the crates, toward the other side of the street. He'd removed his hat, and he was all but concealed by the crates. Stringbean wouldn't have seen him if he hadn't seen the sunlight glint off the Henry's brass breech.

Stringbean quickly followed the barrel of the rifle toward the other side of the street. Marshal Mannion was just then approaching the jailhouse. Mannion's bay, Red, was tied to the hitchrack and looking toward its approaching master. Rio Waite was standing on the jailhouse's stoop, talking to Mannion who gave Red's snout a quick pat then turned to climb the porch steps, removing his hat and running a big hand through his hair.

Stringbean jumped to life, yelling, "Marshal Mannion —get down! *Ambush!*"

That last word had just cleared his lips when the stranger's Henry roared.

Stringbean clawed his old hog-leg from its holster too late. The stranger had already recocked the Henry and was swinging it toward him, knocking the top crate off the pile before him, an enraged look in the man's bulging, dark eyes.

The Henry stabbed smoke and flames toward String-bean a quarter eye blink before Stringbean triggered his Remington at the stranger, seeing his slug rip a chunk of wood out of the unpainted siding of the building flanking the man. At the same time, Stringbean felt the burning pain of the stranger's bullet in his right side.

The bullet knocked him backward, twisting him around. He tried to get his boots set beneath him.

"*Stringbean!*" came a shout just before Stringbean's knees buckled and he struck the boardwalk, inadvertently triggering his Remy into the wood a foot from his right knee.

There was a fierce spatter of gunfire and then, as Stringbean watched the sun-seared, gray boards of the walk rise quickly toward him, so that the cracks between them grew as large as the breaks between two business buildings on Main Street, everything went dark.

CHAPTER 17

Mannion had just gained the top of the porch fronting his office and jail when the shouted warning vaulted at him from the other side of the street. The second call hadn't entirely left Stringbean's mouth before a bullet curled the air off Mannion's right ear to *thunk!* into the porch support post before him.

He ducked and swung around, reaching for the Russian holstered for the cross-draw on his left side. As he did, he saw the barrel of a Henry rifle swing toward where Stringbean stood on the boardwalk fronting Dunham's Tonsorial Parlor. Before he could get the Russian steadied, the Henry spat flames. Stringbean gave a cry and lurched backward, swinging hard to his right, dropping to his knees, and firing the Remington in his right hand into the boardwalk beside him.

"*Stringbean!*" Rio Waite bellowed behind Mannion.

Crouching, Russian extended straight out before him, Mannion cursed through gritted teeth and triggered three quick rounds toward where the shooter crouched behind packing crates between the barber shop and a leather goods store. The man, sensing Mannion's move, had just pulled his head and rifle down behind the crates, so all Mannion's bullets did was chew into the crates though he hoped one or two caromed all the way through to strike the son of the devil behind them.

None must have, because the Henry suddenly appeared again, resting atop the crates. Mannion cursed again and emptied the six-shooter into the crates. After his first two rounds, the Henry had disappeared and then the shooter appeared, rising from behind the crates and running back through the break toward the far end, crouching, holding the Henry in one hand, a brown hat in his other hand.

"Who in blue blazes?" yelled Rio.

Leaping down the steps and into the street, Mannion shoved the empty Russian into its holster and reached for the one on his right thigh. He ran across the street without worrying about the traffic, for the traffic had stopped on the street between the jail and the barbershop when lead had started flying.

"Is he alive?" Mannion yelled to the barber, John Dunham, who'd come out of his office and was now on one knee beside the unmoving deputy.

Dunham shot a glance at Mannion, his spectacles glinting. "He's breathing!"

"Get the sawbones!"

Dunham straightened with a flash of his teeth and hurried off down the boardwalk, half-jogging.

Mannion paused beside Stringbean, who appeared to be coming around, moving his head a little and blinking his eyes. Blood shone on his right side, between his hip and his ribs. "Easy, son!" He turned to regard Rio Waite moving as fast as his arthritic knees would allow through the break in the traffic along the street. "Stay with Stringbean! I'm going after that devil!"

Mannion leaped down off the boardwalk, hurled several crates that his bullets had scattered, and ran down the break toward the far end, kicking empty bottles and airtight tins. He stopped at the rear of the barbershop, pressed his shoulder up against the wall, and peered around the corner to his left, the direction he'd seen the shooter flee.

Seeing the Henry's barrel poking out from around the far rear corner of the third building up the alley in that direction and seeing two dark eyes peering down the barrel toward Mannion, Joe pulled his head back. A bullet plunked into the corner of the building where his head had been a second before, peppering his face with wood slivers. He blinked them from his eyes then snaked the Russian around the corner, narrowing an eye as he aimed down the barrel.

His target was gone.

He ran forward along the barber shop's rear wall and kept running. When he gained the building corner from which the man had last fired at him, he ran into the break, raising the Russian. The man wasn't here, either.

Mannion ran, emerging from the break at Main Street. He looked to his right just as the man who'd fired at him casually mounted the boardwalk fronting the Three-Legged Dog Saloon. He glanced over his shoulder at Mannion, smiled, and touched two fingers to the brim of his hat just before he disappeared behind a fine coyote dun tethered at the hitchrack there.

Mannion ran forward, wincing at the pain that remained in his bullet-burned temple.

"What's up, Marshal?" asked a man standing outside the saloon on his right, just as the shooter swung the coyote dun around and put the spurs to it.

"That's the son of a buck who shot my deputy!"

Mannion ran into the street and swung to the south, raising the Russian but holding fire. The rider had just galloped around a big freight wagon parked in front of the mercantile. Mannion saw the man angle back out into of the middle of the street. The Russian bucked and roared. Mannion missed his target as the man wove back into heavy traffic. One of Mannion's bullets evoked a shrill scream from a portly, brown-haired lady in a large red picture hat and red shawl who'd just then been making her way across the street with a large paper shopping bag in her hand, a good block away.

She looked down at the hem of her dress splattered with dirt from Mannion's bullet then cast a glare toward Mannion himself.

"Christ, Marshal!" This from none other than the mayor, Charlie McQueen, standing outside a dentist's parlor not far from the woman Mannion had soiled. He, too, cast an angry-eyed stare toward Mannion, who cursed and ran back up the street to the north.

By now, bystanders were yelling, inquiring what all the shooting had been about, and a small crowd had gathered in a semi-circle in the street near where Rio Waite was just then helping the younger deputy sit up against a ceiling support post. Mannion pushed through the crowd, telling everybody to go about their business, the shooter was gone.

Rio looked at him. "He get away?"

"Not for long," Mannion said. "How's the younker?"

"Took it in the side, but he's comin' around. Wanted to sit up."

Stringbean turned to Mannion who dropped to a knee beside him. "S-sorry, Marshal...I...tried..."

"What the hell are you talking about, Kid?" Mannion said. "You took a bullet that was meant for me." He shook his head and patted Stringbean's shoulder. "Don't worry—I'll get him." Quick footsteps sounded on the boardwalk behind Mannion, who turned to see the doctor hurrying toward them, his medical kit in his hand. "Treat him right, Doc." He glanced at Waite. "Stay with him."

"Get him, Joe!"

"Intend to."

Mannion rose and hustled off through the sparse crowd remaining to gawk at the wounded deputy. He jogged over to where Red was tethered to the hitchrack fronting the jailhouse, untied the horse, swung up into the saddle, turned the bay south, and put the steel to him.

He weaved through the traffic that was still mostly stalled because of the shooting, men palavering over what had happened and casting Mannion curious looks as the lawman galloped past them, hunkered low in his saddle, hat pulled down. In the corner of his eye, Mannion saw Charlie McQueen still giving him the wooly eyeball from outside the dentist's parlor.

Mannion didn't turn to look at the mayor. He had bigger fish to fry than Charlie McQueen.

Soon he was out of town. He slowed Red where several secondary trails diverged from the main one, near a large cottonwood standing in the V between the left-forking trail and the main one, its leaves touched with the yellow of the coming fall. The fresh prints of a fast-galloping mount scored the trail angling off to the right, in the direction of the San Juans lumping up big and blue-green in the south, the highest peaks mantled with the dirty cream of last winter's snow. Mannion swung Red onto the secondary trail and was soon climbing into broken, shelving country, the trail twisting between rocky dikes jutting up like the spines of half-buried dinosaurs.

He kept one eye on the trail ahead and one eye on the freshly scored hoof prints, which weren't hard to make out, for this trail was less traveled than some around Del Norte, leading as it did only to one abandoned mine. When he saw the sprawling log housing of the mineshaft on a ridge a quarter mile ahead, he slowed Red and noticed that the man he was trailing had slowed his own mount here, too.

Mannion jerked the bay to a sudden stop and reined him to the right, behind a sprawling cedar jutting up from the base of a sloping dike. Since this was for all intents and purposes a box canyon, with no way out other than the way in, the shooter had likely led Mannion in here to bushwhack him.

Again.

Mannion shucked the Yellowboy from its sheath, swung his right leg over his saddle horn, and dropped to the ground. He pumped a live round into the Winchester's action, set the hammer to half-cock, and edged a look around the left side of the cedar, staring up the two-track trail gradually rising toward the sun-grayed logs of the mine and the gray rock tailings littering the slope below it. The stamping mill lay to the left of the mine, all derelict now, a large golden eagle just then lighting on the peaked roof of the mine and giving its shrill, ratcheting cry.

Other than the sighing of the breeze blowing down from the craggy ridge behind and above the mine, that was the only sound.

The devil was here somewhere, Mannion thought, tapping his thumb against the Yellowboy's hammer. *Waiting to clean me off his trail once and for all. Likely feeling rather sore about having been interrupted by the kid. Damn fool move Stringbean made. His life for mine? What the hell kind of a lopsided deal was that?*

Mannion patted Red's neck. "Stay, boy," he whispered, knowing the shooter was here somewhere, probably near, waiting to line up his sights on his target once more.

Mannion stepped around Red and climbed up into a deep V-notch in the dike wall. Staying low and keeping an eye peeled on the higher ground around him where the shooter was likely on the lurk, he continued through the notch then, when he came to the dike's opposite side, clambered down to low ground.

He dropped to a knee and looked around at the rocky, cedar- and pine-studded terrain lumping up around him. He jerked with a start when a loud CAW-CAW-CAW! sounded on his right. He turned to see a crow sitting on a fire-blackened branch of a lightning topped birch standing alone and black and dead on a barrel-shaped bluff, the formation's near side bearing the deep dimple and tailings of an exploratory mineshaft.

The crow gave its indignant cry again, stretching its large, black wings.

It wasn't looking at Mannion. It was looking at something ahead of Mannion, beyond where a deep notch curved around the side of another dike maybe fifty, sixty yards ahead.

The bird saw something up there. Some intruder it didn't like?

Mayhaps...

Mannion moved ahead along the crease, following it to the left and then the right between rocky walls. He followed it left again then straight on for about a hundred feet. He stepped over a long-discarded pick with a rusty head and splintery handle and kept moving slowly, taking one step at a time, keeping his eyes skinned on the higher, rocky ground above him.

He was here. Mannion could smell the shooter. He could hear the pulse pounding in the devil's ears.

Likely getting nervous. Likely knowing that since he'd left a clear trail, Mannion should be here by now.

Likely coming to the conclusion the lawman was onto his intention to bushwhack him again...

Mannion took another step, then another, squeezing the Yellowboy in his hands.

To his right, a slender shadow slid out from the shadow of the dike rising on his left. Mannion threw himself forward just as a bullet spanged off a rock three feet to his right and was followed by the hiccupping report of a rifle. Mannion rolled then half-sat up, raising the Winchester up at a slant and firing three quick rounds, the thundering reports echoing shrilly.

The shooter, standing fifty feet up the dike, stumbled back against the rock wall behind him. His hat fell forward and rolled down the dike toward Mannion. The man threw his rifle back against the stone wall and dropped it. It slid down the slope toward Mannion, loosing gravel in its wake.

The shooter, a tall, dark-haired man with dark eyes and a thick, dark mustache, looked down at the three holes in his chest—two up high near his right shoulder, the other in his upper left chest. He gave a deep sigh, dropped to his knees and rolled forward. Over and over, he rolled, arms and legs flopping, before he dropped over a steep shelf and piled up on the ground before Mannion with a heavy grunt.

His eyes were closed but his chest rose and fell quickly. He was grunting and groaning miserably.

Mannion pointed the maw of his Yellowboy at the man's head. "Who are you?"

The man opened his eyes bright with pain. He coughed, said in a deep, gravelly voice, "Go to hell."

Mannion knew on sight most of the regulators who worked this neck of Colorado. This man must either have come in from out of the territory or he did his best to keep out of sight. If so, he'd taken a foolish chance by trying to kill Mannion in town. He must have been right desperate to get his man.

That he was a regulator there was little doubt. Mannion knew who most of his enemies were, and this man wasn't one of them. He had the hard, cold eyes of a gun for hire.

That he'd taken the risk of shooting Mannion in town told the lawman something else about him. He'd likely been hired by Garth Helton. Helton was an impatient man. Likely even more impatient after Mannion had shot his son.

"Helton sent you," Mannion said.

The man coughed again, winced with a pain spasm, his chest a bloody mess. "He'll send more. What you did to his son—that's gonna have to be accounted for."

The man twisted a crooked smile, gave his head a single, slow shake. He turned his head to one side so that he was staring up over Mannion's right shoulder, and the light of life left his eyes.

"Yeah, no doubt," Mannion said, thumbing his hat up on his forehead.

CHAPTER 18

THREE DEAD MEN TWISTED AND TURNED IN THE COOL, early autumn breeze.

At least, Mannion figured they were men. Judging by the tattered clothes remaining on their bloated, putrefied bodies, they were men. Their faces were almost gone, eaten away by birds. They hung side by side from a stout branch of a sprawling cottonwood just inside Garth Helton's Spur range.

A plank sign hung around the neck of the man in the middle. In painted red letters, it read:

WE WERE CAUGHT RUSTLING HELTON BEEF

Mannion gave a dry snort then reined Red on up the trail in the direction of the Spur headquarters. He led the regulator's horse along by its bridle reins. He'd wrapped the dead man in his blanket roll and tied him belly down across his saddle after he'd found the dun languidly grazing not far from where the lawman had shot its rider.

The dead man would be his calling card at the Spur headquarters.

It was late in the day when he rode over the last hill and then through the portal proudly emblazoned with the Spur brand and the Helton name in its crossbar. Several men were working on a corral gate to the left of the house where it sat aloft on a low hill. A man holding a Winchester carbine stood just inside the yard, before a bench on which a canteen sat, under a willow tree offering shade. As Mannion rode in, the man stepped forward and held up a gloved hand.

Mannion checked his mounts down. The guard sized him up distastefully before turning his head and calling loudly to the house, "Rider, Mister Helton!"

Mannion turned to the big house ringed by a broad veranda. Presently, a second story door opened onto a balcony, and Garth Helton stuck his big head out. "Who is it?"

"Mannion," the guard called.

Helton just stared down into the yard toward his visitor. As far as Mannion could tell from the distance of maybe seventy yards, his face was expressionless.

Finally, he said, "Send him up!"

He turned, saying something Mannion couldn't hear to someone else in the room.

The guard—Richards was his name, Pete Richards— grinned lopsidedly up at Mannion then clamped his carbine under his right arm and used his hands to form a shape the size of a grapefruit. "You must have *cajones* this big, Mannion."

Mannion clucked Red into motion, and the bay started walking up the hill toward the house, the pack horse clomping doggedly along behind. When Mannion pulled Red up to one of the hitchracks fronting the veranda, he heard at least two sets of heavy footsteps inside the house. The sounds grew louder until the front door opened and Helton stepped out onto the stoop.

His ramrod, Quint Wayne, stepped out beside him. Helton wore his traditional black shirt and black vest with silver tipped bolo tie and black corduroy trousers. Wayne, as usual, was dressed for the trail. He had a worn-out look and sweat-matted hair—the end of another long day at Spur. Both men held a drink in one hand, a fat stogie in the other hand.

Now as both men, roughly the same height, one considerably older and paunchier than the other— silently considered their visitor and their visitor's spare horse, Wayne cracked a devilish grin, lifted his stogie to his mouth, and gave it several thoughtful puffs, the smoke wreathing his face.

Mannion stared back at him flint eyed.

"Brought your killer," Mannion said flatly to Helton. He drew the dun ahead until it stood up beside him and Red and then he tossed the reins over the hitchrack before him.

Helton just stared up at him, his eyes hard, face stony, his broad chest rising and falling heavily as he breathed. Wayne still had a crooked grin on his lips as he puffed the stogie, slitted eyes glinting mockingly.

Finally, Helton said, "Tell me—what brings you here, Joe?" He glanced at the pack horse. "I've never seen that man before in my life."

He returned his flat, defiant gaze to his visitor.

Mannion gave a grim, knowing smile at that. The dead man was concealed by his own tightly wrapped bedroll.

Face hardening again, Mannion said, "I'm here for your son, Helton."

Helton appeared to consider this for a time as he

regarded Mannion still sitting the fine bay lazily switching its tail. Finally, the rancher said, "Why don't you come in and have a drink and a good cigar, Joe? I don't think in all the years you've been marshal of Del Norte we've ever sat down together, have we?"

Mannion said nothing. Helton knew they hadn't sat down together.

"Come on in," Helton urged Mannion, turning toward the door standing half-open behind him. "Let's discuss the matter like civilized men."

"There was nothing civilized in your son's treatment of my daughter," Mannion said. "But yeah...sure...all right." He swung down from Red's back and looped the reins over the hitchrack. "We'll discuss the matter."

"Good, good," Helton said with a stiff, slit-eyed smile.

Mannion turned a glance toward the yard. A good dozen of Helton's riders were slowly making their way toward the house, gazing incredulously—some grinning shrewdly, muttering bemusedly to each other—at their boss's unexpected guest. They moved in a slow, loose-jointed, leisurely way that owned the air of bullying threat, dusty chaps flapping, whang strings jostling, guns bristling on their hips or thighs.

Mannion stepped around Red and shucked his Yellowboy from the saddle sheath. "Don't mind if I pack this, do you?" He glanced at the gun-hung cow punchers still making their way up the hill, strung out in a loose, wolfish pack. "Wouldn't want it to get stolen."

"It's a fine rifle," Helton said. "I wouldn't, either." He glanced at his men, then, too. "Who knows? You might even need it."

He gave Mannion a coyote grin then beckoned.

Mannion glanced at the Spur riders once more then climbed the steps to the veranda where Helton held out a hand for Mannion to enter first. Mannion moved on through the door. He wasn't worried about getting a knife or a bullet in the back. Not here, and not by Helton's own hand. Not by his foreman's hand, either. Oh, they killed rustlers and nesters all the time—two years ago a dead Basque sheepherder had been found dead on Spur range—but not men of importance like Joe Mannion.

That wasn't Helton's way. He preferred to hire out that kind of work to men like the one Mannion had killed. That way, he kept his hands clean. He'd killed many men that way, mostly rival ranchers or rival businessmen or just men he felt had crossed him in some personal way, maybe by having beaten him at one too many hands of cards.

"Upstairs and to the left, Joe."

Mannion climbed the stairs, swung left, and ducked through the open door of Helton's office—a badly cluttered but smartly appointed room.

"Have a seat," Helton said, entering the room in front of Wayne and using his hand to indicate one of the two visitor chairs arranged before the massive desk all but hidden by books and papers as well as cigar ashes and half-smoked stogies. There were several dirty goblets and a couple of empty Irish whiskey bottles, as well.

Mannion sat down in the chair. He had not taken off his hat and would not. He owed Garth Helton not one ounce of respect. In fact, he wished he'd had cow- or horseshit on his boots but did not.

While the foreman sank into the chair to Mannion's right, Helton walked to a liquor cabinet and grabbed a clean goblet and removed the glass stopper on a cut glass bottle.

"No drink," Mannion said. "No cigar. This isn't a social call."

Helton chuckled. "Do you ever make social calls, Joe?" Chuckling again, he set the goblet back down on the cabinet and walked around behind his desk and sank with a heavy sigh into his chair, sort of flopping back and casually draping his arms across the chair arms.

He canted his head to one side and cast Mannion a sour expression. "My son is a devil, I'll grant you that. But he's still my son, and he's gravely wounded. He may not live."

"If you thinking I'm going to say I'm sorry to hear that, you're mistaken."

"He's my son, Joe. Whatever he may be, he is a Helton. One day, when he grows up, I intend to turn this spread over to him. He's my only son."

"He and his demon buddies burned my house and raped my daughter. She hasn't spoken since the attack. I want him."

Wayne glanced at him with that jeering, glint-eyed grin again. "You think you're gonna try him? No judge will try a Helton?"

"Phelps better, or I'll try him myself." The Honorable Homer J.P Grayson was the circuit court judge who made the rounds to Del Norte and other points south around the Sawatch and the San Juan Mountains.

Wayne turned to his boss and sucked air through his teeth, making a surprised whistling sound.

Mannion stared stonily across the desk at the lawman.

"Ten thousand dollars, Joe."

Mannion scowled.

"Ten thousand dollars to let this go. I'll pay to send your daughter to a good doctor in Denver."

Mannion felt the burn of rage turned up several notches inside him. Tightly, flaring his nostrils, he said, "I oughta kill you."

Wayne turned to Mannion again, closing his hand over the bone grips of the Colt jutting on his right thigh. "Now, now, Marshal Mannion."

"Twenty thousand," Helton said, his face still expressionless. "I'll even build you a new house."

"You have three days to bring him to town," Mannion said.

"Or *what*?" Wayne said.

"I'll come and get him myself," Mannion said. "Whether he makes it to town or not is anyone's guess."

Now Helton cracked a smile. "Tall odds even for you, Joe. With Quint here, I have twenty-five gun-handy men. You know that!"

"I'll kill them all and then I'll kill you and your son last, and I'll burn your house to the ground." Mannion placed his hands on the chair arms and heaved himself to his feet. "Three days."

Mannion walked to the door.

Helton stopped him with: "You've threatened me in my own home now, Joe. That means the rules have changed."

"Three days." Mannion left the office and tramped down the stairs and walked out onto the stoop.

The Spur hands stood in a loose group out front of the house, about ten feet off Red's left flank. They stared at Mannion insinuatingly, threateningly. Mannion cocked his Winchester one handed then, extending it straight out from his right hip, he walked down the porch steps, grabbed Red's reins off the hitch rack, and mounted the bay on the horse's left side, snaking the rifle across his belly, aiming the gun at the hands on his left.

He gazed back at the hard-faced riders as he backed Red away from the hitchrack, quartering to his own right, away from the men staring at him with open threat. He'd arrested them all at one time or another, mostly for drunk and disorderly in town. He was in their territory now, and they wanted to make sure he realized that.

When he and Red were a good fifteen feet back away from the hands, who'd turned to follow him with their cold or sneering gazes, he backed Red down the hill, keeping the Winchester trained on the men grouped before him, making sure none reached for iron. Of course, if more than one tried it, he likely wouldn't make it, but he doubted they'd do anything their boss hadn't ordered.

They might be tempted but they respected and feared old Garth.

Twenty feet down the hill, Mannion turned Red around and spurred him into a trot across the yard and out the gate and through the entrance portal. When he'd ridden maybe a hundred yards back along the trail that would take him to Del Norte, he checked Red down suddenly.

He'd heard a dog barking and another sound he'd couldn't identify.

Now he identified it. A girl and a big, shaggy, black and white dog were running around a spruce tree maybe fifty yards off the trail's left side. The girl was blonde, barefoot, and clad in a tight cream dress and short, denim jacket. She held flowers in one hand, and she was laughing as she ran around the tree, the dog barking and jumping up beside her.

"Stop, Ivanhoe, you're making me laugh soo hard!" she laughed.

When she came around the tree again, she stopped suddenly and gasped in surprise, eyes widening. Her gaze had found Mannion on the trail. The dog stopped beside the girl and raised its hackles.

"Stop, Ivanhoe," the girl admonished the dog, placing her hand on his head. "That's impolite."

She looked at Mannion again, and suddenly she smiled.

Mannion was so taken aback by the expression that he returned her smile with a genuine, unguarded one of his own. A rare one.

The girl was a little older than Vangie but not by much. Helton's daughter. An odd one, too. Not like the rest of the Heltons at all, it seemed.

Go figure.

Maybe a little like Vangie. Different. Not a pack animal.

Mannion reined Red around and put him into a trot, wanting to get back to see his own daughter now very badly, indeed.

But before he was back to the main trail to town, the thuds of several sets of galloping riders rose behind him. Helton's words sounded again in his ears: "You've threatened me in my own home now, Joe. That means the rules have changed."

CHAPTER 19

JANE FORD WAS SITTING AT HER DESK IN HER SUITE ON the third floor of the San Juan Hotel & Saloon when a not so light knock sounded on the door.

She winced with annoyance and cast a look at the bedroom door behind which Vangie Mannion was recovering. There were two bedrooms in the roomy suite so having Vangie occupy one was no imposition. In fact, Jane was glad the girl was here where she and the five girls Jane had working here as percentage girls could keep an eye on her.

Over the past seven months that she and Joe had considered themselves a couple, Jane had gotten to know Vangie well and had become quite close to her, which wasn't hard to do. Jane had never known a young lady sweeter or more endearing than Vangie Mannion, and it horrified her to think what that demon Whip Helton and his goatish, fiendish men had done to her.

It was hard to believe that Joe Mannion could have spawned such a sweet child, but Jane thought it reflected well on the man. She knew that Joe's heart was a lot softer than he let on or wanted anyone, including her, to know. That cold exterior was his defense against the harsh world he'd lived in most of his life. Jane knew that he loved his daughter more than life itself.

Maybe that was part of the reason she'd found herself loving him, though she had to admit always having been attracted to rough men despite that she'd had a rather genteel, moneyed upbringing in St. Louis. Maybe it was the influence of the rough riverboat men who'd populated her father's docks.

Jane set down the ink pen she'd been signing checks with and walked to the door, frowning, as the knock came again louder than before. Jane opened the door quickly to see the Mayor, Charlie McQueen, as well as the banker, Morgan Howell and the mercantiler, Wilfred Drake, standing in the hallway. Jane scowled at the dapper, bespectacled, little McQueen.

"Mister Mayor, do you mind?" Jane scolded the man in a loud whisper. "Evangeline Mannion is recovering in my bedroom!"

"I do apologize," McQueen said, removing his crisp brown bowler hat and holding it over his chest. "I'd forgotten she was recovering here. How good of you to take her in."

Jane stepped into the hall and quietly latched the door behind her. "What can I do for you men?"

Howell, a rotund, bald man but with a thick, gray walrus mustache and long side whiskers, removed his own gray bowler. Keeping his voice down, he said, "We apologize for the intrusion, Miss Ford, but we'd like to have a word with you."

Wilfred Drake, a tall, very thin man with a pencil line mustache and, like the mayor, always wearing a smarmy smile, had already removed his own straw, silk banded planter's hat. He said, "It's about a rather pressing matter,

I'm afraid. Could you leave the girl for just a few minutes, Miss Ford? Maybe we could talk downstairs...over a drink?"

"It's too early for me," Jane said, not liking the overly ingratiating air of the men standing before her, for she sensed they were up to something. All three were on the town council, and they were always meddling in something, mostly out of bald greed.

Drake said, "As I said, Miss Ford, the matter is quite pressing."

Jane sighed. "I have a girl in the room with Vangie. I suppose I can spare a few minutes."

"Please..." McQueen said, extending his hand toward the stairs.

Jane led them downstairs where roughly a dozen customers sat at tables or stood at the bar now in the mid-afternoon and ordered the afternoon barman to bring a good bottle of brandy and three glasses. When Jane had poured each man a drink and returned the cork to the bottle, she shook her long, curly red hair back behind her shoulders and leaned forward to cross her fine, pale, freckled arms on the table.

"Now, then, gentlemen," she said, "tell me about this pressing matter you wanted to talk to me about."

The men glanced at each other a little nervously and then Mayor McQueen fidgeted with his shot glass, cleared his throat, and said, "Miss Ford it has to do with, well, Marshal Mannion."

"Marshal Mannion."

"Indeed," said the banker, Howell, smoothing his thick mustache with thumb and beringed index finger. "Marshal Mannion."

He looked at the mayor, prompting the man to continue.

McQueen said, "You see, Miss Ford, we and the other businessmen here in Del Norte are a little concerned about his behavior."

"Haven't you always been a little concerned about his behavior?" Jane said with a knowing smile. "We all know how uncompromising Mannion can be. That's why Del Norte is as quiet and safe as it is. Before Joe came five years ago, I considered closing this establishment because I couldn't keep the place from being smashed to matchsticks every Saturday night not to mention keep glass in the windows."

"It's undeniable," said Wilfred Drake, sitting directly across the table from Jane. The mayor was on her left, the banker on her right. "Del Norte has become a different, far more civilized town over the past five years. Now, however..." He gave a pained looked, bunching his apple red cheeks as he looked down at the table as though looking for the right words with which to continue.

McQueen helped him out. "We're a little afraid that the marshal is standing in the way of progress."

"In the way of *progress*?" Jane asked, stitching her red brows. "Joe *brought* progress to Del Norte. Before he came, this was little more than an outlaw encampment."

"Yes, we've been through this, Miss Ford," said Howell, his tone becoming impatient. "We all agree Mannion has settled down the town and made it a much more prosperous place than it was before, but don't you think he's become a little, uh...well, *unhinged* since this incident with Whip Helton and his daughter?"

"Yes, angrier," McQueen said. "More uncompromising."

"I mean," said Drake, "he rode out there and shot those men who kidnapped his daughter without giving them a chance to give themselves up. We have it on good word they'd had a change of heart about what they'd done—all four were three sheets to the wind at the time —and had decided to return Mannion's daughter to Del Norte the very next morning."

"You have it on good word," Jane said with a skeptical arch of a brow. "Who, may ask, did this good word come from?"

The three men shuttled their dubious gazes around to each other.

McQueen gave his shot glass a nervous spin, cleared his throat again, and, frowning down at the glass, said, "From, um...Garth Helton."

Jane laughed and slapped the table. "And Garth Helton's word is good about anything much less about his devil of a *son*?"

She'd said this louder than she'd intended—she had to admit to having a little trouble restraining her own emotions at times just as Mannion did—and every head in the room swung toward her. She didn't care. She continued with: "And who, pray tell, told Helton about what happened in the cabin that night?"

The three councilmen shuttled looks around at each other again. A tad sheepish ones this time.

"Well," said the banker, also fingering his glass, "Whip himself."

"Whip himself," Jane said, barely able to keep from screaming the name at these popinjays. "Well, we all know how good Whip's word is, now, don't we?"

"Mannion shot him," McQueen said. "Didn't announce himself or anything like that, just kicked in the door and started shooting. Wounded but believing he would be killed if he didn't flee, Whip fled out a window and ran for his life. He's gravely wounded and could very well die."

"Poor thing!"

"Look, Miss Ford," McQueen said. "What Mannion did is against the very laws he swore to uphold."

"If you remember correctly, Mister Mayor, that's exactly how he cleaned up Del Norte in the first place. I don't remember any of you complaining back then."

Drake spread his long, pale hands. "Yes, but now he's antagonizing the Heltons."

"*Mannion* is antagonizing the *Heltons?*" Jane said, trying very hard to keep her wolf on its leash but having one hell of a time of it. She turned to the bar. "Fred, bring another glass—will you, please?"

The barman smiled his understanding and said, "Coming right up, Miss Ford."

When the apron had brought the glass, Jane filled it, threw back half the shot, wiped her mouth with the back of her hand, and looked at each man directly, angrily, as she said, "Whip Helton and his three vile friends raped Mannion's daughter. Vangie is so traumatized she hasn't said a word since it happened. She's awake and eating but not enough, and she hasn't been out of bed other than to use the chamber pot. Her eyes are utterly haunted. She is no longer the sweet, innocent girl she was before those animals kidnapped her after burning her and her father's house to the ground!"

"Please, Miss Ford," said McQueen, placing his hand on her wrist. "A little less emotion, please. We came here to have a *reasonable* conversation with you."

"Yes, we thought you were a little more rational than your gentleman friend," Drake said with a deeply offended air.

"Yes, *reasonable*, as well," offered Howell.

"*Reasonable?* What man would be reasonable after his daughter was so badly ravaged? After the father of one of the men who ravaged her sent a regulator to town to kill him, which he would have done if Mannion's young deputy hadn't intervened."

"Yes, how is Stringbean?" McQueen asked, the question sounding rote.

"The doctor thinks he'll mend. I have him upstairs, as well. Thank you for your concern, Mister Mayor."

"Miss Ford, please!" said Drake, again with a deeply offended air. "Please, your tone..."

Jane laughed throatily. She loved how men were so sensitive to women's tones. They could overlook a rape but not a tone.

"Besides," said the banker, "it has not been proven that the regulator or whoever he was, was actually employed by Garth Helton."

"Who else would have done it?"

McQueen shrugged. "We all know that the good marshal has his share of enemies."

"You think it was just a coincidence?" Jane said, her voice still heavy with sarcasm, "That someone came to kill Mannion so soon after he shot Whip Helton?"

"It very well could be," Drake said. "Nothing has been proven either way."

Jane studied each man, speechless.

Finally, she fell back in her chair, closing her hands over the edge of the table and said, "So, what do you gentlemen want me to do here—stop seeing Mannion?" As if she would do that just because they wanted it. Temper or no temper, his tactics admittedly dubious and often illegal, Mannion was ten times the man all three of these tinhorns would be put together if they lived a thousand more years.

"No, no, no," Howell said. "Who you choose to have in your life is certainly none of our business, Miss Ford."

"No, it's not."

"All we ask is that as someone who has Mannion's ear, so to speak—"

"And has at least some influence on him..." Drake added.

"We merely ask that you try to *reason* with him," McQueen said. "Settle him down as best you can. What this town does not need is to get crossways with Garth Helton."

"Oh, I see." Jane threw back the last of her brandy then sat back in her chair and crossed her arms on her low-cut, white bodice that accentuated the burnt orange of her gown as well as her hair. "That's what this is about. Helton."

"The man has done as much or more than Mannion to have brought progress to Del Norte."

"Right," Jane said tonelessly. "And he intends to bring a rail line."

"Exactly," said Drake. "Which would mean more business for your saloon, hotel, as well as your young ladies upstairs, Miss Ford."

"I'm doing fine without the railroad and the crime that would bring." Jane frowned across the table at Drake. "Doesn't Helton have a half interest in your mercantile, Mister Drake?"

"That's neither here nor there," Drake said, indignant.

"Helton has as short a fuse as Mannion," McQueen pointed out. "If those two go head-to-head, the town could get caught in the crossfire."

"And Helton might pull his money out of Del Norte." Jane gave a lopsided smile.

"Exactly," the banker said with a fateful sigh.

"So, you gentlemen expect Mannion to just forget that Helton's firebrand son raped his daughter."

"Mannion will be compensated," McQueen said. "Helton has assured us. Besides, his son took a bullet."

"An *illegal* bullet," Drake put in.

Jane was so stunned by what McQueen had said that she could only stare at him, speechless. When she was certain she'd heard what she'd thought she'd heard, she said, "If you think Joe Mannion will accept money to forgive what Whip Helton and his cohorts did to his daughter, then you know very little about Mannion, Mister Mayor. And, I might add, you'd be a very, very silly man, indeed!"

Again, she slapped her hand down on the table, making every head in the place turn toward her. She reached for the bottle, popped the cork from the lip.

"Maybe you've had enough, Miss Ford..." the banker suggested, regarding her reprovingly from beneath his shaggy, gray brows.

"Hah!" Jane splashed brandy into her shot glass.

"Let me just say this," said McQueen and loudly filled his lungs with air. "You getting Mannion to pull his horns in and to consider the matter with the Heltons settled would be doing him a favor."

"Oh, really?" Jane said, eyes flashing her sarcasm once more. "You'll fire him for not insisting that man be punished for raping his daughter?"

"In a word, yes," Drake said. He slid back his chair and donned his bowler.

"That's about the size of it," McQueen said, doffing his own hat and carefully adjusting it. He slid his own chair back and rose.

Howell gave Jane a grave look then rose heavily from

his own chair, the effort turning his face even redder than its natural pallor.

The three men made their way to the door and were gone, the batwings swinging into place behind them.

Jane saw the bartender looking at her grimly, sympathetically from behind the bar, slowly shaking his head.

"I'm taking the bottle to my suite, Stewart," Jane said, grabbing the bottle off the table and heading for the stairs.

"Shall I send a steak up for supper, Miss Ford?" Stewart called.

"No," Jane said, starting up the stairs. "Just the bottle will do."

She thought she'd heard it all. Obviously, she hadn't.

CHAPTER 20

WHIP HELTON OPENED HIS BEDROOM DOOR AND stumbled out into the hall, a crutch wedged under his left arm, holding a pistol in that hand.

He turned to peer through bloodshot eyes toward the stairs on his left, his broken nose still making it hard to see at times. His left hand throbbed as though a badger was chomping down on it. Now he had a wounded side to add to his miseries. He'd just heard Bloody Joe leave his father's office and walk down the stairs and outside.

Young Helton's right hand trembled with fury, making the gun shake. He chewed his lower lip and caressed the hammer. Down the hall near the top of the stairs, on the hall's right side, the door to his father's office opened and Quint Wayne stepped out, setting his big Stetson on his head. He turned to see Whip standing ten feet away, propped on the crutch, blood showing through his long-handle top low on his left side, where Mannion had shot him.

Flesh wound but it hurt like hell.

Wayne stood studying the younger Helton with a grim little twist of the foreman's lips.

"What're you lookin' at?" Whip snarled.

Wayne gave a disapproving chuff then crossed the hall and started down the stairs, boots clomping loudly, spurs ringing.

Grinding his teeth with anger and against his sundry agonies, Whip hobbled down the hall and turned into the door of his father's office. The old man sat at his desk, looking at Whip from over his reading glasses, an envelope in one hand, the Barlow knife he'd used to open it in his other hand.

"What're you doing out of bed?"

"I heard Bloody Joe's ultimatum." Whip raised the gun in his hand. "Why didn't you blast him right then and there?"

The old man kept that wide, blank stare on his son from over the top of his reading glasses. "Maybe he should try you and hang you. That's the punishment in this territory, you know."

"*What?*"

"What you did is unforgiveable. You're a Helton. Taking a girl by force is beneath you. At least, it should be beneath you." The old man pointed the folding knife at him like an accusing finger. "I should have gone ahead today and let him take you and kill you and dump you in a ravine. It would have been no less than what you deserve."

"I'd have shot him!" Whip was so unsteady on the crutch because he'd been drinking to kill the pain that he stumbled violently to one side, ramming up against a bookcase, knocking over an ambrotype. If the bookcase hadn't been there, he'd have fallen in a pile on the floor.

"Good God!" the old man said. "Look at you. Drunk and it's still daylight. And if I'd let Mannion take you, he'd have taken you, all right. You're no match for him.

Maybe late at night after you've set his house on fire and he had his daughter to look out for..."

Glaring, old Helton shook his head with revulsion. "How in the hell I ever sowed such seed as you is beyond me. Well, I know." He glanced at the open doorway as though the boy's worthless mother were standing in it. "I got a daughter who's soft in the head and a son who's a backshooting rapist!"

"I told you, we was drunk!"

"No excuse!"

"An' look what he did to me!" Whip raised his bandaged left hand to indicate his bandaged nose, which was still twice its usual size and the color of a ripe plum. The skin around his eyes was the same color mottled sickly yellow.

"If you were gonna try to kill Bloody Joe Mannion, then you sure as hell should have done it!"

"I done tried!"

"He was just here!"

"The man's got nine lives, I swear!"

The old man pounded the end of the fist holding the knife on his desk, his broad face swollen and red with rage. "*Worthless!*"

"I ain't worthless!" The effort of yelling so loudly caused Whip to stumble back in the direction of the door and nearly fall again.

"That cinches it!"

Old Helton heaved his bulky frame out of the chair, marched around his desk and into the hall. Whip turned uncertainly on the crutch and hobbled out the door. His father was heading down the hall on Whip's left.

"Where you goin'?"

"To this pit of a room of yours!" Garth's stentorian voice thundered around the hall.

"What's going on up there?" came a woman's thin, raspy voice from the bottom of the stairs.

"Stay out of this, woman!" Helton shouted from inside Whip's room.

From the room issued the clattering of what sounded like bottles.

"What're you doin', Pa?" Whip shouted.

The only response was more clattering bottles.

Then Garth bulled out the door and into the hall, his arms full of whiskey bottles with various amounts of tangleleg in them. "I'm drying you out!" He swung around and headed toward the door at the far end of the hall. He dropped a bottle while he fumbled the door open, stepped out onto the second-floor landing, and heaved all the bottles in his arms over the rail.

They landed in the yard with a loud *crash!*

"No!" Whip bellowed like a poleaxed bull. "That my liquor, damn you!"

The older Helton crouched down and followed the first bottles up with the bottle he'd dropped on the floor.

He closed the door and turned back to Whip leaning unsteadily on his crutch and glaring at his father, pulling back the hammer of his pistol then depressing it then pulling it back again and depressing it. He showed his teeth like a rabid cur.

Footsteps creaked on the stairs and then Whip's mother, Berenice, stepped into the hall beside her son. She was dressed the way she always dressed—ratty nightgown and bathrobe, a cut glass goblet in her hand. Thick, red velvet, gold-trimmed slippers on her feet. Her gray hair was down around her long, craggy face, giving her a witch-like air.

"What is going *on* up here?" she said in her smoker's

raspy voice, the hand holding the glass trembling so that the whiskey threatened to spill over the sides.

"I got rid of this hellion's liquor!" Garth intoned, marching back toward his son and his diminutive drunk of a wife. He stopped before Whip and raised his arm and jutted a commanding finger at him. "You're gonna stay here and you're gonna dry out, and then I'm gonna once and for all make a cowhand out of you!"

"What?" Whit cried, exasperated. "You know I ain't a cowhand!"

"Oh, Garth, no," pleaded Berenice, face scrunched in sympathy for her boy. "You know he's too sensitive to work around your rough men."

"Sensitive, huh? That's what you've always said about him, woman. That's always been your excuse why he could never make a hand. The truth is he's a pampered, no-good drunk just like you!"

Rage burned hotly in Whip.

Again, he showed his teeth as he raised the pistol in his hand. He aimed it straight out from his right shoulder at Garth's craggy face. "How dare you talk to Ma like that! How dare you trespass on my room and throw away my liquor! You're the reason I ended up the way I am. You always wanted me to prove. *Prove! Prove! Prove!* Only, there's no way I could ever prove a damn thing to you, even after I broke my first colt!"

"You left the grain bin open and let it founder!"

"So I made a mistake! It wasn't cause for you to make me spend the whole damn night in the old well pit!" Whip raised his voice even louder and the gun shook in his hand like a leaf in the wind. "I was fourteen years old!"

"Oh, son!" Berenice cried, raising a hand to her face as she stared in horror at the gun her son aimed at his father. She turned to her husband. "He's right, though. Garth! You know he's right! You're a hard, cruel, cruel man!"

"I am, am I?" Garth said, glaring at Whip over the top of the trembling gun in his son's hand. "Apparently I wasn't hard and cruel enough! This is what I get for building a ranch to be proud of...one I intend to leave you and your sister. If you're man enough to own it, that is." He smiled savagely. "After you dry out, you're gonna have to prove it. You're gonna have to *prove* you can run it and command men. Real men. Not penny-ante thieves and maulers of cork-headed girls!"

"I'm warnin' you, Pa!"

"You are, are you?" Suddenly, Garth reached up and closed his hand around the gun and ripped it out of Whip's hand.

Whip screamed as he stumbled forward, rammed into his father's left shoulder, then slammed against the wall before hitting the floor with a *boom*!

Holding the gun by its barrel, Garth glared down at him. "If you were gonna shoot me, you'd have done it by now. You're not even man enough to do that!"

"Garth, how dare you!" Berenice shambled forward, teeth gritted, and tossed her drink in his face.

Garth's eyes widened to the size of silver dollars. A forked vein in his forehead turned dark blue and throbbed. He hardened his jaws and gritted his teeth, swept his right hand back behind his left shoulder, and thrust it forward in a blur of fast motion.

Crack!

Berenice screamed as the blow picked her slight body up off the floor and thrust her several feet back before slamming her down onto the varnished puncheons.

"Ma!" Whip howled.

He crawled wildly over to her, clutching his wounded side. "Ma, you all right? You all right, Ma?"

When she blinked her eyes a few times, Whip cast a glare of pure, raw, unadulterated hatred over his left shoulder at his father, the bandage on his nose glowing in the shadows. "I may not have killed you today, old man. But someday I will."

Garth smiled down at him. "When you're man enough to do so, Spur will be yours."

He turned toward the stairs then stopped and turned back to Whip. "I sent men after Mannion. He won't leave Spur range. Ever." He pointed a commanding finger again at Whip. "That's a note you owe me, kid. Dry out and make a man of yourself."

He headed down the stairs.

CHAPTER 21

As the thunder of his pursuing riders grew louder, Mannion reined Red off the trail's left side. He quickly dismounted, tore a limb off one of the willows sheathing the trail, and used it to rub out his tracks where he'd left the trace.

He swung up onto Red's back and put the horse into a gallop. He was in a broad, sage-stippled bowl with white-faced cattle peppering the graze, a larger herd gathered along a creek to the north. Mannion rode south, scattering cattle bearing the Spur brand clumped here and there, grazing or lounging, and climbed a tawny-grassed rise. At the top of the rise, he reined Red to a halt and turned him back to face the trail.

From here he could see the riders coming along the trail to the east, obscured by the willows and pines, dust rising and turning pink in the late light. He'd half-expected the entire Spur payroll, but he was wrong. Only five riders were galloping hell for leather along the trail.

Maybe they weren't after him. Maybe they were on their way to town with extra jingle in their pockets...

Mannion waited there atop the rise and watched the five riders pass the spot where he'd left the trail and continue on to his left, disappearing behind a stone outcropping, the thudding of their hooves dwindling to silence.

Not for long.

Only a few minutes later, he picked up the rataplan again.

It grew louder until all five riders reappeared, galloping out from behind the outcropping. As they approached the place where Mannion had left the trail, the third man back in the pack turned his head toward Manion then lifted an arm and pointing finger, and said, "*There!*"

All five reined in, disappearing for a few seconds in their own billowing dust.

Why only five?

Mannion smiled. All twenty-five would have been a compliment. Helton wasn't given to compliments.

The five riders galloped through the willows then checked their horses down, looking up the rise at their quarry and then turning to each other, conferring. Mannion could hear them speaking in the quiet of the early evening, but he couldn't make out what they were saying. They sat there, stirrup to stirrup, spaced ten feet apart, considering the situation.

Mannion grinned and shucked his Yellowboy from its boot, cocked it, and rested the barrel on his saddle horn. He raised a gloved hand to his mouth and shouted, "What are you waiting for, you damn tinhorns? Fish or cut bait!"

All five looked at each other. Then they all shucked their own rifles from their saddle boots, cocked them, and put the steel to their mounts, galloping across the sage-carpeted flat toward Mannion's rise. Mannion touched spurs to Red's flanks.

"Hy—*yahhh*, boy!"

The horse whinnied and lunged off its rear legs, hard-charging down the rise toward the five riders spaced out ahead, a hundred yards away and closing fast. One of the riders wearing a tall cream Stetson raised his rifle to his shoulder and snugged his salt-and-pepper bearded cheek up against the rear stock.

Mannion had already taken his reins in his teeth. Now he squeezed the Yellowboy's trigger and watched in satisfaction as the man in the cream Stetson fired his own rifle wide, the bullet buzzing over Mannion's head. The man dropped the rifle and rolled back in his saddle before disappearing over his galloping horse's arched tail. The cream hat shot up from the ground and was swept away on the breeze.

The others fired then, too, smoke and flames stabbing from rifle barrels.

The bullets caromed, screeching and buzzing around Mannion's head before plunking into the ground behind him. He was within thirty yards of the Spur riders now. Separating slightly into two groups, two on one side of Mannion, two on the other, they recocked their own Winchesters.

Chomping down hard on the bay's reins, Mannion set his rifle's butt plate against his shoulder, aimed, and fired.

The man riding on the far right of the now four-man pack gave a yell and dropped his rifle as he fell down the left side of his horse. He yelled again as his boot got caught in the stirrup, dragging him. He lost his hat and acquired a terrified look as he bounced along the ground beside his galloping horse, his blue neckerchief blowing up over his mouth.

"Oh!" he said. "*Oh-ahhh!*"

That distracted the other three riders long enough that, while one triggered lead at Mannion, the bullet sizzling just off the lawman's left cheek, he managed to get another shot off before the three manned horses, two on his right, one on his left, galloped past him. The man nearest him on his right, wearing a palm leaf sombrero and serape—that would be the Mexican Luis Salazar—flinched and slapped his right hand to that cheek.

Meanwhile, the fourth rider, still being dragged behind his horse—horse and dragged rider heading straight for Mannion, gave a shrill scream just before his mount swung sharply to Mannion's right to avoid a collision. The rider, his foot still firmly ensconced in the stirrup, flew up off the ground and sideways—straight into Red's galloping hooves.

Red screamed.

Mannion cursed as the flying rider cut Red's legs out from under him. Red struck the ground on his knees, throwing Mannion up over the horse's head. Mannion turned a full somersault in the air above and beyond the horse, yelling now himself, "Ohhh—*whoahhhhh!*"

The lawman hit the ground and rolled and looked up in horror to see Red flying up over him, the horse's wide, brown eyes meeting those of its rider—horse and rider sharing similar expressions of horror. One of the saddle stirrups whipped down from the saddle and brushed across Mannion's left cheek before the stallion landed six feet away from him with a heavy grunt, on Mannion's left.

Ears ringing and head spinning from his unceremonious meeting with the ground, Mannion regarded the horse in mute exasperation and fascination at them both still being alive.

Especially himself.

He'd come within three feet of being hammered flat by a good three-quarter ton of horseflesh.

A bullet blew a branch off a sage plant to his right.

The rifle's screech reached his ears.

He turned to see the three remaining riders, roughly fifty yards away, just then turning their horses around toward Mannion.

The big man in a buckskin shirt and leather hat had just fired at Mannion while turning his rangy buckskin. That was Hector Plowson, a tough, surly Texan and one of Helton's most pugnacious hands—a big, shaggy-headed, shaggy-bearded man with eyes set too close together beside a wide wedge of a sunburned nose. Mannion had always thought he'd had an animal air about him. When Mannion had had him in jail, it had taken him a day or two to rid the cell block of the man's stench. He didn't know how the other Spur riders lived with him.

Mannion looked around for his rifle. It lay fifteen feet ahead of him and to his left.

He hustled to his feet, vaguely astonished that he didn't seem to have any broken bones, and ran toward the rifle, the three galloping riders firing, plunking bullets into the ground around him. Mannion dropped to a knee beside his Yellowboy, picked it up, cocked it, and planted the butt against his shoulder and cut loose, triggering and cocking, triggering and cocking, evoking one yell after another as the three riders within thirty yards now, either flew off their horses to hit the ground and rolled or, in the case of Plowson, sagged forward in his saddle clutching his right shoulder but still holding his Henry repeater with that hand.

Plowson galloped past Mannion, who cocked the Yellowboy and swung around to face his remaining antagonist. He fired, but just then Plowson's horse stopped and turned left. Mannion's bullet blew up fawn-colored grass and dirt beyond his target. Plowson sat up straight in the saddle, threw his shaggy head back, and loosed a grizzly like roar of pain and rage to the darkening sky, blood oozing from his upper right chest.

He opened his eyes and turned to Mannion who lined up his sights on the big man's chest again and fired.

The Yellowboy's hammer dropped benignly, empty.

"Hah! Hah! Hah!" Plowson roared, pumping a fresh round into the Henry's chamber.

He put the spurs to his buckskin's flanks and the horse lunged into a gallop toward Mannion.

Plowson fired. Mannion winced as the bullet cut across his right ear.

Mannion dropped the Yellowboy and shucked both Russians, raised them, clicked the hammers back.

He fired the right-hand gun. The bullet blasted a ragged hole through Plowson's buckskin shirt over his right shoulder.

Mannion fired his left-hand gun. That bullet blasted a ragged hole through Plowson's buckskin shirt just below and to the left of his left shoulder.

Roaring like an enraged lion, Plowson cocked the Henry again, aimed at Mannion. He was twenty feet away, so close the lawman thought he could smell the man's feral stench.

The Henry roared just as Plowson galloped past Mannion's right side.

Both of Mannion's Russians roared at the same time,

both bullets smashing into Plowson's left thigh and the right side of his belly, respectively.

Plowson gave a loud, coyote-like wail as he galloped on past Mannion then checked his horse down to a halt, curveting the mount. The big man sagged forward in his saddle, eyes closed, chin dipped to his chest. He could have been praying. But he wasn't.

He was dying.

Mannion straightened, clicking both Russians' hammers back.

Plowson must have heard. He straightened in his saddle, opened his eyes, and turned toward Mannion, who could feel blood dribbling down his left ear. He was a little disoriented from his and Red's plunge and roll as well as the frantic lead swap. He blinked once, hard, focusing.

Plowson reined his horse toward Mannion, booted it into a walk.

Mannion held both Russians down low by his sides. Plowson was in no condition to raise the Henry again. He held it loosely in his hands. His buckskin shirt was nearly all blood.

The big, smelly man reined the buckskin to a halt before Mannion.

He glared down at the lawman through weird, gray-blue eyes, showing the whites around them, and roared, "Damn you to hell, Bloody Joe! Kill me now and be done with it!"

"You got it, Heck."

Mannion raised both Russians and blew two bullets through the big man's brain plate.

Plowson's head jerked back, and he toppled to the ground, hitting with a heavy thud on his chest and belly, quivering as he died. The buckskin jerked with a start and ran off, trailing its bridle reins.

A loud whinny rose behind Mannion.

He jerked with a start to see Red standing twenty feet away, looking no worse for the wear though his saddle hung down one side. The horse looked a little indignant, however. He was standing near the badly crumpled and bloody body of the man who had tripped him.

Mannion chuckled.

Wearily, he removed his hat and ran his hand through his thick, salt-and-pepper hair, smoothed his mustache with thumb and index finger. As he did, he looked around at the five dead men lying broadly scattered, their horses standing a ways off, idly grazing.

"Well, Red," Mannion said. "He's down to twenty. That's manageable."

He looked at the horse. The horse looked back at him skeptically.

"Yeah, maybe not," Mannion said with another dry laugh. "I do get myself into shit—don't I, Red?"

Red pawed the ground with one front hoof.

Mannion went over and straightened and adjusted the saddle then swung up into it, wincing at the sundry aches in his weary old carcass.

Forty-five minutes later, he rode into Del Norte. It was good dark.

Jane Ford was standing with a drink on her balcony, smoking a cigarette in a long black holder. She watched him as he rode up to the hitchrack. The roar of laughter and the jangle of a piano sounded from inside her fine establishment. Shadows slid across the lamplit windows framed by guilt-edged, green velvet curtains.

Light from burning oil pots illuminated the street with here and there a flickering orange glow.

Mannion stopped Red and looked up at her.

He must have looked as bad as he felt.

"God, Joe," she said, shaking her head, making her long, thick red hair dance about her bare shoulders. Rings flashed on the fingers wrapped around the drink in her hand.

That's all she said.

CHAPTER 22

"HOW YOUR BIG, OLD CARCASS TAKES ALL THE ABUSE you give it is beyond me," Jane said as she ran a coarse brush across his back, using both hands and leaning into her work.

Mannion had his knees up in the bath water. He had his elbows on his knees and, smoking one of the fine cigars Jane kept a supply of just for him, he watched the soapy water lap up against the sides of the copper tub. She'd cleaned with whiskey and a soft cloth the bullet burn on his left ear and his cheek and a few more he'd taken without realizing it, one across his hip, another across the back of his neck. They burned, and his head still ached from the bullet Whip Helton had shot across his temple, but the bath helped shove those sundry miseries away.

So did Jane.

He groaned luxuriously at the good scrubbing she gave his back. In sharp contrast to the coarse bristles of the brush, he felt the ends of her hair dance across his wet skin, giving him pleasure chills. Occasionally, she leaned lower and placed a tender kiss on his cheek and gave his ear a bewitching nibble.

"Beyond me, too, darlin'," Mannion said as he blew a smoke plume over the room divider to the big, four-poster bed on the other side of it.

Earlier, when he'd first entered the suite, he'd gone into Jane's second bedroom to check on Vangie. A girl named Candy had been with her, reading an illustrated magazine. Vangie had been asleep, curled in a tight ball under the bed covers. Candy had said Vangie still hadn't spoken a word. When she'd been awake, she'd simply stared off into space.

Thinking of his poor dear daughter now, Mannion's mood soured.

Would she ever come back to him?

Vangie and Jane were the only two grace notes in his otherwise crude, rough and tumble life. Without them, that's all he had. That wasn't enough anymore. When he'd been younger it had been, but the older he got, it wasn't. He'd never tell anyone that, of course. They'd see it as a weakness. Wolves would come to call...

"What are you thinking about?" Jane asked, shoving her hands and the brush under the water to scrub the small of his back, grunting with the effort. Her hair buffeted against his cheek.

"Wolves." He gazed through the smoke at the canopied bed but what he saw was his daughter and the visages of both Garth and Whip Helton.

Jane straightened and set the brush in the washbasin on the bench beside her. She'd rolled the sleeves of her white blouse up her freckled arms. Breathless, she sat on the chair, shook her hair back, and frowned down at him. "What happened today?"

"I ran down the bushwhacker who shot Stringbean."

"Who was he?"

"Don't know."

"He'd dead, of course."

"Oh, yes."

"How'd you get the burns?" Jane poked the one on his ear none too gently, making him wince.

"Helton," Mannion said, blowing another smoke plume toward the window now where light from oil pots danced shadows across the face of the false-fronted buildings on the other side of the street.

"It's started, then…"

Mannion looked at her. "What?"

"The war. The one with Helton."

"It started two weeks ago, my dear Jane."

She grimaced then rose, set the washbasin on the floor, and sat down in the chair, smoothing the skirts of her long gown across the backs of her thighs. Gazing down at him thoughtfully, she removed each silver earring in turn then, holding them in her cupped hands, leaned forward, resting her elbows on her knees.

Her lowcut bodice pulled down to reveal her deep, alluringly dark, freckled cleavage.

"The town is scared, Joe."

"The town?"

"At least, the mucky mucks on the town council."

"Ah, they visited you," Mannion said.

"McQueen, Drake, and Howell."

He crooked a knowing smile. "Sure, they did."

"If you keep pushing so hard against Helton, they're going to fire you."

"Not before the job is done."

"I knew you were going to say that."

"What else would I say? What else would *any* man say?"

"I knew you were going to say, that, too." Jane leaned forward, wrapped her arms around his neck, and pressed her cheek to his temple, hugging him, kissing the top of his wet head. "And I don't blame you, Joe. It's just that, you see, you'll die if you go up against Helton."

"I didn't die today."

"How many did he sic on you?"

"Only five."

"He has more, Joe," she said, her arms still wrapped firmly around his neck, hugging him tightly and with deep affection. "The town is too scared and divided on Helton to help you. You have only Rio. Stringbean will be out of commission for a couple of weeks, Doc says."

She removed her arms from around his neck and frowned down at him, cupped hands holding the earrings extending out from her knees, palms up, over the spruce green silk of her gown. "We could leave here, Joe. We could take Vangie and leave, start a new life elsewhere."

"And what about what he did to her?"

"You killed the others, gave him a bullet. Isn't that enough?"

Mannion shook his head and stared across the room again. Rage burned in him. It had been burning since the night they'd burned his house and ravaged his daughter. He just wasn't aware of it all the time. But now he was aware of it. It was a fire he couldn't have put out even if he'd wanted to. They'd taken one of the only two people who meant anything to him.

"Joe...?"

He turned his head, looked up at her.

She smiled sympathetically, regretfully. "You'll die."

Mannion twisted his own grim smile. "I know." He turned away to stare at the bed again. "It can't be helped."

"What about Vangie?"

He turned to Jane again. "You'll care for her?"

"Of course, but she needs her father. Now more than ever."

Mannion sighed then took another deep drag off the stogie, blew the smoke out toward the curtained window beyond which the dull light and shadows from the oil pots danced. Out there somewhere, a man was laughing hysterically, drunkenly. "I know that, too. But I can't stop it, dear Jane. I just can't stop it."

He turned his gaze to her again, frowning with genuine befuddlement. "Why do you put up with me? Why do you toil over me so? You have a business to run, men to entertain downstairs."

He could hear the rumble of conversation below, even feel the reverberations through the floor beneath the tub. Someone was playing the piano and a girl was singing "The Mossy Oaks of Southern Georgia", in a bittersweet Southern accent. One of Jane's girls, a Southerner named Melody Flowers.

Jane often sang late at night. The men waited all night long for her to take the stage on the far side of the drinking hall from the bar where often a three- or four-piece band played.

"I don't know, Joe." Jane reached out and placed a hand on his cheek, ran her thumb down the long, broad line of his nose. "Maybe I'm a fool, but I love you."

She leaned down and kissed him. He wrapped his arms around her and returned the kiss. They held the kiss for a long, passionate time. Still holding it, Mannion heaved himself up out of the tub. Her lips against his, Jane gave a start. She laughed, stretching her lips back from her teeth, holding him tighter around the neck as he picked her up in his arms and stepped out of the tub.

"Oh, God—Joe, your back!" she cried, laughing.

"Everything else hurts," Mannion said, dripping wet. "Why not my back, too?" He stepped out from behind the room partition.

He carried Jane over to the bed and dropped her onto it.

She gave an "Oh!" when she hit the mattress and then she laughed and rolled onto her side, facing him.

"You're getting the floor all wet! Towel off, you brigand!" She smiled as with one hand she began unbuttoning the bodice of her shirtwaist. "And I'll make myself more comfortable."

———

MANNION WOKE AS THE FIRST DAWN LIGHT TOUCHED the room's two curtained window to his left. Jane lay curled in sleep beside him, breathing softly through slightly parted lips.

Mannion slowly slid the covers back. He hadn't gotten them far when Jane woke suddenly and placed her hand on his arm.

"Do you have to go?" she asked, her voice throaty with sleep.

"I should start the day."

She gave him a seductive smile. "Just a few more minutes. Wake me up...?"

Mannion smiled and rolled toward her. She rolled onto her back and spread her legs and wrapped her arms around his back.

When they finished, he kissed her. "Thanks for taking such good care of Vangie."

"I love her, too, Joe. She's a very special lady."

"She is. I hope I get her back."

Jane wrapped her arms around him and gave him a direct look. "You will. I'll work with her. The girls will work with her."

"Thank you, darlin'." He kissed her lips then rolled off her and rose to quietly dress as the deepening dawn light washed through the windows.

He donned his hat and grabbed his Winchester. Jane had been so quiet that he thought she was asleep. That's why he didn't say goodbye but only walked quietly to the door. Just as he wrapped his hand around the knob, she said, "Joe?"

Mannion looked at her over his shoulder. "Yes, Jane?"

"I know why I love you."

He arched his brows. "Oh? Why?"

"Because what other woman would?"

Mannion chuckled.

"I'm joking," Jane said, kicking her legs around beneath the covers. She rolled onto her side, propped her cheek on the heel of her hand. The covers slid down, giving him an alluring view of her rich, full, freckled breasts, still mottled red from his manipulations. "I love you because you have a big, big heart, my darling."

"Now, that's something I've never been accused of before."

"Maybe no woman has gotten to know you as well as I have."

Mannion thought of Sarah and thought that what Jane had said was true. That had been his fault, not his wife's.

"You have a big, tender heart, Joe. That's your secret, isn't it?"

He frowned at her, a little befuddled. Was it his secret?

"Your problem is it's bigger than most everyone else's,

so you feel you need to protect it. You go overboard, protecting it."

Mannion considered that, chewing his mustache, nodding slowly.

"Have a good day, Joe. I'm always here for you, you rapscallion."

Mannion smiled and pinched his hat brim to her. "Goodbye, my dear Jane."

He opened the door, stepped out into the hall, and closed it quietly behind him.

He went downstairs into the main drinking hall lit by only a few scattered hurricane lamps casting as much shadow as light. He stopped halfway down the steps. He recognized a shadowy figure sitting at a table near the front door, which was closed over the batwings, for the mornings were growing chilly at this altitude. The young man was chowing down on a big plate of ham, eggs, and fried potatoes. A stone mug of coffee steamed on the table before him. He was the only customer in the place.

The morning bar tender sat at a table near the bar, reading a newspaper.

"What in holy blazes are you doing out of bed, String-bean?" Mannion continued down the stairs.

Stringbean turned to him. Around a mouthful of food, he said, "Mornin', Marshal."

"Don't 'mornin', Marshal' me." Mannion crossed the room to the kid's table. "What are you doing out of bed? The doc said you needed a good two weeks to recover."

"Unless I remember wrong, he said the same thing about you," Stringbean said around another mouthful of food.

"Don't get smart with me. You look like hell."

Stringbean grinned, still chewing. "You do, too...uh,

no disrespect, Marshal!" he added quickly then took a sip of his coffee.

"Stringbean, look—" Mannion stopped when the front door opened, and Rio Waite stepped into the saloon.

"Ah, Joe—there ya are. Figured you'd be up." Rio frowned when his gaze landed on Stringbean. "What's the younker doin' up?!"

"That's what I've been asking?"

"Fit as a fiddle," Stringbean said, wiping his plate with a scrap of buttermilk biscuit.

"You look like hell, Junior!" Waite said, walking slowly into the room, scowling at the junior deputy.

"It's just a flesh wound," Stringbean said, then belched and reached for his coffee cup. He turned to Mannion. "I promise, sir, that if I start to feel poorly, I'll go on back to the boardin' house. I can't keep imposin' on Miss Ford's generosity. I got my own digs."

"She wants to keep an eye on you, Jane does. Just like she does Vangie."

"She's a good woman, Miss Jane." Stringbean smiled then sipped his coffee. "But, nah, nah...I gotta get back to work. If I keep layin' around like English royalty, I'll get sores on my butt."

"You're puttin' sores on *my* butt," Rio said, still glowering down at the younker.

Mannion regarded the kid with concern. He knew why Stringbean was up. He still felt as though he had something to prove after turning tail the other day. Mannion wanted to assure him that there was no need. Hell, the kid had distracted the would-be assassin and taken a bullet meant for Mannion. But he didn't want to talk about the other day in front of Rio. As far as

Mannion was concerned, the other night would remain between him and Stringbean.

Mannion looked at Rio. "How was the night?"

"I have a coupla fellas—punchers from the Kitchen Sink—locked up in the basement. Drunk and disorderly, broke a mirror over at the Purple Elephant. Otherwise, all quiet. Except..."

The older deputy looked with gravity at his boss.

"Yes...?"

"Helton just rode into town with five other riders. He's over at the mayor's office."

"McQueen?"

"One and the same."

Mannion raked a thumbnail down his unshaven jaw. "Well, this is likely to get interesting."

He walked to the batwings, pushed through them, and stood on the broad veranda, peering north along the main drag. The oil pots had burned out. While a pearl glow grew in the east, most of the street was in shadow.

But he could see six horses standing at the hitchrack fronting Charlie McQueen's law office. McQueen was an early riser. He'd be in there, palavering with Helton.

McQueen was gutless. So were most of the rest of the businessmen in Del Norte. Mannion knew what this visit from Helton meant. They'd stand with him in good times. Bad times were another thing.

He turned to face Stringbean still sitting at the table, and Rio Waite standing beside the table, facing Mannion. Both men wore grave, vaguely dreadful expressions.

"Look," Mannion said. "This isn't your fight. Either one of you. You're fired."

CHAPTER 23

RIO'S FLESHY FACE BUNCHED AND TURNED RED. "THE hell you say!"

Stringbean heaved himself to his feet, albeit a little uncertainly, favoring his wounded side. "Yeah, Marshal. I stand with Rio. The hell you say!"

"I'm firing both of you. I don't want either one of you taking another bullet meant for me. Helton has twenty men remaining on his roll. They'll be coming. And when they do—"

"When they do, we'll be backin' your play, Joe," Rio said with quiet assurance, his face grave beneath the brim of his battered Stetson.

"What Rio said, Marshal. You've backed us. We'll back you."

Rio drew a deep breath, puffing out his chest. "This isn't just your fight, Joe. It's our fight, too. Hell, it's the whole town's fight. It's a matter of what's right and what's wrong. What Helton did to you—burnin' your house, takin' Vangie. That there is dead wrong, no matter what cause he thought he had."

Mannion studied them both. He felt a tightness in his

throat. They'd back him, all right. They didn't have to. But they'd back him, just the same.

He cleared emotion from his throat. He was feeling more and more of it lately; he didn't like it. "I reckon you two deserve raises."

Rio and Stringbean looked at each other hopefully then turned back to Mannion, shrugging.

"Forget it," Mannion said.

He turned and pushed through the batwings. He walked through the morning's thinning shadows to his office. Buster was lounging on the porch rail. A dead rat lay on the puncheons before the door.

"Ah," Joe said. "More evidence of what a good hunter you are." He chuckled and ran his hand down the cat's stout, furry body. Immediately, Buster started purring. "But you know, Buster," Joe added, "we already knew that. You don't need to keep trying to convince us."

Buster meowed and curled his tail.

Joe chuckled again then picked the rat up by its tail, tossed it over the rail into the brush beside the building, then tripped the latch and went into the office. Rio had built up the fire in the stove and had put a pot of coffee on for him.

He leaned his rifle against the wall by the door, pegged his hat, found a clean mug, and filled it with the black, piping hot brew, enjoying the smell wafting up with the steam. He gave a weary groan. It had been a long couple of weeks, and he hadn't gotten much sleep. He and Jane had stayed pretty busy last night under the sheets.

He'd needed that. He could tell she'd needed it, too.

He walked around behind his desk and slumped into his chair.

From down the street, voices rose, and boots

thumped on a boardwalk. He recognized the deep, angry baritone of Garth Helton. He also recognized the wheedling voice of Charlie McQueen. Presently, hoofs thumped.

"*Hyah!*" Helton barked.

The hoof thuds dwindled into the distance.

A door closed.

Silence.

Joe drew a breath and sat back in his chair, tapping his thumb on the rim of his mug, waiting. Finally, just as the sun rose above the horizon and bathed the main street outside the window in golden morning light, the crunch of footsteps rose outside, amidst the rising din of business traffic.

"Here we go," Joe said to himself.

Footsteps sounded on the porch steps, then on the porch.

On the door, two light knocks. The door opened a foot. Charley McQueen smiled through the crack. "Oh, hello there, Joe. Got a minute?" He stepped in, smiling unctuously, then quietly closed the door behind him.

"Charlie, for you, old friend, I always have a minute. Sit down and take a load off." Mannion indicated the spool back, hide bottom chair angled in front of his desk.

"Thank you, Joe. I appreciate it." McQueen doffed his bowler and sat and rested the bowler on his knee.

"Now, then," Mannion said, sipping his coffee and purposefully not offering any to the dapper, little mayor with his tailored three-piece suit, glinting glasses, and counterfeit smile. "What can I do you for?"

"Well...I hate to say this, Joe." Holding his hat with one hand on one thigh, McQueen ran his other hand up and down his other thigh. "But...uh...but, uh...

"Yes, Mister Mayor?"

"I'm afraid..." McQueen drew a deep breath, let it slowly, heavily. "We're gonna have to let you go."

"Let me go."

"Yes."

"Let me go where?" Mannion was toying with the popinjay now.

"No, no—you don't understand. We're letting you go. As in..."

"I'm fired?"

"Well, um...yes, I'm afraid so."

Mannion lifted his mug slowly to his lips and took his time taking a sip, gazing over the mug at McQueen, who sat squirming in his chair and looking like a man who'd eaten something that wasn't setting right.

Mannion set the mug back down on his desk. "On what grounds?"

"What grounds?"

"Yes. You have to have a good reason to fire me, Charlie. You can't just fire me without a reason, you know. That's against the rules." Mannion wasn't sure about that, but he had a feeling McQueen wasn't sure about that, either. And he had no real grounds for firing him. Mannion had only been doing his job.

"To be honest, Joe, while I really appreciate what you've done for the good people of Del Norte over the past five years...it's this thing with Garth Helton."

"I see. You're talking about the father of the man who burned my house, kidnapped my daughter, and raped her."

"Yes...well, be that as it may..."

"Be that as it may?" Mannion's right eye twitched as he felt his muscles and sinews tightening, his heart throbbing in a growing fury.

"Yes, be that as it may...it seems...it just seems you've gone too far."

"How far is too far?"

"Well, you shot three men *and* Whip Helton without good cause. You just busted into the cabin and shot them."

"Yes, well, they had my daughter, you see, Mister Mayor, and I didn't want to give them a chance to kill her before I could kill *them*. Any man...even any *law*man...would have done the same thing in my situation. You might even have done it that way, too."

McQueen smiled and tugged nervously at his neatly cropped, chestnut beard.

"That being said, I would have killed them like I did even if Vangie's life hadn't been in danger. Because that's how I work. And you knew how I worked when you hired me five years ago. That's *why* you hired me."

"I'm afraid it's just not as simple as that anymore, Joe. Things aren't the way they were five years ago. Now we have to recognize laws and go about doing things in a lawful manner."

"Bullshit."

"What's that?"

"It's bullshit. Your laws might have changed...or you've suddenly decided to recognize them and enforce them, Mister Mayor, but people around here, on the wooly Western frontier, haven't changed. Men like Garth and Whip Helton haven't changed. They're the same way they were five years ago when I came in here and cracked heads to settle things down and you congratulated me for it. Even invited Vangie and me over to your house to have dinner with your family one Thanksgiving, if I recollect."

"Oh, we were happy to have you, Joe. We were happy to have you." McQueen was really rubbing his thigh now.

"It's just that...well, hell, Joe...you rode out to Helton's and accused him of siccing that rifleman on you without any real evidence." Suddenly, he raised his voice, pitching it with exasperation. "And then you shot five of his men! That's Garth Helton we're talking about here, Joe. He's a major investor in this town, and if he *keeps* investing, we could be as large and as prosperous as Leadville. That would be good for all of us!"

"And what about my daughter?"

"Helton said he offered you good money—"

Mannion thrust his hand over his desk, palm out. "Don't finish that sentence, Mister Mayor, or I'm gonna have to shoot you."

McQueen appeared to swallow something large. "Now, Joe."

"Let me get this straight," Mannion said, raising his own voice now, the fury growing in him though he was trying to keep it on its leash. If he hadn't done that so far, McQueen likely would be sitting there sporting a third eye—one he couldn't see out of. "You want to fire me because I killed three men who raped my daughter, and shot the fourth one. And because I accused Helton of sending a rifleman for me, though that's all I did—accuse him. I didn't arrest him. And you want to fire me for killing the five riders Helton sent to kill me."

McQueen stared back at him with a constipated look. He opened his mouth and dragged his tongue across his thick lower lip them closed his mouth and said, "Joe...Joe, it's Garth Helton you're talking about. You're putting your own interests ahead of the town's."

"Why, you chicken-livered dog." Mannion had set it very quietly, but his voice was pitched with steel. His cobalt eyes burned in their sun-seasoned sockets.

Again, McQueen swallowed.

"Get out of here," Mannion said.

"Joe," McQueen said tentatively but insistently. "We're letting you go. I'm sorry, but..."

"I'm not going anywhere, Mister Mayor." Mannion leaned forward across his desk and hooked a defiant smile. "I'm gonna stay right here until Whip Helton has been tried and convicted for the kidnapping and rape of my daughter. Only then, after he's hung from the gallows out on the street behind you there, will I turn in my badge." He gave his head a single shake. "After that, I'll be glad to do it. But not before." He sat back in his chair and lowered his arms. "Unless you want to take it off me, Mister Mayor? Do you want to do that?"

McQueen just gazed across the desk at him, hang jawed. His lips moved and he muttered something Mannion couldn't hear.

"What's that, Mister Mayor? Speak up. I couldn't hear you."

Again, McQueen swallowed. He shook his head. "N-no." Again, he shook his head. He rose slowly from his chair, kneading the brim of his bowler with his pale, little fingers.

He walked sullenly to the door, stopped, and glanced back over his right shoulder at Mannion. He put some steel in his voice and anger in his eyes, and he pointed a finger at the lawman. "But this isn't over, Joe. You just threatened me, and that will not stand, damn you! I'll be meeting with the rest of the town council tonight, and something will be done about you and this...this...*war* of yours with Garth Helton. Rest assured!"

With that, he fumbled the door open, his face puffed and red with anger. He went out and slammed the door behind him. Footsteps faded.

Mannion threw back the last of his coffee.

———

LATER THAT DAY, MANNION WALKED OVER TO THE SAN Juan Hotel & Saloon to see his daughter. He dismissed the girl Jane had stationed there, and the girl silently picked up her knitting, smiled sympathetically up at Mannion, and said with none too much confidence, "She'll get better, Marshal. I'm sure she will."

"Thanks for saying so, Candy."

Candy went out and Mannion found himself alone in the room with his daughter. Vangie was in a day dress Jane had bought for her. Jane or one of the girls must have done her hair, too, because it was pulled back in the French braid Vangie had preferred after seeing that her mother had worn her hair like that in photographs. She looked freshly scrubbed. The only difference was how thin she was, and pale. And how quietly she sat in a brocade chair to the right of the bed, angled to partly face one of the room's two windows.

"Hi, honey."

He hated the way she looked at him when he greeted her. As though she were momentarily afraid of him. She jerked her head toward him, opened her eyes wider, then, apparently recognizing him but not feeling any emotion about seeing her father, simply turned back to gaze out the window, though he doubted she saw anything out there.

Her eyes... They were like her mother's eyes before she...

Mannion shook his head to rid himself of the thought.

But another one, just as chilling, came to replace it. He saw the eyes of the woman who'd tricked him into killing her.

No, not Vangie now, too.

Again, Mannion shook his head, wincing against the emotional bite.

He set his hat on the bed and walked over to Vangie, gently placed his hands on her shoulders. He felt her muscles tighten against his touch and then loosen slightly. Only slightly.

Sorrow welled in him, fairly exploding.

He bowed his head and sobbed.

CHAPTER 24

IN THE TOWN MARSHAL'S OFFICE, STRINGBEAN POURED himself a cup of piping hot black coffee and winced at the hitch in his side. Just lifting the coffee pot was a strain on his bullet wound though it was just a burn, really. The bullet had gone all the way through, missing everything important but grazing a rib.

"Dang!" he said, blowing ripples on the coffee. "What a fool I was..."

Once again, self-recrimination assailed him. He should've just shot the devil with the Henry repeater, and that would have ended it right then and there. But he'd frozen again. Leastways, he *thought* he'd frozen. He couldn't remember exactly, but for some reason he'd decided to call the warning to the marshal first and *then* shoot the son of a buck with the Henry.

Instead, the shooter had still gotten off the shot, and Stringbean's own shot had flown wide as the gunman swung toward him.

And shot him.

At least grazed him. Not a terrible wound but Stringbean had still passed out from the pain and from the blow of his head hitting the boardwalk.

"Damn fool," he said, blowing on his coffee again and walking around behind the marshal's desk. "I thought you were good, Henry McCallister. But suddenly you've turned into an incompetent coward!"

He sat down in the marshal's chair and looked down at the desk where he had a game of solitaire laid out. He shouldn't be sitting at the marshal's desk. He had no business over here. He should be at his own, smaller desk abutting the wall to the right of the basement cell block door. He liked the marshal's desk better, though. It was larger, making it easier to lay out his cards. And the marshal's chair was more comfortable.

Still, Stringbean didn't belong over here. A coward of an inept deputy didn't—

The click of the door latch cut off his thoughts. He looked up to see Molly Hurdstrom poke her pretty head in the door. "There you are, Henry. I've been so worried about you!" She came in and, closing the door, said, "I heard you'd been shot. Pa wouldn't let me visit you in the San Juan. Said it was no place for young ladies. I talked to the doctor, though, and he said you were on the mend. I saw Mister Waite on the street earlier, and he said you were back on the job."

She stopped in front of the desk and placed her hand on her hip, elbow jutting straight out to her side. Her pretty, gray eyes were large as buttons. "Against doctor's orders, I might add!"

"Oh, it was just a flesh wound, Molly," Stringbean said, having scrambled to his feet when she'd entered. "I gotta get back on the job. Marshal Mannion needs me."

Did he really? was the question in the back of Stringbean's mind. Did anyone need a no-good deputy. Mainly,

Stringbean had wanted to get back to work so he wasn't just lying around in bed, feeling sorry for himself when he wasn't berating himself for his foolishness and worthlessness.

His cowardice.

"You have your health to think about, Henry McCallister!"

Stringbean couldn't help smiling. He liked it when she called him by his given name, and he liked it that she seemed genuinely concerned about him. He also liked the pretty gray and white gingham dress she wore with puffy sleeves and a matching, gray felt hat. The gray in the hat and the dress matched the gray in her eyes.

Lovely chestnut sausage curls hung down to caress her peaches and cream cheeks.

"What are you smiling about?" she asked him, frowning curiously.

"You sure are pretty," Stringbean said before he even realized what he'd been about to say. He felt his cheeks warm with sudden embarrassment.

Molly smiled and canted her head to one side. "Why, Henry, you've never told me that before."

"I'm...I'm sorry if I was bein' too forward..."

"You weren't being too forward at all. I liked hearing you say it."

Stringbean blanched a little under the girl's gaze. His chest was heavy, and his heart was suddenly beating fast. He had something he had to tell her before they went any further than they'd already gone, though he knew that wasn't far. But she somehow seemed to expect more from him now.

But he wasn't worthy of this pretty girl.

He had to tell her why. She deserved to know the truth.

"Molly, would you please sit down for a minute?" Stringbean asked her, looking gravely at her from across the marshal's desk.

She frowned again, this time with concern. "Sure, sure," she said, sitting down in the guest chair to String- bean's right, smoothing her long skirts against her back- side. How gracefully she sat down intrigued him, though that was only one of the many things that intrigued him about her.

What he found himself especially liking about her now was that she genuinely seemed to like him when he knew she had so many more, better-bred, better mannered, and better-looking suitors than he. Her father owned a large freighting business, and the Hurdstroms lived in a big house on the edge of town by a creek, and they drove to church every Sunday in a red-wheeled, leather-seated chaise carriage. Molly's father had a thick, black walrus mustache and used a fancy walking stick, and her mother, who also worked in the business, was tall and beautiful and was the president of several women's groups around Del Norte.

Stringbean had no idea what had possessed him to call on Molly that first time, but he knew he'd likely lost a good ten pounds in weight from sheer nervous energy before he'd worked up the gumption to do so. He'd been admiring her in church and walking around town, shop- ping with her mother, for over a year.

There was so much he liked about her. And now he had to let her go and disgrace himself before he did.

What a sad state of affairs Stringbean McCallister's life had become!

He'd likely be laughed out of town after this. He'd likely spend the rest of his life living alone in some long-dead fur trapper's cabin in the mountains, never to be seen or heard from again by anybody. Maybe he'd adopt a dog. There were plenty of strays running around the streets of Del Norte. A dog might put up with him.

But not this girl. Not after she heard his confession.

Maybe he shouldn't tell her. Just end it. Keep his dignity.

No, he had to tell her. He wanted to tell her. He *needed* to tell her.

That was the only way to salvage at least a scrap of his dignity.

He walked around the desk and sat in the guest chair beside Molly, facing her.

"What is it, Henry?" she asked softly and with a puzzled look.

"I have to tell you something."

She dipped her chin slowly, her eyes becoming very serious. "All right. Go ahead."

Stringbean slid his chair a little closer to her, until his knees were nearly touching hers. He reached out and took her hand in his, gave it an affectionate squeeze. He did this automatically, too, just freeing himself and letting him do what came naturally, and that's what had come naturally to him.

It also felt natural, for some reason, to tell her what he had to tell her. He couldn't wait to get it off his chest. It must be like how a Catholic felt when giving confession to a priest.

"You know the posse I took out...after Whip Helton...?"

Molly placed her other hand over the one of his holding hers. "Yes, I heard. You alone survived. I thought you would maybe tell me about it when you were ready." She paused, canted her head to one side, and gave him a deeply sympathetic look. "Are you ready to tell me, Henry?"

Stringbean was staring down at his hand ensconced in both of hers. Now he swallowed down his hesitancy and lifted his gaze to meet hers directly. "The reason I survived is because I froze and ran."

He stared at her. She gazed back at him, unblinking.

"You see...I went crazy with fear when Mister Hennessey was shot right in front of me. I dropped my rifle and ran up the mountain. When I started down the other side, I fell into a mineshaft. That's what saved me. There was enough cover in there that Helton's bullets didn't reach me 'cept a graze or two. The marshal came along the next day and fished me out."

Stringbean couldn't hold the girl's gaze anymore. It was just too much—what he was telling her and what she must be feeling about him now. "I wanted him to just leave me. It's the God's truth I wanted to die down there instead of havin' to face the world with..." He forced himself to lift his chin, to meet Molly's clear-eyed gaze once more. "Havin' to face the world with my cowardice."

She gazed back at him, wrinkling the skin above the bridge of her nose, long, deep lines cutting across her forehead. Her eyes searched his and then suddenly tears washed into them. "Oh, Henry!" she said, and leaned toward him and wrapped her arms around his neck. "Oh, Henry—my dear Henry!"

A little stiffly, Stringbean wrapped his arms around Molly, not one bit surprised at how warm and soft and supple she felt pressed against him, their hearts beating together, chests pressed together, hearts only inches away from each other. She squeezed him tightly and sobbed against his neck and ran one of her hands up and down his back.

She held him like that, and he held her like that, for several minutes, until the din on the street and several dogs barking in the distance and a mule braying over near the freight office seemed a long way away. Until he couldn't hear them anymore but could hear only Molly's faint sobs and feel the wetness of her tears against his neck, dribbling down under his shirt.

Finally, she pulled away but kept her face before his, their noses only inches apart.

"I thought I should tell you," Stringbean said. "You deserved to know. I reckon...I reckon I won't be showin' up to sit on your porch with you anymore."

"Don't be silly," she scolded him, laughing suddenly and brushing tears from her cheeks with the backs of his hands.

He frowned curiously at her. "What...?"

"Oh, Henry, you're no coward. All right, so you ran. You got caught off-guard and you ran." Molly sniffed and wrapped her arms around his neck again and smiled at him affectionately. "The fact that you told me makes you the bravest man on earth."

Again, he frowned at her, taken aback by her reaction, not sure what to make of it.

"Besides, everyone in town knows you saved the marshal's life the other day. Why, that's how come you got shot. You warned the marshal, and the shooter shot you instead!"

"Nah, nah. I messed that up, too. You see, I—"

She cut him off with: "You know what, Henry?"

"What?"

"You don't give yourself near enough credit. You look at yourself and all you see are your faults. I look at you and I see a very brave young man. A brave, polite, ,humble, and caring young man. So unlike those other young men who come calling on me and want to take me walking out by the creek just so they can get me away from my parents, and..." She chuffed in disgust. "Well, you know."

"You don't...you don't think I'm just a disgustin' coward? You don't think I should just get a dog and go live by myself in the mountains?"

"Of course not!" Molly took one of Stringbean's hands in both of hers and leaned close to him again. "It's time for you to start believing that now, too, Henry!"

Just then, running footsteps sounded outside the office. A figure rushed past the two front windows and then the door burst open. A bearded man in a bullet-crowned black hat and a black cloth vest over a hickory work shirt poked his head into the office and said, "The marshal around?"

"He's over to the San Juan with his daughter," Stringbean said. "What can I help you with, Anton?"

The man—a mule skinner named Anton McBride—hooked his thumb over his shoulder. "Three toughnuts are robbin' the Powderhorn Saloon even as I speak!"

His heart quickening, Stringbean turned to Molly.

She smiled and squeezed his hand reassuringly.

"That tears it!" Stringbean said, rising quickly from his chair and grabbing his hat off a wall peg. "I'll be over there in two jerks of a cow's tail, Anton! Molly, you stay here in case there's shootin' out on the street!"

He ran out onto the porch and leaped into the street.

CHAPTER 25

STRINGBEAN TRIED JOGGING NORTH ALONG THE MAIN drag, but it grieved his burned side and his game hip too much, so he slowed to a fast walk. The Powderhorn wasn't far from the marshal's office, anyway.

Anton McBride was dogging his heels, breathlessly saying, "I was in the backroom layin' in a fresh supply of beer kegs when I heard the commotion. I cracked the door to the main hall, and three rannies had closed and locked the front door, pulled the shades down. They were robbin' the place!"

"How well armed, are they?"

"They each have a shotgun. That well enough for you, Stringbean?"

"Yeah, that's well enough." As Stringbean rounded the corner of Fourth Street and Main, he glanced over his shoulder at the lumbering, bearded McBride, who hauled beer for a local brewery, and said, "Best wait here, Anton. Thanks for the tip. I'll take it from here."

"Don't you need some help?"

"Doesn't look like I have any help. Rio pulled night

duty and like I said, the marshal's with his daughter. Now, wait here!"

Stringbean headed west on Third, toward the Powderhorn Saloon—a long, deep, adobe brick building with a slate-tiled roof that sat on the street's right side all by itself, only a livery barn and a lumber yard beyond it, and the creek and its sheath of cottonwoods and aspens beyond them. The saloon lay only half a block away from the main drag.

Five horses stood at the hitchrack fronting the place as well as three freight teams strung out along the saloon's side of the street, each with a hitch of six mules. The Powderhorn was a hole in the wall, but the freighters loved it both for the whiskey and grub the Mexican owner of the place served downstairs and the kind of girls—mostly Mexicans with one black girl, Stringbean had heard—Otero served upstairs. The place was either dead or hopping at any time during the day depending on when a train of freight wagons pulled through.

Right now, it appeared to be hopping.

That's likely why the "rannies" had decided to rob the place.

Stringbean was walking at a slant across the street toward the Powderhorn when the front door opened suddenly and three men stormed out onto the boardwalk —three big, bearded, roughhewn characters Stringbean had never seen before. The first two each carried a gunnysack by its neck. The third one had one big arm wrapped around the waist of a Mexican doxie clad in a black and blue satin corset and bustier, with black feathers in her hair, long black gloves and very high-heeled black shoes. Stringbean thought they were called stilettos.

The whore was screaming and crying and trying to fight the man as he and the other two started for the horses tethered at the hitchrack.

Stringbean froze, his hand on his holstered six-shooter. The middle of the street with no near cover was not exactly where he'd wanted to encounter the three shotgun-wielding toughnuts. But here he was, so...

Make up your mind, Stringbean. What would Marshal Mannion do?

A gun blasted from inside the place and the big hombre with the girl shoved the girl to the ground and swung around, raising his barn blaster to fire back through the open door.

"Deputy Town Marshal—hold it!" Stringbean shouted, raising his old model Colt, crouching and extending the cocked piece straight out from his right shoulder. "Drop them gut-shredders or you're all three gonna be snugglin' with the diamondbacks!"

All three swung around as though attached to the same swivel.

The man on the left—shorter and stockier than the other two and wearing a long, red wool coat—gritted his teeth and raised his shotgun, yelling, "*Kill him!*"

Stringbean's heart skipped a beat as he lined up his Colt on the red-coated man's chest and fired a half second before the red-coated gent's double-bored shotgun blossomed rose-colored flames. Fortunately, Stringbean's bullet knocked the man back as he fired, so both rounds of likely double-aught buck caromed, buzzing like bees, into the air several feet over String-bean's head.

Seeing the other two also leveling their shotguns at him, Stringbean threw himself hard left and rolled just as two big fists of dirt and ground horse apples were kicked up just beyond where he'd been standing a second before. His bullet-burned side howled like a dog runover by a freight wagon. He rolled onto his belly, firing the Colt quickly, thumbing the hammer back and firing again, then again, and was astonished to see that all three of his slugs hit what they'd been aimed at.

Both shotgunners flew back against the front of the Powderhorn.

The man on the left dropped. The one on the right, bounced off the wall, got his feet under him, then reached over to where the Mexican doxie lay sprawled on the ground to the right of the open door. He was the tallest of the three. He wore a broad-brimmed canvas hat, a long, green canvas duster, and buckskin pants. Sprouting blood from his right arm and left shoulder, he dropped his shotgun and pulled a big, wide-bladed Bowie knife from a buckskin sheath on his right hip.

He pulled the girl to her feet, jerked her around in front of him, and held the curved point of the Bowie to the tender underside of her chin.

"Drop that hog-leg or I'll gut her like a fish, kid!" the man bellowed.

"No!" the girl cried.

She turned her head sharply right, leaving the man's broad, bearded face a clear target. The man's blue eyes snapped wide, flashing fearfully, and he opened his mouth to yell just as Stringbean's pistol roared. The bullet plowed through the man's right cheek, just beneath that eye, knocking him backward. From inside the saloon, a gun roared hollowly. It roared again, both bullets ripping through the man's back and out his chest, shredding his shirt and knocking him forward.

"*Bastardo!*" came a fierce cry from inside the saloon.

The gun roared again, and the bearded gent released the girl, dropped the Bowie with a clatter, and stumbled farther forward and slumped down over one of the two hitchracks fronting the place. His long, thick arms hung straight down over the rack to the ground.

Stringbean stood extending his smoking Colt from straight out in front of him, both hands wrapped around it, as a short man with distinctly Mexican features and wearing a grimy blue shirt and white apron emerged from the shadows inside the Powderhorn. He was nearly bald on the top of his head, and ears protruded like jug handles.

The Powderhorn owner, Ramon Otero, met String-bean's gaze and grinned a gap-toothed grin.

He lifted his own smoking revolver and blew at the end of the barrel then grinned again and gave Stringbean a salute by tapping the barrel to his liver-spotted right temple.

Stringbean lowered his Colt and returned the Mexican's smile. "Glad to be of help, Senor Ramirez."

He holstered the Colt and turned just as Molly Hurdstrom approached at a dead run, Anton McBride walking along behind her.

"Henry!" Molly cried, throwing herself against his chest and wrapping her arms around him. She looked up at him, eyes bright with concern. "Are you, all right?"

Stringbean frowned thoughtfully and held up his right hand. It wasn't shaking. His left side hurt like the blazes. He thought he might have opened it up again. But at least he hadn't lost his nerve.

He looked down at Molly, frowning. "You know—I think I am!"

She laughed. "That was some crazy shooting, Henry! Just crazy!"

Stringbean shrugged nonchalantly. "All in a day's work, Molly. All in a day's work."

He looked at Anton McBride.

McBride winked at him.

CHAPTER 26

GARTH HELTON LED HIS PACK OF TWENTY GUN-HUNG riders into Del Norte at full gallop—a proud, black-clad general leading his troops into battle. His red, neck-knotted bandanna blew in the wind back behind him.

Helton threw his head back and loosed a wild coyote howl.

The other men behind him followed suit as they hard-charged their way through Main Street traffic, scaring some horses so badly they leaped hitchracks while others broke loose from their tethers and ran away, buck-kicking.

Pedestrians screamed and ran for their lives.

Mule skinners had to stop their teams and set their wagon brakes to keep their mules from running full out to get away from the crazed horde of howling gunmen led by the fearless, pugnacious Garth Helton himself and followed close off his right flank by his hard-faced fore-man, Quint Wayne.

The men behind them whooped and hollered and waved their hats in the air. Several pulled pistols and fired skyward, further causing a panic with horses, mules, and people all up and down the main drag.

Men on the boardwalks cursed and shook their fists.

Dogs barked and babies cried.

One of the Helton riders leaped over a small farm wagon, making the overall-clad man and boy on the driver's seat pull their heads down quickly, yelling.

Finally, Helton reined up outside of Mannion's office and both of Mannion's deputies, the young one wielding a Winchester, the older, lumpier one holding a double-barrel shotgun, came down off the porch fronting the place to stand in the street before the rancher and his riders. A racoon-sized, black and white cat with a fur necktie sat on the railing, staring incredulously through its amber eyes at the newcomers.

The deputies blinked against the riders' thickly rolling dust.

Behind Helton's gang, the street became almost eerily quiet in the wake of the howling horde though several men were still cursing quietly and conversing angrily amongst themselves. One man was trying to coax his horse down off the boardwalk fronting the grocery store, where it had fled the frenzy of the crazed Spur riders.

It was nearly twelve-thirty, a half hour past Mannion's deadline for bringing his son, Whip, to town. Helton inwardly smiled at that. His being late was part of the calculation.

He had no intention of turning Whip over to Mannion, of course.

Now it was time for Mannion to get straight just who *really* was in charge around here if Helton had to take bullwhips to the man right here on Main Street to do it. (In fact, three of his men were, indeed, armed with bull-whips on their saddles.)

Helton leaned forward, spat to one side, and glared down at the two deputies staring back at him. "Where's Mannion?"

The two deputies glanced at each other before turning back to Helton. The lanky one called Stringbean shrugged a shoulder. "Haven't seen him."

"Haven't seen him?" Helton said. "What're you talking about? He wanted my boy in town by noon. Surely, he's around."

"I don't see Whip with you," said the older deputy, Rio Waite. *Some crop of deputies Bloody Joe has. One still wet behind the ears and dumb-looking and the older one way over the hill and gone to seed.*

But who else would Joe find to work for such a man as himself?

Inwardly, Helton smiled at that, too. Outwardly, his face was a granite mask of barely bridled rage.

"That's because he is *not* with me!" Helton barked. "That's what I want to see Mannion about. It's about damn time he and I get a few things straight. He might think he's tough, but I'm tougher. This is *my* town. Not his!"

The two deputies looked at each other again.

Then Stringbean turned back to Helton and said in his mild, diffident way, "Well...I reckon we'll relay the message when we see the marshal again."

"When will that be?" asked Quint Wayne, booting his horse up beside his boss.

Rio Waite spat to one side and used one hand to pull his baggy denims up higher on his broad hips. "Hard to say. You'd think a man like Joe would keep a better schedule than he does, but..."

"Yeah, we're not sure when we're gonna see the marshal again," said Stringbean.

"What's this about, Mister Helton?" This from the town's so-called mayor, Charlie McQueen, who'd walked sort of tentatively up the street from his office a half a block farther north. He walked slowly, nervously, smiling deferentially behind his glasses.

"*Mister* Mayor," Helton said, mockery in his gravelly voice. "Just wanted to have a little chat with the man you don't seem to be able to fire."

Again, McQueen smiled his constipated smile. "Ah. I see. Uh...I guess you didn't bring Whip with you, did you?"

"Of course, I didn't. He wouldn't get a fair trial in Mannion's town."

McQueen smiled at that, too. He didn't respond.

"Where is he?" Helton asked the mayor. "Don't tell me he's hiding." He gave a coyote grin.

"Oh, I don't think he's hiding," Waite said and gave a crooked little smile.

Exasperation was building in Helton. He looked around angrily and yelled to the onlookers grouped on both sides of the street, "Anyone seen Mannion? Anyone know where Bloody Joe is?"

One man in a group of five gathered outside the Three-Legged Dog Saloon, said, "Seen him ride out of town a couple hours ago."

Helton hipped around to stare back at the man, his eyes narrowed, brows beetled with incredulity. "Ride *out of town?*"

"Which way was he headed?" Wayne called.

"I think south," returned the man.

"South," Helton repeated to himself.

He turned suddenly to Wayne. He blinked. Wayne looked directly back at him, unblinking. The foreman was thinking the same thing Helton was thinking.

"He's heading for Spur!" the rancher yelled, reining his horse around sharply and putting the steel to it. "Come on, you men—*he's after my boy!*"

———

SLOWLY, MANNION WALKED UP THE REAR STEPS OF THE Helton house at the Spur headquarters. The risers creaked beneath his boots. That was all right. Since all the Spur riders had gone to town—Mannion had watched them leave Spur from a distant ridge through his field glasses—that left only possibly, aside from Whip, Helton's aged cook out in the bunkhouse or cook shack, and Helton's wife and daughter.

They would be no trouble.

Still, to avoid a ruckus, he'd like to be able to get Whip out of the house without any of them knowing. He kept moving slowly up the stairs until he reached the door at the rear of the second floor. He twisted the knob and shoved on the door, but it wouldn't budge.

Locked.

Mannion slid his cross-draw Russian from its holster and fished a red handkerchief out of his back pocket. He wrapped the hanky around the end of the gun butt then with just as much force needed tapped it against the glass in the door's upper panel, on the bottom right corner. The glass broke, a shard a little larger than the butt of the gun tumbling onto the floor inside the house with a dull, crunching ping.

Mannion winced, waited, listening.

All remained silent inside the house.

Mannion reached through the hole in the glass panel and unlocked the door. He opened it, stepped inside, and closed the door behind him.

Now to find Whip.

Depending on how badly he was injured, he could be anywhere. Mannion hoped he was alone but even if he was with his mother or sister, Mannion would take the son of Satan. He would not be denied. He had plenty of time. It was nearly an hour's ride to town and back. He had at least an hour.

He moved down the hall, opening doors and peering into bedrooms. He opened the second door on the right and froze. A wasted-looking woman in a nightgown, pink robe, and pink slippers lay on a large, canopied bed, sound asleep. She lay on her side, head resting on her arm, a drink in the hand stretched up toward the bed's left front corner. Mrs. Helton snored softly, opening her mouth with every breath.

Mannion studied the woman. Hardly anything was known about Berenice Helton. She was never seen in town. Now Mannion knew why.

He eased the door closed then checked the next one.

Another vacant bedroom that, judging by the pantalets, corsets, camisoles, and other articles of female clothing strewn over nearly every inch of the bed and floor, was the girl's.

Mannion closed the door then checked the room on the opposite side of the hall.

Again, he froze as he stared inside, heart quickening.

He glanced up and down the hall then stepped very quietly into the room and gentled the door closed behind him. Whip Helton lay on a bed ahead and right, under a window angling bright, lemon light onto the newspaper Whip was holding up to his face, one bare foot hiked on the upraised opposite knee. He wore only red long-handles.

Mannion moved slowly toward the bed.

He winced when a floorboard creaked.

The paper came down and Whip Helton frowned up at him, the bandage over his nose appearing grimy in the bright sunlight. The frown quickly became a hang-jawed look of exasperation.

"Hey—"

Mannion clipped the firebrand's cry with the butt of his Russian laid resolutely across Whip's right temple. Whip dropped the paper to the floor as he lay back against the pillow and turned his head to one side and gave a long, ragged sigh—out like a blown lamp.

Five minutes later, Mannion was descending the rear outside stairs with the barefoot, longhandle-clad body of Whip Helton draped over one shoulder, like a hundred-pound sack of potatoes. His two horses—Red and a mount he'd rented from the livery barn—waited at the bottom of the stairs, well out of sight from the yard but not from anyone who might look out a window on this end of the house.

It was a chance Mannion had been willing to take. He had Whip sewn up and Mrs. Helton appeared to be three sheets to the wind. The daughter—Landry, Mannion believed was her name—was probably out frolicking like some forest sprite.

Seeing her out there the other day, playing with her dog, had reminded him of Vangie—a solitary girl who enjoyed playing by herself or with one of the dogs she'd had in the past, or her horses. At least, that's how Vangie *had been* before Landry's brother had mauled her. No telling if she'd ever be back to her old self again.

Mannion wasn't scared of much, but he was scared to death his daughter would never be her old self again...

He was none too gentle tossing the unconscious Helton over the saddle of the spare horse and tying his wrists and ankles together beneath the horse's belly. He tied his hanky over Helton's mouth for a gag in case the firebrand woke up before they were out of the yard.

He reined Red around and, leading the spare horse by its bridle reins, headed up the timbered ridge south of the house. On the ridge's other side, he followed a creek west. By now, Helton had come awake and was groaning and grunting through the gag.

"I bet that's a might uncomfortable," Mannion said with grim satisfaction.

Louder groaning and grunting issued from behind him.

Manion did not look back at the firebrand. He kept riding.

When he gained the main trail, he swung north and headed for Del Norte, keeping an eye skinned on the trail ahead threading the gaps between shelving, cedar-stippled dikes. Mannion knew that Helton would be riding hell for leather back toward Spur as soon as he figured out that Mannion wasn't in town. When he figured that much out, he'd put two and two together and figure the rest out.

When he heard the distant drumming of hooves coming from straight ahead, Mannion checked Red down, ground-reined him, and went back and cut Helton loose. He pulled him down off the saddle, Helton grunting and cursing and glaring at his captor, who let him drop to the trail where he piled up with even louder complaints through the gag.

Mannion saw the firebrand had left blood on the saddle.

He looked down at Helton lying on his side on the trail, knees drawn up toward his chest. Blood shone through the longhandle top where Mannion had shot him low on his left side. His long, girlish brown hair lay in a dirty, tangled mess across his shoulders and down his back.

Mannion pulled him to his feet. "Climb up on my horse."

Helton tugged the gag down away from his mouth. "You're crazy, Mannion!"

Mannion gave him a hard shove toward Red, who craned his neck to watch with dubious interest the pair behind him, slowly switching his tail. "Be that as it may, climb up on my horse."

Helton reached up and grabbed the horn. He turned to glare back at Mannion and said through gritted teeth, "You're a dead man. You know that? A dead man!"

Ahead, the rataplan of the oncoming riders grew louder.

"Be that as it may, climb up on my horse or I'll pistol whip you."

Cursing, Helton shoved a dirty bare foot into the left stirrup and pulled himself into the leather. Mannion grabbed Red's reins, pulled Helton's foot out of the stirrup then toed it himself, pulling himself up onto the bay's back behind his prisoner. He'd leave the spare horse here, send someone out from town to retrieve it later.

"Don't look so sad," Mannion said as he clucked Red ahead along the trail. "We're about to see dear old dad."

CHAPTER 27

HELTON CURSED MANNION AGAIN AND SAID, "HE'S gonna kill you. He's gonna kill you hard." He turned his head to one side to look at the man behind him. "Only, he'll take his good time doin' it. Believe me, I know the old man. His worst enemies suffer a long, long time, and you're definitely one of his worst enemies, Joe."

"Now, ain't this a coincidence? The feeling's mutual," Mannion said.

He kept Red to a walk.

Ahead, dust shone on the other side of the next rise, a thick cloud of it wafting skyward. The hooves drummed louder until the black hat of the first rider appeared, and then Helton's broad face and chest and heavy shoulders and then the head of Helton's fine, wide-eyed buckskin stallion. Helton wore a long, brown corduroy coat over his traditional all-black attire save the red neckerchief.

As Helton galloped down the near side of the rise, his passel of gun-hung cow punchers rode up the rise behind him, tightly grouped, filling up the entire trail. When Helton was halfway down the rise, he lifted his chin to peer ahead and immediately tugged back on the buck-skin's reins.

"*Whoah! Whoah! Whoah!*" yelled his foreman, Quint Wayne, riding ten yards behind him, holding up his right hand to stop the others while tugging back sharply on his own reins with his left hand.

When the entire group of Spur riders had checked their mounts down on the near side of the rise, behind their boss, Helton stared straight ahead toward Mannion walking Red toward him. Mannion took the reins in his left hand and drew his cross-draw Russian from its holster with his right hand.

He raised the gun to Whip's head, pressed the barrel against his scalp just behind his ear, and thumbed back the hammer.

"Make way, Helton," he called.

Helton hardened his jaws and drew the big Colt .45 from the black leather holster seated high on his right hip.

Thirty feet from the base of the rise, Mannion halted Red and looked at Helton. "No, no. Put it back in its holster." He shoved his Russian's barrel harder against Whip's head.

"*Ow*damn you!" Whip complained, leaning away from the gun though Mannion kept it pressed hard against it.

The older Helton glared at him through the dust still wafting around him and the other riders clumped on the trail behind him and Quint Wayne.

"Don't give me more reason than I already have to blow his brains out, Helton," Mannion said, his low, even voice thick with menace.

Helton studied him, his broad chest rising and falling heavily. He glanced at the other riders behind him. They, too, had drawn either revolvers or Winchesters. "Holster 'em," Helton said, and shoved his own Colt back down in the leather.

When the others had returned their own weapons to their housings, Mannion smiled and nudged Red ahead. "There—that wasn't so hard now, was it?"

Mannion slowly closed the gap between him and the Spur riders.

"Make way," he said when Helton sat the buckskin defiantly before him, the other riders stubbornly following suit, blocking the trail.

Mannion kept Red walking straight ahead.

When he was eight feet from Helton and the buckskin, Helton reined his mount to one side and called behind him, "Make way, make way!"

Grudgingly, scowling at Mannion, the others moved their horses to either the left or right, cutting a narrow trail between them. Keeping his cocked Russian pressed taut against Whip's head, Mannion followed the narrow trail, cleaving the Spur group in two.

"Pa, you gotta get me away from this madman!" Whip implored his father.

"Shut up," was the older Helton's curt reply.

When he was beyond them, Manion said casually, not looking behind him but keeping his eyes on the trail ahead, "Don't even think about back shooting me. This Russian has a hair trigger. Just the tiniest nudge and Whip'll look funnier than he already does—without his head and all that pretty hair on his shoulders."

He chuckled dryly to himself as he put Red on up and then over the rise.

At the bottom of the rise, he glanced behind him. Garth Helton just then topped the rise followed by Quint Wayne and then the others, as well. Mannion grinned then turned his head back forward, hearing the slow clomping of the Spur riders' horses as they followed from fifty, sixty yards behind, keeping pace.

They followed him into Del Norte.

As Mannion and his unwilling charge rode down the busy Main Street now in the late afternoon, heads turned toward him, eyes widened in shock, and held on him before turning still more to watch the Spur riders trailing Mannion and Helton's half-naked, barefoot son.

The street emptied quickly around Mannion and the Spur riders, for surely hell was about to pop. Good God —Bloody Joe rode out to Spur and nabbed Helton's son right out from under him!

As Mannion continued along the street in his slow, plodding fashion, Red dubiously twitching his ears at the astonished reactions of onlookers on both sides of the street, traffic stopped ahead of him. Wagon drivers and horseback riders pulled quickly to one side, faces blanching when they saw the strange, deadly procession heading toward them.

As Mannion approached the San Juan Hotel & Saloon, he cast his gaze to the second-floor balcony that opened off Jane Ford's suite of rooms. Probably hearing the sudden hush that had descended upon the street, Jane just then stepped out through her open French doors, wearing a lovely green gown and pearls, her hair immaculately coifed and ready for the night crowd, a long, black cigarette holder in her beringed right hand.

Her curious gaze settled on Mannion and young Helton and, as she set her free hand on the balcony rail, her red lips parted. She turned her head to see the Spur riders following Mannion. Her rouged cheeks paled a bit, and then her gaze returned to Joe.

She gave a grim, knowing half-smile and then a slow, fateful shake of her head.

Mannion turned his head forward to see both of his deputies, Stringbean and Rio, step down off the porch fronting the marshal's office and jailhouse and come out into the street to turn and face Mannion. Stringbean held his 1878 Winchester carbine up high across his chest. Rio held his double-barrel Greener in the same fashion, each man's face cast gravely though a little twitch of ironic humor tugged at one corner of Rio's mouth.

"Get your man again, Joe?" Rio said as Mannion drew Red to a halt before him and Stringbean.

"Don't I always?"

Manion swung down from Red's back and aimed the Russian up at Whip. "Come on down. Slow."

Whip glanced over his left shoulder. His father and his father's men were approaching, slowing. Helton's face was a stone mask of barely restrained fury. Not only fury but humiliation. Bloody Joe had hornswoggled him. Helton was a proud man. No one hornswoggled him.

Joe had.

And the whole town had witnessed it.

Whip swung heavily down from the saddle and stepped barefoot onto the street. He turned to his father.

"Pa...?"

Helton said nothing. He sat his horse thirty feet away. Wayne sat his own mount beside him. The other riders flanked them, looking around at the astonished, fearful onlookers a little sheepishly. They, too, were embarrassed to have been so badly buffaloed.

Rio stepped up and said, "Got a room all reserved for your prisoner down in the Hotel de Manion, Marshal."

Mannion was facing the Spur riders. "Good, good," he said loudly enough for Helton to hear. "Take him down, lock him up, and keep that shotgun on him at all times. If anyone tries to spring him, scatter his damnable brains all over the cellblock!"

"You got it, Marshal," Rio said, pulling Whip forward by his left arm then giving him a brisque shove toward the jailhouse.

"Pa!" he wailed over his shoulder as he stumbled along barefoot.

When Rio and his prisoner were gone, Helton put his horse forward and stopped ten feet from Mannion. He sat up in his saddle, drew a deep breath, then settled back down in the leather again.

"All right, Joe—you won this round. I'll give you that." Helton raised his voice as he turned his head to encompass the entire Main Street with his pugilistic gaze. "But hear this, good citizens of Del Norte! I'm giving you three days to work up enough spine to free my son. I'll be back in three days at high noon to take Whip home. If he's not free at high noon on Thursday day, I will sack the entire town!

"I will burn every building—*and I mean every church and saloon and hurdy gurdy house and*"—he turned to John Dunham standing out front of his tonsorial parlor— "*every barbershop*"—he turned to Charlie McQueen standing out front of his own place of business—"*and law office in town!*" He turned to where the tall, thin, aproned Wilfred Drake stood on the loading dock of his own store— "*Every mercantile included, and*"—he turned to Jane Ford standing on her second floor balcony, gazing somberly into the street—"*every damn hotel and restaurant, to boot—not excluding the San Juan, Miss Ford!*"

His stentorian voice fairly rocketed around the street, chased by its own echoes as he punctuated the harangue with: "*And I will sift the ashes!*"

He reined his buckskin around. *"Three days!"* he bellowed.

Then he put steel to his mount and his men scrambled to make way for him as he charged through them like a bull through a chute, heading back the way he'd come.

The Spur riders, including Wayne, looked at each other in their own brand of excited astonishment, brows raised, then reined their own mounts around and followed their boss out of town, howling like moon-crazed coyotes anticipating fresh meat.

———

The next day, Mannion sat on the stoop fronting his office, tipped back in his hide bottom chair, boots crossed on the porch rail before him.

He had his rifle across his knees. He absently flicked his thumb against the hammer as he studied the faces of the men and some women passing in the street before him.

Every one, to the man and to the woman, gave him a dark, insinuating, accusing stare.

He couldn't blame them.

But he was sure as hell not going to release Whip Helton. By rights, he should kill him. As it was, he was doing the man a favor by having called in the circuit court judge to hold a fair trial. The Honorable Homer J. P. Grayson should arrive on the morning stage in four days. One day after Garth Helton's deadline for having his son released.

The judge might be visiting a burned-out town.

Mannion would just have to wait and see.

If Helton came to town and tried to raze the place,

he'd be sacrificing his son. Cutting off his nose to spite his face. But then, he probably knew that. And deep down didn't care. He was a stubborn old devil. Mannion would give him that.

Mannion knew something about stubborn.

He would not, could not relent.

Even if it meant sacrificing the town?

The answer was decisive.

Yes.

He kept seeing the eyes of his poor, wretched, silent, sullen girl...

She still had not uttered a single word. Sometimes Mannion thought she recognized him when he entered her room in Jane's suite. Other times, he thought she didn't. He thought possibly most of the time she didn't recognize much of anything around her, so inward had her attention turned.

To the horrible, haunting, eminently painful memory of her being taken by five drunken louts.

Mannion squeezed the neck of the Winchester with his right hand until the knuckles bulged and turned bone white.

"Joe?" The voice had come from far away—from the far end of a deep, dark tunnel. "Joe?" the voice came again. "Hello there, Joe. Say, Joe!"

Suddenly, Mannion's eyes focused. A man in a gray suit and gray bowler hat sat a cream mare in the street before the office. He was waving a black-gloved hand to get Mannion's attention. He was a slovenly gent in his sixties with a potbelly, bowed shoulders, and blunt nose and chin. Long white-silver hair hung down from his bowler to well below the collar of his suit coat. He wore a two-day growth of beard stubble the color of steel filings.

He smiled an unctuous smile at Mannion, showing one gold eyetooth.

Pinned to the left lapel of his suit coat was a county sheriff's star.

Well, well...if it wasn't the great, baby-kissing politician himself—Sheriff Titus T. Willoughby.

Mannion smiled to himself. Willoughby hardly ever made it out this far into the tall and uncut. That's why Mannion had a deputy sheriff's commission. So he could run down owlhoots in the country beyond the Del Norte city limits and leave Willoughby to his ice cream socials, Odd Fellows parades, horse races, and Civil War Veteran Days where he could shake hands and pass the proverbial hat for contributions to his next campaign.

Mannion did not get up or even switch positions.

"Sheriff," he said wearily, "to whom do I owe the honor?"

Again, Willoughby smiled his oily smile. "Joe, do you mind if I light an' sit a spell? Long ride out here from St. George." St. George was the county seat a good sixty miles away, on the Arkansas River.

As if paying Mannion a visit was not his sole reason for riding out here.

"Sure, sure," Manion said, surveying the older, smaller man's pudgy frame. "Need help?"

Willoughby chuckled as he swung heavily down from the saddle, his face turning red with the effort. "I can make it just fine." He whistled out a sigh, doffed his hat, and batted it against his thigh. "Although I have to admit, I don't ride as often as I once did. That saddle does start to pinch after a while!"

"They will do that," Mannion allowed.

Willoughby laughed a nervous laugh and set his hat

carefully on his head, making sure to get the angle just right.

He came up and set his small, right, black booted foot on the porch's bottom step and leaned against that knee. "Joe, I…"

"I know why you're here, Sheriff."

Willoughby arched a brow in surprise. "You do?"

Mannion smiled coldly. "Helton sent you."

Willoughby frowned with deep indignation. "Joe, if you're suggesting that—"

"You're in Helton's pocket?"

Willoughby blinked, his face turning red behind the sunburn he'd gotten on the ride out from St. George. "Joe, you have no right to talk to me that way. The reason I'm here is because there have been several, um, complaints. From Del Norte. People seem to think you've gotten…well…a little out of control, Joe. Shooting down Main Street when innocent bystanders could very well take a bullet…"

"You're here for my deputy sheriff's badge."

Willoughby sighed and drew his mouth corners down. I, uh…I am, Joe, yes. I think it's time. I've documented quite a few complaints over the past several months, and —well, don't you think it's time, too, Joe? Five years is a long time in this line of work."

Mannion studied him with his cold smile in place.

Helton had gotten to him. Probably the mucky mucks from Del Norte, too. Certainly Charlie McQueen. But Helton was the real reason he was here. Old Garth probably gave Willoughby's reelection campaign a very healthy inoculation, indeed, to ride out and run Mannion out of the country.

As if some bought and paid for, baby-kissing politician could run Mannion out of anywhere…

"Helton's son raped my daughter."

"I, uh...I heard that Whip was seen in the area when she was taken, yes."

Mannion leaned back in his chair, studied the oily son of a buck through gimlet eyes. "You heard he was in the area..."

"Yes, I heard, Joe. By the way, how is Vangie doing, anyway?"

"Better than you if you don't get your ass out of my town."

Willoughby frowned in astonishment. "What?"

"You heard me, Titus. Get your ass up on that horse and ride back the way you came." Mannion pulled his cross-draw Russian, clicked the hammer back.

Willoughby watched the move in horror. "Uh, Joe..."

Mannion aimed down at the step the sheriff's little boot was on and sent a round into the wood an inch to the right of the boot, the sudden roar making Willoughby jump nearly a foot in the air.

"Joe, for chrissakes!"

Boom!

Another bullet plumed dirt three inches from the man's other foot, again making the sheriff jump nearly a foot in the air.

"You're nothing but Helton's grocery boy, Sheriff!"

Boom!

That bullet punched into the ground a foot behind the sheriff as the little man lunged for the reins of his cream horse, which was dancing away from the gunfire, backing into the street.

"For Godsakes, Joe—have you lost your *mind?*"

Boom!

Willoughby grabbed the cream's reins just as the next bullet smashed into the ground, throwing dirt over both boots. The horse reared suddenly, and Willoughby went flying forward to strike the ground hard on his chest and belly. Somehow, he'd managed to cling to the reins. The horse dragged him forward.

"Best climb aboard fast, Sheriff," Mannion said from his perch on the porch, clicking the Russian's hammer back once more. "I'm beginning to lose patience!"

Boom!

"*Ohh!*"

The cream half-dragging him, Willoughby scrambled to his feet. He'd lost his hat and his silver-white hair was mussed and dirt streaked. He grabbed the cream's horn and clambered into the saddle, his right foot leaving the ground just as Mannion's next bullet—*Boom!*—landed where the foot had just been.

The hatless, wild-haired, glassy-eyed Sheriff Willoughby leaned forward in his saddle and extended his left arm and pointing finger at Mannion. "This will not stand, Joe!"

Boom!

The bullet tore into the street just right of the cream's right front hoof. The horse whinnied shrilly, rearing, before swinging around abruptly, lunging off its rear hooves, and galloping off down the street in the direction from which it had come, the sheriff leaning forward to cling for dear life to the saddle horn.

Still sitting the hide-bottom chair with his boots crossed on the rail before him, Mannion broke open the Russian. He removed the spent shells, letting them clink onto the worn puncheons below, then replaced them with fresh ammo from his cartridge belt. He filled all six chambers, snapped the gun closed, clicked the hammer back, and extended the piece straight out from his right shoulder, aiming over the porch rail.

Boom!

The bullet tore into the sheriff's bowler hat, blowing it high in the air. The wind caught it and bounced it off down the street to the south before the large, iron-shod wheel of an ore wagon smashed it flat.

Mannion returned the smoking Russian to its holster, snapped the safety thong in place over the hammer, then leaned back, crossed his arms on his chest, and pulled his hat down over his eyes.

Time for a nap.

Buster leaped out of nowhere to settle onto the lawman's lap, purring, for a snooze of his own.

CHAPTER 28

AGAIN, IN THE INKY DARK OF NIGHT, WITH MOST OF the oil pots on Main Street having burned themselves out, Mannion was at his post in the hide-bottom chair on the jail office's front porch. He brought a quirley to his lips, inhaled deeply, and blew wobbling smoke rings out into the darkness.

He'd decided to take night duty now that the town had turned against him. Leastways, judging by all the wooly eyeball stares he'd been getting, it seemed like at least *most* of the town was against him. He didn't want Rio or Stringbean taking anymore lead meant for him, or to incur any violence due to the wrath directed at him.

This was his fight. Not theirs. They'd insist on backing him when the time came, because that's the kind of men they were. But he didn't want them out here in the dark when gunmen were more likely to be on the lurk, possibly gunning for all three town lawmen.

Main Street was quiet and dark, only starlight offering a dull blue ambience. The moon was not up yet. A couple of all night saloons were still doing business, and Mannion could hear the prattling of distant piano music in the south and the crooning of a girl singing somewhere to the east, probably over at the Powderhorn, to the strumming of a slow guitar.

The Powderhorn.

Mannion smiled. He'd heard about Stringbean's foiling of the three toughnuts who'd robbed the place. He hadn't heard it from Stringbean, of course, but the entire town had known about it within a few minutes of it having occurred. Mannion had heard about it from Rio Waite, who'd relayed the news with the grin of a proud uncle, which the older fellow was in a way to the junior deputy.

Mannion hadn't been surprised. True, he'd hired Stringbean because he'd needed a man, damn near any man, but the former horse gentler had proven his worth. Best of all, he commanded respect the way good-natured men often can and was often able to stop trouble before it started. That wasn't Mannion's way.

Joe was more like a bull in a china shop that way. Because of his temper and out of habit—back in Kansas and Oklahoma during the 1860s and '70s, a lawman had to be every bit as vicious as the most vicious men he faced every day on the streets or in the saloons—he often unwittingly made a bad situation worse.

Stringbean had also proven himself with his old Colt and Winchester. Mannion didn't know what had happened the other day with the posse, but he'd seen men panic before. Hell, a few times he'd almost turned and run himself when the chips were down—back when he was younger, around Stringbean's age and even a little older.

Fear was natural. Sometimes it was good to go ahead and get it out of your system.

He was glad and proud that Stringbean had handled the

Powderhorn situation so well, because it had returned the gleam to the young man's gaze and the spring to his step. It had, however, cost him a visit to Doc Bohannon, because when he'd hit the dirt to avoid buckshot, he'd opened up his wound. Bohannon had had to replace several sutures and give the lad a talking to about caring for the wound.

Stringbean had insisted on returning to the job, but he was on permanent guard duty downstairs with Whip Helton now, where he could sit back on a cot, Rio's shotgun close to hand, reading the illustrated newspapers and dime novels he favored. Buster was likely down there with him, putting a natural check on the mouse and rat population.

Faint footsteps sounded on his left.

Mannion turned his gaze to the south along Main. He couldn't see anyone for the deep darkness, but the crunching footsteps were growing louder. Someone was heading toward him.

He kept his gaze on the south until a moving shadow formed against the deeper darkness of the night-cloaked street. The figure was small, slender. The walk was decidedly feminine. When starlight angled over a low building on the west side of the street, it limned the red in the visitor's hair, the folds of a long dress buffeting about the woman's legs.

Suddenly, she stopped.

"Joe?" Jane called softly. "That you over there?"

Mannion rose from his chair, flipped the quirley into the street. It landed with a spark. "Yep. That you over there?"

She lowered her chin and continued walking. When she approached the jailhouse, he saw that she wore a simple dress, slippers, and a thick, knitted brown shawl around her shoulders. Her thick, curly red hair was pinned loosely up on her head, tendrils dancing against her cheeks.

"Shouldn't be out here, Jane."

"No?" she said, climbing the porch steps. Her breath frosted in the cool air before her.

"One of my fellow townsman is liable to shoot me. Hell, you're liable to shoot me. Can I frisk you?"

Jane stopped before him and showed the white line of her teeth in the darkness as she smiled. She held her arms out. "Frisk away."

He frisked her lovingly, kissed her.

"Hold on."

He opened the office door and came out a few seconds later with a second chair. He set it beside his own then gestured to it with his hand. "Light an' sit a spell."

"Thank you."

"Want a drink?"

"No."

When she sat, leaning forward, holding the shawl close about her, Mannion sat, as well. "Can't sleep?"

"God, no."

"What's wrong?"

She turned to him, frowning. "You know what's wrong. Can you sleep?"

Mannion looked down at his hands. "I sneak a few minutes here and there."

When she didn't say anything for nearly a minute, but just stared out into the street, he turned to her again and said, "Do you want me to let him go?"

Again, she turned to him, frowning. "God, no!"

"You don't?"

"Good Lord, Joe, he raped your daughter and burned your house!"

"I know, but—"

"Don't think that just because a few of these yellow-livered bastards on Main Street want you to back water for Helton that I do, too. Not all of the town does, Joe, though I'm sure it likely seems so to you." Jane leaned toward him, kissed his shoulder. "Don't think I do. Hell, I'll be protecting my place with a Winchester. If Helton intends to burn me out, it's going to cost him! You keep that scoundrel locked up and shoot him before his father can spring him!"

Mannion smiled. "God, I love you, woman."

She smiled back at him, reached over and slid a silver lock of his long hair back behind his ear. "That's the first time you said it."

"Might be the last."

"Do you think you're gonna die?"

"I might."

Jane lifted her head and took a deep draught of the cool night air. "There's been some talk, Joe."

"I'm sure there has."

"Some people are pulling out tomorrow. Leaving. They said Helton has hired more riders. Gun men. Might've added another ten or fifteen to his roll. That means he really does figure on sacking the town."

"I guess it does. If I can shoot him first, cut the head off the snake, the others might not be quite so agreeable about fulfilling that crazy fool's wishes."

"You know his men, Joe. They're savages—all of them. They'll enjoy it."

"I know. Tall odds."

Jane stood, took another deep breath then leaned down and kissed Mannion's cheek. "Stick to your guns,

Joe. Don't mind the town. They're just scared. Scared and greedy. Bad combination."

"The worst," Mannion said.

"Good night, Joe."

"Good night, Jane."

She'd taken one step when a girl's shrill scream sounded from along the street to Mannion's right, the south. Jane gasped and slapped a hand to her chest.

Mannion rose quickly. "Stay here, Jane!"

Mannion unholstered his right-side Russian and leaped down the steps and into the street. He took off running, vaguely noting that the bullet crease to his temple no longer ached like it had, and for that he was grateful.

Ahead, the girl screamed again, louder.

A man said something in what sounded like an anger-pinched voice. There was the sharp crack of a hand smashing flesh.

Mannion could make out jostling shadows ahead and on his left, in a break between two buildings a half a block away. One of the buildings was an all-night hole-in-the-wall appropriately if unimaginatively called The All-Nighter, that catered mainly to blacks and half-breeds who were generally unwelcome elsewhere. A seedy little place with bad hooch and cheap doxies.

"Ow—damn you, woman!" came a resonant yell from the break as Mannion approached. "You bit me!"

Mannion entered the break just as a tall man slammed the back of his right hand against the cheek of a blonde young woman in a striped blanket coat leaning up against the side of The All-Nighter.

"Hey!" Mannion yelled. He holstered the Russian, stepped up to the tall gent, grabbed his right shoulder to turn him around, and slammed his right fist into the man's face twice hard.

The man grunted and staggered back against The All Nighter, to the left of the sobbing girl, who turned her head sharply left, toward the mouth of the break, and screamed, "What're you waiting for? *Shoot him!*"

Mannion turned just as a gun flashed. The bullet whipped past his right arm. The man he'd just punched gave a yowl. The shadow of a long-haired man in a bullet-crowned black hat stood at the mouth of the break before Mannion, starlight glinting off the smoking revolver in his outstretched right hand.

The man staggered backward and tried to level the gun once more.

Mannion ripped his right-side Russian from its holster and shot the man twice. The long-haired man stumbled backward off the boardwalk, got his feet tangled up, and fell, groaning.

Mannion whipped around just as the tall man, holding his left arm across his belly, extended the gun in his own right hand. It flashed brightly; the crashing report banged around inside Mannion's head. He wasn't sure if he was shot or not. He raised the Russian again and drilled the tall man once before the man gave another yowl and took off running down the break, tripping over trash. He twisted around and his gun flashed and banged again and then Mannion's flashed and banged two more times.

The tall man grunted, took two more lunging strides forward and then fell forward and rolled. A cat gave a startled cry and ran off through the brush beyond the break.

Mannion turned to the girl. She stood facing him, eyes wide, one hand over her mouth. She lowered her hand slowly and said, "I'm...I'm s-sorry," she said. "Marshal...I..."

"You armed?"

Slowly, keeping her hand over her mouth, she shook her head. "They gave me ten dollars..."

"To lead me into a trap."

Eyes still wide, she nodded.

Mannion turned to the tall man. He wasn't moving.

He walked up to stare down at the man in the street. He was aware of faces staring out the saloon's window behind him. He looked around quickly to make sure no one was about to shoot him, then looked down at the man in the street. He lay on his back, groaning, writhing in pain.

He was a half-breed hostler who worked at one of the livery barns. His name was Dwight Six Crows. Mannion had had him over to Hotel de Mannion more times than he could count on both hands.

"Who hired you, Six Crows?" The man was no killer. Just a desperate drunk.

The man stared up at him darkly, moving his lips. Only grunts came out. Then his mouth fell still along with the rest of him, and his eyes rolled back in his head.

The girl came up to stand beside Mannion. She was sobbing, her hand over her mouth.

"Who hired the three of you?"

She shook her head, said in a pinched, little girl's voice, "I don't know. These two just said they'd give me ten dollars to lead you over here. Someone must have paid them good money because they were drinking the good stuff tonight. Neither one of 'em ever has more than two dimes to rub together."

Mannion hooked his thumb over his shoulder to indicate the rear of the break. "Who's the tall gent?"

"Kylee Franklin."

"Ah. Figures." Franklin was a white man, but he was a regular at The All-Nighter, as were most drunks in town whatever color they may be. "Both easy marks."

Mannion looked along the street to his right. Jane was jogging toward him, hair hanging tumbling down from the loose bun to hang over one shoulder.

"Joe," she said, breathless as she approached. "What happened?"

"Nothing I wasn't expecting."

He cast his gaze off down the street as though looking for the man or men who'd sicced these two desperate vermin on him. Two Crows and Franklin sure hadn't planned this themselves.

McQueen?

Dunham?

Drake?

Howell, possibly?

Maybe all four had.

The doxie, whose name Mannion didn't know, cleared her throat and said thinly, dreadfully, "Marshal...?"

Mannion turned a cold eye to her. "Go to bed."

"I...I..."

"I said go to bed!"

She wheeled and hurried into the saloon, the bell jangling over the door.

There was no point in throwing her into Hotel de Mannion. She was just a desperate wretch not unlike the two men Mannion had killed here tonight. No point in fooling with her.

Again, he gazed off down the street. The night seemed thicker, darker. It was closing in on him. He could feel the hair sticking up at the back of his neck.

Enemies...

They were everywhere.

Jane was gazing up at him, her eyes searching, concerned.

"Are you all right, Joe?"

Mannion hooked his arm for her. "Come on, Miss Ford. I'll walk you home."

CHAPTER 29

THURSDAY MORNING—THE MORNING OF HELTON'S deadline to release Whip—Mannion knocked twice on Vangie's door.

He twisted the knob, shoved the door open, and stepped into the room, doffing his hat.

Jane stood on the left side of the rumpled bed, in front of an orange brocade armchair that had an open book laid face down on it. She was staring at Vangie standing on the other side of the bed, peering out a window while slowly brushing her hair. Vangie wore a cream day dress.

It was the first time Mannion had seen her in anything but a nightgown since the night she'd been taken. She was brushing a shine into her hair.

Mannion frowned curiously at Jane. "What's going on...?"

Jane's eyes shown with pleasant surprise. "She dressed herself. Climbed out of bed, retrieved the dress I bought her from the closet, and put it on. Now she's staring out the window and brushing her hair as though she has somewhere to go."

"Has she said anything?"

Jane shook her head. "No."

Holding his hat, Mannion walked haltingly toward his daughter. "Good morning, Vangie."

She stopped brushing and turned her head to regard him over her shoulder. She looked at him flatly for a brief moment, the way she'd been looking at him lately, without recognition. But now she smiled suddenly. Not a big smile but a smile, just the same. And her eyes shown with the light of recognition.

She knew who Mannion was!

She turned her head to stare back through the window and continued brushing her hair.

Mannion walked up to her, stood beside her. "What is it, honey? Is there something you're looking at out there?"

She glanced at him again and smiled then continued to gaze out the window and into the morning-bustling street below, brushing her hair.

Mannion glanced at Jane then returned his gaze to his daughter. "Would you...would you like to go out there, Vangie?"

She turned to him quickly, eyes wide, startled. Then her gaze grew pensive as she stared at him, wrinkling the skin above the bridge of her nose. It was as though she were considering the question.

Again, Mannion cast a conferring look to Jane, who widened her eyes and gave a hopeful shrug.

Mannion rested his left hand on Vangie's right shoulder. "I'll take you out there if you want. We'll go for a walk...see the town." He knew he shouldn't be out on the street with Vangie, for last night's incident had convinced him beyond a doubt that he had a target on his back. But if Vangie was trying to break out of the shell she'd been in, it might be worth the risk. He certainly couldn't deny her. This was the first time in weeks her eyes had lit up with the joy of living.

They were no longer her mother's eyes in those last days.

No longer the eyes of the woman who'd tricked Mannion into killing her.

Now if she'd only speak...

Mannion looked down at Vangie's feet. She had ankle boots and stockings on.

Hope grew in him.

She was ready to break out of here.

Mannion squeezed her arm. "I'll take you outside, honey...if that's what you want..."

Again, Vangie turned to him, gave him that pensive, rather consternated look again, then turned to the window. She turned back to him and smiled.

Mannion smiled, as well, his heart growing lighter. He hadn't realized how heavy it had become over the past couple of weeks, like a large stone in his chest. "All right, then."

He stepped back. Vangie set the brush on the bedside table and then walked slowly around the bed toward the door.

"Hold on," Jane said, placing her hands on Vangie's shoulders, halting her at the foot of the bed.

Jane walked to the closet and returned with a black, hooded cape.

"Lift your arms, honey."

Vangie lifted her arms and Jane dropped the cape down over her head. She raised the hood and smiled into Vangie's eyes. "It's chilly outside. No longer summer but fall."

Vangie smiled.

"Do you like fall?" Jane asked her.

Smiling, Vangie nodded.

"I do, too," Jane said and turned her hopefully smiling eyes to Mannion.

"All right, honey," he said, placing his hand on Vangie's back.

She walked tentatively forward. He stepped ahead of her and opened the door. She seemed to hesitate before walking through it, and when she did, she looked around carefully as though scouting for a possible threat.

"It's all right, honey," Mannion said. "You're safe here. You're safe with me."

But she hadn't been safe with him the night she'd been abducted, had she? No, that night he'd been dead drunk.

But he wasn't drunk now. He'd never get drunk again.

Mannion extended his hand. She looked at it, seemed to think about it, then slowly raised her hand and let Joe wrap his around hers. He led her slowly to the door to the hall, opened it.

"Go easy, Joe," Jane said behind him, nervously fingering her gold necklace. "Don't take her out too long. Might be too much."

"We'll just take a short walk," Mannion said, and led Vangie out into the hall.

She was as skittish as a newborn fawn as he led her down the hall and then down the stairs. There was a dozen or so customers seated at tables or standing at the bar. One of Jane's girls, Margie, a short, plump brunette, was sitting with a couple of cattle buyers from Chicago. All faces turned to Mannion and his daughter and the conversational hum dwindled quickly.

Vangie looked around, wide-eyed, still skittish, hesitant, as Joe led her down the stairs. The girl seated with the cattle buyers, clad in the skimpy outfit of her trade, feathers in her hair, rose slowly, staring hopefully across the room at Mannion and his daughter. Margie entwined her hands before her, sort of squeezed her shoulders together, and smiled brightly, optimistically.

Mannion smiled back at the girl, pinched his hat brim to her in thanks for all she and the other girls had done for Vangie—always sitting with her, never allowing her to be alone. He continued to lead Vangie down the stairs then even more slowly across the drinking hall to the batwing doors.

She stopped in front of the doors, stared at them, biting her lower lip.

"If you want to go back upstairs, honey," Mannion said, "we can do that. Just let me know. You don't have to do anything you don't want to do."

He gave her hand a reassuring squeeze.

She looked at him and smiled, gave her head a quick shake then released his hand and stepped forward, pushing her way through the heavy oak doors. She took a bold step forward and stood staring out into the street, lifting a hand to shade her eyes from the bright morning light. She smiled almost rapturously.

Mannion followed her out and glanced to his right.

Charlie McQueen, John Dunham, George Howell, and Wilfred Drake, all clad in business suits and bowler hats, stood in quiet conference, soapy beer mugs in their fists, raw eggs lolling at the bottom. Howell glanced toward Mannion and his daughter, caught the other men's gazes, and canted his head to indicate the father and daughter standing in front of the batwings, the girl casting her dreamy, innocent, little-girl's gaze out into the street, swinging her head from left to right and back again, eyes fairly flashing her delight in reentering the world.

The four businessmen to Joe's right stared at Vangie, looking a little shaken. Clumsily, they doffed their hats and averted their gazes, cheeks coloring sheepishly.

Mannion stepped forward. "Are you coming, honey?"

Vangie looked up at him. The smile left her face. It was replaced by that troubled, consternated look again.

Mannion put one foot down on the top step and half-turned to his daughter. "It's all right, honey. We don't have to go any farther. Just if you want to."

Vangie looked around again, taking in the street.

She looked at her father, drew a deep, steeling breath and, pinching her skirt up above her ankles, slowly descended the steps. Mannion offered her his hand, but she didn't take it. She wanted to do this alone.

Inside, he smiled. So far, so good. He just wished she would say something.

He walked along beside her, ready to grab her if she should fall. She looked frail and moved a little unsteadily.

When they reached the bottom of the steps and stood on the boardwalk facing the street, Mannion realized that wagon traffic had nearly come to a standstill. Foot traffic had, as well, except for those pedestrians moving closer to see what had grabbed so thoroughly the attention of those nearer the San Juan. Slowly, all around Mannion and on the boardwalks on the opposite side of the street, crowds were gathering.

A hushed silence like that which had descended on the saloon a few minutes ago now settled over the street.

Vangie looked around, again hesitant.

"We can take a walk," Mannion said. "But only if you want to, honey."

Vangie looked around, considering, then slowly

reached out for her father's hand. Joe took her hand in his and slowly led her forward. The small clumps of people who'd stopped to watch Mannion and his daughter made way for them as they walked slowly, hand in hand, along the street to the south.

Vangie seemed to be fascinated by everything she saw —the displays in the store windows, the mules hitched to a large Pittsburg freight wagon parked out front of Drake's Mercantile, a chunk of red rock candy stuck in the boardwalk cracks at her foot, three stray dogs, each of a different size, running barking along the street, two following the shaggy, fawn-colored one with a knuckle bone in its jaws.

She pointed the dogs out to Mannion. Joe chuckled. He couldn't help remembering Helton's daughter playing with her dog. "I bet you'd like one of those again," Joe said, smiling down at Vangie

She stopped suddenly with a gasp.

Mannion followed her gaze to three men in rough trail garb standing outside a beer parlor two buildings down on the right. The men were talking amongst themselves, two smoking, all holding beer schooners, one sloppily eating a ham and cheese sandwich on thick, crusty brown bread.

Mannion looked at Vangie. Her suddenly troubled gaze was on the man eating the sandwich. Mannion knew why. The man was roughly Whip Helton's height and build, with a soft, round face with several days' growth of beard stubble, flat eyes, and long, girlish brown hair hanging straight down his back.

Mannion placed his hand on his daughter's arm. "Vangie, it's all—"

She wheeled suddenly and started walking very quickly, holding her arms straight down at her sides, fists clenched until they turned white, back in the direction of the San Juan.

Damn, Mannion thought. *Damn, damn, damn...*

————

LYING ON HIS COT IN THE BASEMENT OF THE HOTEL DE Mannion, Whip Helton dug in the pocket of his black denims for his monogramed, silver-washed timepiece. He opened it with his right hand. His left hand was still useless thanks to Bloody Joe, and he didn't think he'd ever breathe right through his nose again, either.

He opened the piece, set it down on the cot beside him, and absently fingered the thick, white bandage on his poor, swollen nose. The time was a few minutes shy of eleven-fifteen.

His father should be along in about forty-five minutes.

Whip looked at the deputy, Stringbean, lying on a cot in the cell on the other side of the cell block from Whip's cell. Stringbean lay with his head resting back on a striped pillow propped against the stone wall. His long, thin, denim-clad legs were stretched out before him, crossed at the ankles.

He had a pile of illustrated newspapers and dime novels strewn about the cot. More were on the square wooden table that sat in the cell block's central aisle, a ladderback chair on the far side of it from Whip. The table was cluttered with the older deputy's playing cards, a cribbage board, a Montgomery Ward & Co. wish book, two overfilled ashtrays and old, yellowed copies of the *Del Norte Bugle*.

A second cell block key ring was on the table, as well. That must be the older deputy's keys. How they got left down here, Helton didn't know. He just knew they were down here, and they were on the desk, partly covered by a newspaper. Stringbean had his own set of keys on his cot with him.

He must not have noticed the extra set of keys on the table.

They had especially captured Whip's attention when the tow-headed kid, Harmon Hauffenthistle, who cleaned the cell block for Mannion, had left his broom leaning against the desk. The key ring and that broom had captured Whip's undivided attention. They surely had.

His heart had started beating like that of a racehorse before a race at high noon on the Fourth of July.

"Hey, kid," Whip called to the deputy, Stringbean, through his locked cell door. "Why don't you fetch me a cup of coffee?"

"I told you not to call me kid," said the long, tall drink of water, his sandy brows knit with indignation. "I'm only a year or two younger than you are."

"Well, you look younger than that."

"Well, I'm not." Stringbean had gone back to reading *The National Police Gazette* that had a drawing of a scantily clad young woman on the cover holding a knife and wielding a menacing expression.

"I do apologize."

Stringbean only grunted.

"Hey, I heard you was a good horse breaker."

Stringbean lowered the pulp rag again, frowning again. "Gentler. I gentled 'em. Never broke a horse in my life. A broke horse ain't no good."

"Again, I do apologize. I heard you were a right good horse *gentler*."

Stringbean, who'd raised the magazine to his face again, merely grunted again.

"What happened? How come you're wearing that star for Bloody Joe?"

Stringbean lowered the magazine and scowled over it at the prisoner. "That's Marshal Mannion to you, fella."

Jesus, when am I gonna stop offending this kid?? Whip scolded himself.

"Again, Deputy, I do apologize. So...as I was askin'...what hap—?"

"Jesus!" Stringbean intoned. "You talk so dang much a fella can't read!" He dropped the magazine on his cot, swung his feet to the floor. "I'm gonna fetch you that coffee so maybe you'll shut up and drink it and let me read!"

Wagging his head in frustration, Stringbean left his cell and strode off down the cell block toward the door that led to the upstairs office, boots clacking and spurs ringing on the lumpy cell block floor.

Whip's heart kicked eagerly as he looked at the key ring and the broom.

The broom was within a stretched arm's length of the door.

CHAPTER 30

"WHAT ARE YOU DOING UP HERE, SIX-GUN HENRY?"
Mannion asked as Stringbean stepped through the door
to the basement cellblock.

Stringbean frowned. "Six-Gun Henry?"

"That's what Rio and I have decided to start calling
you."

Leaning against the wall by the open front door, Rio
grinned. He held a steaming cup of coffee. So did
Mannion. The marshal was perched on the end of his
desk, drinking the coffee, his Yellowboy leaning against
the desk to his right.

Helton's high-noon deadline was looming.

Stringbean blushed. "I don't understand..."

"When were you going to tell me about the three
hardcases who tried rob the Powderhorn...and that you
took down with such aplomb? Aplomb was the word that
Miss Molly Hurdstrom has been using to describe it to
most of the town. Probably all of the town by now."
Mannion sipped his coffee and glanced at Rio. "The girl
gets around."

"Here, I thought she was shy," Stringbean said, filling

a cup of coffee. "To answer your first question, Marshal, this is for Helton."

"He don't deserve any coffee," Rio grumbled.

"I'm just tryin' to get him to shut-up so I can read," Stringbean said, returning the pot to the range. He looked at Mannion. "To answer your second question, Marshal, I done wrote it all up in my report. It's on your desk there. I think your newspaper's on it."

"Oh, we're all official now," Mannion said, winked at Rio, and took another sip of his coffee.

Stringbean looked down at the cup steaming in his hand. "I reckon I don't have anythin' to brag about. I'm your deputy, and that sort of thing is expected of me. I'm sure I'll screw up again soon enough."

He walked to the open cellblock door.

Mannion stopped him with: "Hey, Six-Gun?"

Stringbean glanced at him, blushing again. "You did good."

"Thanks, Marshal. I am a might proud of my efforts. But like I said, I'll screw up again."

"We all screw up, kid," Rio said and took another sip of his coffee. He smacked his lips and added, "Even me from time to time."

He grinned.

Stringbean chuckled then headed down into the basement, closing and locking the door behind him.

———

HE DESCENDED THE STAIRS, WINCING AS THE HOT coffee sloshed over the rim of the cup, burning his hand.

"Galldangit, Helton," he said, as he clacked and jangled back along the stone floor toward the far end of the cellblock where Helton was housed. The rest of the cells were empty. "You made me burn my cottonpickin' ha—"

He stopped dead in his tracks, staring wide-eyed into Helton's cell.

It was empty.

A shadow moved along the floor to his right. A furtive tread sounded behind him.

"Night-night, Deputy!"

Stringbean felt the crushing blow of a gun butt laid across the back of his head.

"*Ohh!*" he said, staggering forward, dropping the coffee cup and trying to keep his feet beneath him.

He tried in vain. The cellblock floor came up fast and hard.

Then it was lights out.

———

RIO LOOKED AT THE BANJO CLOCK ABOVE THE WINDOW, on the same wall he was leaning against, the front one, and glanced at Mannion.

It was high noon.

"How you wanna play it, Joe?"

Mannion came down off his desk, walked slowly across the office to the open front door. He stood in the doorway, staring into the street that had become more and more quiet over the past half hour. Now there wasn't a soul on the street. Only a few wagons parked here and there. As far as Mannion could see, only one saddled horse stood at a hitchrack fronting a saloon. It was drawing water from the stock tank on the other side of the hitchrack, tail arched.

It suddenly lifted its dripping snout from the water and craned its neck to peer around behind it, as though it had sensed the tension hanging over the town and was affected by it now, too.

Mannion sipped his lukewarm coffee. "I don't know, Rio. I reckon if they start shooting, we shoot back." He glanced at his thick-set deputy standing to his right, Rio's right shoulder pressed up against the wall.

The older man gave a grim nod.

Mannion turned back to face the street. "For what it's worth, I'm sorry, Rio. If this goes the way I got a feeling it's going to, that is." He turned to him again. "I'm sorry. I'd like to send you and Stringbean both home, but I won't insult you again. I realize you're as much a part of this thing as I am." He turned to face the street again. "But it's my fault."

"You got that wrong, Joe." Rio stepped over to place a thick hand on Mannion's shoulder. "It's the fault of the Heltons."

"You sound like Jane."

"Smart lady, Miss Jane."

Mannion looked down at his cup as he ran his thumb around the rim. "There are other ways I could've played this." Slowly, fatefully, he shook his head. "Just wasn't in me."

"When they mess with your family, that's when you become a bare-knuckle fighter."

Mannion gave a dry chuckle. "I've always been a bare-knuckle fighter."

Rio chuckled then, too.

Mannion looked at him, his eyes serious again. "If they take me out first, kill Helton. At least kill Helton."

Rio nodded. "You got it."

A sharp whistle sounded from down the street to the south. Mannion looked that way to see the tow-head Harmon Hauffenthistle standing at the mouth of a break between two buildings a block away. Young Harmon canted his head to the south then stepped back into the break.

Mannion looked south. A dark, jostling smudge lay far back along the trail, growing gradually in size.

"Here they come." Mannion turned and walked over to his desk. He set his cup on it, picked up the Yellowboy, and jacked a round into the chamber. He moved to the cellblock door and called through the small, barred window down into the murky shadows, "Be ready, String-bean! They're coming! If anybody but me or Rio opens this door, blast that devil to hell and gone!"

"Got it, Marshal," came Stringbean's hoarse reply.

The kid must be a little scared. Understandable. Mannion had to admit his own guts were a little tight themselves.

He turned to see Rio standing on the stoop, his double-barrel shotgun in his hands. His Winchester repeater leaned against the railing to his right.

Mannion walked out onto the stoop and cast his gaze to the south. The smudge had defined itself into individual riders approaching Del Norte at a dead run.

The drumming of the horses' hooves rose, growing louder.

As the riders entered the town and stormed down the eerily deserted Main Street, Mannion glanced at Rio. "Stay up here. Remember..."

"I know. If they take you down first, kill Helton."

"You got it."

Mannion walked down the porch steps and strode out into the street as the thunder of the approaching riders rose to a near roar. He could hear tack squawking and bridle chains jangling. The Spur riders were halfway between the south end of town and Mannion's office and closing the gap quickly, a thick cloud of dust roiling around them.

Helton was in the lead, Quint Wayne behind him, the others grouped loosely behind Wayne. They were a larger group than they'd been before. Sure enough, Helton had added a good ten, maybe fifteen men to his roll.

That meant he'd keep his word here today. If Mannion didn't release Whip, Helton would lay waste to the town.

Wearing a long, brown, corduroy coat over his otherwise all-black attire, Helton galloped up to within twenty feet of Mannion and drew rein, his fine buckskin stallion digging its hooves into the finely churned dirt and horse manure of the street and sliding, curveting slightly, whickering. Wayne and the others drew hasty rein behind their boss, and Mannion blinked as the dust roiled over him, powdering his hat.

Back along the street behind the Helton riders, the lone horse at the hitchrack gave a long, shrill, nervous whinny as it cast its frightened gaze toward the Spur riders. It stood parallel to the hitchrack.

Helton thumbed his black hat up his broad, ruddy forehead and blinked once as he stretched his gaze from Mannion to Rio standing on the porch then back to Mannion again.

He leaned forward, resting his left elbow on his saddle horn. He leveled a direct, commanding gaze on Mannion. "Bring him out here."

"Not a chance."

Helton's eyes turned hard and mean. "Don't play games with me, Mannion." He cast a quick glance over his right shoulder. "I've added to my roll. I have thirty-three men here today. You don't have a chance." He glanced around at the street, as deserted as the street of any long-abandoned ghost town. "This pitiful town doesn't have a chance!"

"Your son doesn't either," Rio said from the stoop. "Stringbean's with him..."

"With orders to blast his ugly hide all over the cellblock if anyone but Rio or I open the cellblock door," Mannion added.

Helton studied the lawman closely, his eyes befuddled. Slowly, he shook his head. "You're willing to sacrifice yourself...this whole town...for my son?"

"He raped my daughter," Mannion said, feeling the burn of rage make its way up from the base of his spine and spreading across his shoulders. He remembered Vangie's reaction to the man who'd resembled Whip. He picked a spot on Garth Helton's forehead where he intended to put the first bullet out of his Yellowboy. It was a large freckle two inches above the bridge of the man's broad nose and slightly left, almost above his left eye. "What kind of man would I be if I let him go free?"

"A living one. A man with a town."

Mannion raised the Yellowboy, held it at port arms across his chest.

Helton hipped around in his saddle, looking south along the deserted Main Street. He turned back to Mannion with a faintly jeering grin crooking his thick, chapped lips. "You're all alone, Mannion. Just you and your fat, old deputy there. You don't have a damn chance."

Rio's face turned red with anger and opened his mouth to give a retort but stopped when the door of the barbershop opened to Mannion's right and John Dunham stepped out, wielding a double-barrel shotgun in his hands. He stepped up to the edge of the boardwalk fronting his place, and said, "I stand with Bloody Joe!"

A click and a squawk sounded behind Mannion. He glanced over his left shoulder to see none other than the bowler-hatted, bearded, suited Charlie McQueen step out of his brick law office and walk this way, holding a pretty Winchester rifle in his hands, up high across his chest. His eyes were not smiling behind his glinting spectacles, like they usually were.

His jaws were set with steely determination.

He came to within twenty feet of Mannion and stopped on the boardwalk near Dunham, squared his shoulders at the Spur riders, and said, "I stand with Bloody Joe!"

"I stand with Bloody Joe!" came a shout from the south.

Mannion turned to see the tall, aproned Wilfred Drake standing on the edge of his boardwalk, facing the Spur riders. His son, Alfred, who took after Drake in length of bone but had a mop of curly sandy hair, stood beside his father, wielding a shotgun.

"Me, too," young Drake called. "I stand with Bloody Joe!"

Another, "I stand with Bloody Joe!" came from out front of the bank, where the corpulent Morgan Howell stood on the boardwalk, wielding a pretty Winchester repeater he used to hunt elk in the mountains every fall.

Footsteps sounded close on Mannion's left. He turned to see Jane Ford step out of the lot between the jail office and the Post Office wearing a black cape over a white shirtwaist, and a pleated blue skirt. Her hair was down and glinting beautifully in the late-summer sun. She cocked the Winchester in her hands and raised it to her shoulder. As she did, she smiled at Mannion and winked then returned her attention to the Spur riders before her.

Garth Helton looked as though he were filling up

with so much blood he'd explode. He looked around, eyes wide, gray-brown brows beetled. The Spur riders were looking around, as well, a few turning their prancing horses this way and that, regarding the shooters lined up on both sides of the street. They all held rifles, but they weren't raising them, and wariness shone in their dark, flat killers' eyes beneath their hat brims.

"How dare you!" Helton bellowed. "Without me, this town would be half its size!" He whipped his enraged look at McQueen, thrust out his right arm and angrily pointing finger. "Charlie, how dare you aim a rifle at me!"

"There's right and there's wrong, Mister Helton," McQueen said, aiming his rifle out from his right shoulder. "What your son did to Joe's girl is just plain wrong. I and the rest of Del Norte—at least, those that count—stand against wrong!"

"The rest of us, too," bellowed the banker, Howell.

The others didn't say anything. They didn't need to. The message was clear in their eyes aiming down the barrels of their rifles or shotguns.

The Spur riders including the foreman, Quint Wayne, all turned their edgy, wide-eyed looks to Helton for guidance then back to the guns bristling at them from both sides of the street.

"Goddamn you to hell—all of you!" Helton shouted, turning his head from side to side to include all the Del Norte citizens backing Mannion, who stood half-frozen in place in shock.

Mannion glanced at Rio. Rio looked back at him, face expressionless except for a slight, surprised arch of both brows.

Mannion could read the rage in Helton's eyes. He wasn't going to back down.

"Don't do it," the lawman said quietly, levelly. "Ride

back to where you came from, Helton. There's gonna be a trial. A fair one."

Helton showed his large, square teeth as he said, "*Like hell!*" He glanced at Wayne sitting his horse to Helton's left. "Kill them! Kell them all and burn the town to the *ground!*"

With that, he raised his rifle to his shoulder and aimed at Mannion, clicking the off-cocked hammer back. Mannion eared back the Yellowboy's hammer, pressed the butt plate against his shoulder, took quick aim at the man's head and then, to his own surprise, pulled the shot slightly left and blew the round through the rancher's left shoulder. Helton jerked to his left as he fired his own rifle, the bullet buzzing over the lawman's left shoulder to break glass somewhere behind him.

The sound was immediately followed by an explosion of gunfire from both sides of the street and from the Spur riders turning their horses this way and that, reins in their teeth or in their hands holding their rifles, returning fire on Jane and the other citizens. Rio cut loose from the porch with his Greener—two quick, cannon-like blasts. Meanwhile, Helton, who'd dropped his rifle when he'd reached for his left shoulder with his right hand, went tumbling down his buckskin's right hip, slamming his head and shoulders against the ground.

His right boot hung up in the stirrup. He hung there, helpless, eyes wide and round with fear.

The buckskin reared, whinnying shrilly, and galloped off down the street past Mannion, dragging its bellowing rider. Mannion held his attention on the riders before him, shooting into the jostling group, blowing one man after another out of his saddle until Mannion had to stop shooting to dodge riderless horses galloping toward him, whinnying crazily.

After a pinto crossed in front of him, nearly slamming him into the dirt, Mannion saw Quint Wayne, one arm bloody, raising his Winchester toward Joe with his right arm, jaws hard, gimlet eyes enraged. He'd lost his hat in the melee, and his sandy blond hair hung in his eyes. Smoke and flames lapped from the barrel of the foreman's rifle but only after a bullet had smashed into the side of his head, slamming him hard to his right.

The bullet he fired blew into the dirt at Mannion's feet.

His horse buck-kicked with an indignant whinny, and the foreman flew over the horse's head to land in the street and roll to a stop before Mannion. He stared up at the lawman, lips stretched back from his teeth, eyes glassy in death.

Mannion turned to see who'd killed the foreman. Jane smiled at him and gave him a two-fingered salute.

Grinning, Mannion cocked another round into his Yellowboy's action and looked for another target.

He held fire.

All the Spur riders were down. They lay twisted in death.

Most of them, anyway.

A few lay writhing in agony while the last of their horses galloped away from the smoke hanging in a thick, fetid cloud over the fallen.

Mannion looked around the street.

None of the Del Norte shooters appeared to have taken any lead. They each stood or knelt on one knee where they'd been standing or kneeling before. Jane included. Rio looked fine, too. He was still crouched atop the jailhouse stoop, aiming his carbine, shifting the barrel around, looking for a target.

Charlie McQueen was on one knee to Mannion's

right, still aiming down the smoking barrel of the Winchester he used to deer hunt. He slowly lowered the rifle now and turned to Mannion.

Mannion gave him a nod.

McQueen gave a single nod back, his eyes grave behind his glinting, dusty spectacles.

A hoarse curse sounded behind Mannion.

He turned to see Garth Helton lying in a heap a half a block away, clutching his apparently injured right ankle with both hands.

He cursed again, loudly, enraged.

Mannion lowered the smoking Yellowboy to his side and walked over to the cursing, grunting rancher. He leveled the rifle at the man's head.

"No!" Helton cried, raising his hands in front of his face.

"Don't worry, you chicken-livered dog," Mannion said. "I'm not going to kill you. You want to know why?" He crouched to pull the rancher's Colt pistol from its holster; he tossed it away.

Helton just stared at him, incredulous, slowly lowering his hands.

"Because you have a daughter. Go home to her."

"End of the line, Bloody Joe," came a menacing voice behind Mannion.

He turned to see Whip Helton walking down the porch steps and into the street. He still wore only his red longhandles, and he was still barefoot. He was extending a pistol straight out before him. Mannion recognized Stringbean's old Colt.

Whip strode toward Mannion, grinning, clicking the Colt's hammer back.

"Whip, holster that thing!" Helton croaked out at his son.

"Nah, nah. I'm gonna kill Bloody Joe. Sure, the others'll kill me, but I'll hang, anyway."

He came to within ten feet of Mannion and stopped, grinning evilly down the barrel of the cocked Colt.

"*No!*" came a girl's cry to Mannion's right. It was followed by the sharp crack of a pistol.

The bullet slammed into Whip's right arm. He yelped and staggered sideways, firing the old Colt into the ground only inches from his father's head.

Mannion turned. His lower jaw dropped when he saw Vangie walking toward Whip, extending a silver-chased Colt revolver in both hands held straight out before her. She wore the cape she'd worn earlier but not the hood. She must have taken the pistol off Quint Wayne. Behind her, the dead man's holster was empty.

She pulled the hammer back and dropped her chin to aim down the barrel, keeping both eyes open, just like her father had taught her.

"No!" Whip cried, suddenly terrified. He'd dropped the Colt and now swung around, holding his right hand straight out before him, pleadingly. "*Please!*"

Orange flames lapped from the big Colt in Vangie's hands.

Whip flew backward with another yelp, slapping his right hand to his bloody left shoulder. He hit the ground on his butt and sat up, regarding Vangie in horror. The girl walked toward him, cocking the Colt in her hands, a determined, sinister cast to her gaze.

"No!" Whip screamed, climbing to his feet, turning, and running. "I don't *wanna* die!"

Again, the Colt roared.

Whip howled, dropped, and rolled. He staggered to his feet again and turned to Vangie, who kept marching toward him, cocking the Colt yet again.

"No!"

"That yellow-bellied fool," Mannion distantly heard Garth Helton growl.

Boom!

Whip flew back into the street again and lay writhing.

Vangie closed the gap between them. Angling the Colt down at the sobbing man's jerking body, she emptied the Colt into his chest. When it clicked, empty, she stood staring down at the dead, bloody carcass before her. Whip's lips were stretched back from his teeth in horror; his dead eyes glistened in the sunlight.

Vangie lowered her hands to her sides. She dropped the gun. It landed at her feet with a dull thud.

Mannion stood frozen in place, heart hammering. "Vangie..."

She turned suddenly. Her eyes widened when she saw him. "Poppa!" she cried and came running.

Mannion dropped the Yellowboy just before she leaped into his arms and wrapped her legs around his waist, burying her face in his neck, sobbing.

Mannion hugged her tight, said into her ear, "You back with me now, my darling girl?"

She nodded against his neck, soaking his neck with her tears. "I'm back, Poppa!"

Mannion turned to see Stringbean and Rio walking toward him. Stringbean was rubbing the back of his head, wincing.

"What happened?" Mannion said.

Rio looked sheepish. He had one hand on Stringbean's shoulder. "You know how I said *I* even make mistakes from time to time?"

"Yeah," Mannion said, still holding Vangie in his arms.

"Well, I made a big one. Left my keys down in the cellblock. Somehow, Helton got his hands on them."

"Don't worry about it," Mannion said. "How's your head, kid?"

"I'll live," Stringbean said.

"We'll leave you two alone," Rio said as he and Stringbean turned around and headed back toward the jailhouse.

Stringbean halted a little when he saw the girl standing near the jailhouse's front porch, waiting for him. Both concern and relief shone in Molly Hurdstrom's pretty, gray eyes.

Vangie clinging to him as though she'd never let him go, Mannion glanced south along the street. The doctor was working his way around to the wounded. The undertaker, Bellringer, was working his way around to the dead, his black wagon parked nearby, a yellow dog sitting on the driver's seat, panting. There were only half a dozen Spur men still kicking, it appeared. The rest lay still in death, scattered as though they'd dropped from the sky. Eventually, the sawbones would get to Helton.

No hurry.

Jane was walking toward Mannion and the still sobbing Vangie, holding her Winchester down low against her right leg.

Her hair glistened in the sunlight.

She was smiling.

A LOOK AT BOOK TWO: REVENGE AT BURIAL ROCK

In this second high-action volume in Peter Brandvold's explosive new western series, Town Marshal "Bloody" Joe Mannion plays cat and mouse with an old enemy...

Joe believes the old regulator, "Long-Shot" Hunter Drago, who did twelve years' hard time because of Mannion, has moved to the town of Del Norte in the Colorado Territory to kill him. But, nearly everyone else in town believes that he merely moved to Del Norte to take over the Three-Legged Dog Saloon and to begin a new, peaceful life for himself.

Mannion, who doesn't believe in coincidences but does know the nature of "Long Shot's" black heart, doesn't buy a word of it.

The rest of the town, including his lover, Jane Ford, thinks Mannion's just being his old, stubborn, bloody self—especially when he catches Drago palling around with his daughter, Evangeline, and beats the old killer half to death on Del Norte's main street for all to see.

Bloody Joe has finally gone too far. The town's powers-that-be believe it's time for Joe to go.

As the game of cat and mouse continues, however, and Mannion finds himself dodging a veritable lead storm nearly everywhere he goes, he finally finds himself in a bloody showdown on the stone mountain called Burial Rock, where he finds that not only his own life hangs in the balance but Jane Ford's life, as well.

He's going to have to move fast and shoot straight to escape a blood bath...

AVAILABLE MAY 2022

ABOUT THE AUTHOR

Peter Brandvold grew up in the great state of North Dakota in the 1960's and '70s, when television westerns were as popular as shows about hoarders and shark tanks are now, and western paperbacks were as popular as *Game of Thrones*.

Brandvold watched every western series on television at the time. He grew up riding horses and herding cows on the farms of his grandfather and many friends who owned livestock.

Brandvold's imagination has always lived and will always live in the West. He is the author of over a hundred lightning-fast action westerns under his own name and his pen name, Frank Leslie.

Made in the USA
Las Vegas, NV
05 August 2023

75684953R00167